NOT IN MY NAME

MICHAEL COOLWOOD

Author's Note & Trigger Warning

Trigger warnings assist people in avoiding trauma triggers. A trauma trigger is a psychological stimulus that prompts recall of a previous traumatic experience. The stimulus itself need not be frightening or traumatic, and may be only indirectly or superficially reminiscent of an earlier traumatic incident, such as a scent or a piece of clothing. Books that contain these triggers cause flashbacks, which make them feel as if the traumatic experience is happening to them in that moment.

I have friends who would not be able to read this book because of specific trauma triggers. I am including a trigger warning for the benefit of my friends and people like them. As such, it contains spoilers. If you do not experience trauma triggers, you do not have to read any further. Please feel free to proceed to Chapter One.

Trigger Warning: Police brutality, rape, sexual assault, emotional abuse and murder.

There are scenes where murder and police brutality are depicted, but not graphically. Rape, sexual assault and emotional abuse are not directly depicted within the text. These elements are alluded to by characters when discussing their backstories, and are directly addressed in the final chapters. The focus in the text is on survivors overcoming trauma, rather than the specific details of the trauma itself. I hope you will agree with me, when you discover the context of these events, that their inclusions are artistically justified, rather than a ploy to build cheap pathos.

For more information on trauma triggers and PTSD in general, please see the information leaflet 'Post-Traumatic Stress Disorder' produced by the Mental Health charity Mind, available from the Mind website or at:

tinyurl.com/NotInMyName2020

Acknowledgements

This book relied on a lot of outside expertise. I am enormously indebted to the work of Helen Gould, who helped both with sensitivity reading, and as a perspective of an activist who has been involved in more direct action than I've been. Al Ross and Sachiko Burton from Salt & Sage also provided sensitivity reads.

Tim Dedopulos helped me with his services as a howling word-ape when I was having trouble writing. He genuinely said that's what he wanted to be credited as.

Rob and Gina Marsh from Clapham Publishing services, and Isobel Lans from Inspired Lines provided editing services. My wonderful publisher, Katie Isbester from Claret Press, also edited the text and worked with me to get the story just right. One memorable occasion saw Katie and me clustered around a white board for four hours trying to establish an exact timeline for the mystery.

Jennifer Cooley and Magdalena Knitter helped me with developing the initial mystery, as well as with subsequent redrafts.

× Table of Contents

× Chapter One

Terror coiled around me as I lay next to my friends on the steps of Birmingham's Victoria Square. It was crushing my chest, making my breathing swift and shallow. The angry white men on the other side of the line of police had been yelling at us for well over an hour, and had just started spitting.

The youngest member of our little group, Cassie, lay next to me. She was eighteen, and habitually wore swirls of black makeup under her eyes. I could only see half of her – she was splayed out, her limbs appearing broken and twisted. An A4 sheet of paper was taped to her chest. On the paper was a printed picture of a casualty of war. A similar picture was attached to my chest.

On my other side was Sefu, a tall man with a kind face and short, clipped hair. If my memory served, his Marilyn Manson t-shirt was currently being masked by a picture of an Iraqi hospital that one of our bombs had flattened.

Just beyond Sefu were Liam and Gus, who were the closest to the police line separating us from the angry white men. My friends' proximity to a mob of people who hated us was only amplifying my terror.

In a die-in, protestors lie down in a public place and pretend to be dead. The idea is the general public don't really understand how devastating wars are so we show them. Extra points are awarded if a die-in takes place in a major intersection so we cause traffic to grind to a halt. But we weren't doing that today. We'd chosen Victoria Square because Birmingham's town hall and council house looked out over it.

"Traitors!" cried the angry white men. "Saboteurs!"

The cops were playing games with us, hoping we'd give up and go home. Every once in a while, they would come up to one of us and carry us away from the square. They'd say they were arresting us, move us past the line of police separating us from the general public and then release us back into the wild. They called this 'de-arresting', which I hadn't known was a thing the police could do. They kept dragging us away from our protest and we kept finding ways to break back through the cop line, back to the steps of Victoria Square.

"Saboteurs!" the angry men yelled again, before someone in their midst with a megaphone managed to organise them into a more complex chant.

"You lost! Get over it!" they screamed. "You lost! Get over it!"

This seemed to energise the zealots at the front of the line who increased their efforts to get at us. The cops were pushed back a few metres, nearly treading on Gus in the process. This seemed to give a couple of men an idea, and they concentrated on spitting on my friends. The spittle rained down on Gus, and some splashed onto Liam. Gus opened his eyes and locked his gaze on to Liam.

I didn't see exactly what happened. All I saw was a furious man in a St George's flag shirt spit at Liam. With a roar, Gus leaped to his feet and swung a punch at the flag-wearer. The flag-wearer went down, but two identical men took his place. Gus dropped another, but his mate struck back. Gus took the blow and didn't seem to notice. The angry men surged forward, furious at Gus's audacity. The cops suddenly didn't know what to do. They were supposed to arrest Gus, but if they broke their line, the mob would attack the rest of us.

Liam scrambled to his feet and tried to pull Gus back, but his scrawny tattooed arms couldn't do the job. Gus swung and swung at the line of identical furious men. He swung until Vince appeared from nowhere. Vince was smaller than Gus, but he placed himself in between Gus and the mob. I couldn't hear anything over the shouts but I saw Vince's mouth move in quick, precise movements.

I knew I should be up on my feet supporting Vince, talking Gus down, but the terror had wrapped itself around my legs and arms. I couldn't move. I heard charging feet from the direction I wasn't looking, and suddenly cops had launched themselves on Gus, Vince and Liam. Gus was seething, Liam was shouting "No blood for oil!" and Vince was holding his head high. He had just stopped a terrible situation from getting even worse.

"Do we make a last stand?" Sefu asked. "Or do we stay put?"

"What kind of question is that?" demanded Xia from just past where Cassie was lying. Xia was a tall woman with greying hair who had been arranging actions like this since the '70s. "The longer we stay here, the more people have to look at us and the more they have to think about what our country is doing. If we get ourselves arrested trying to free our friends, the authorities win and we lose."

I'd been waiting for Xia to say that, all the while hoping she wouldn't. My hands clenched and unclenched as I saw the cops dragging my three friends off with them. I wish actions like this were as effortless for me as they were for Xia.

"Phoebe!" My sister Mel called down to me. She was just

up the steps from where I was lying, her voice calm and warm. The muscles in my jaw loosened. "Think about what they'd want. They'd want us to carry on."

Mel was right, as always. Our parents had always insisted I defer to Melissa, but it was when she'd discovered her softer side and started calling herself 'Mel' that I found someone actually worth listening to.

I relaxed my hands. The stone beneath my back felt less cold. "Cassie," I said, trying not to move my lips. "How are you doing?"

"I'm alright," Cassie said, "but the last cop who arrested me told me that he was going to nick me properly if I tried this again."

They'd told me the same thing. "You okay with that?"

Cassie rolled her eyes to look at me, although her face still stared serenely towards the sky. "Duh. Can anyone see Paula?"

"I made her promise she'd go home after the third time she got hauled out," Sefu said, "so she climbed onto the statue of the Floozie in the Jacuzzi and started hanging a banner. You didn't see that?"

A battle-hardened grin flashed onto Cassie's face. "I think I was trying to break back through the cop line then."

"You didn't see it, Phoebe?" Sefu asked me.

I grunted a sort of 'no' noise. I was trying not to think about the cops or the mob of men who'd beat us to within an inch of our lives if they could get at us. As part of not thinking, I had been steadily working through an Evian bottle I'd filled with vodka and lemonade. I'd initially been using it to settle my nerves, and since it seemed to be working, I'd carried on.

"So there's five of us left?" Sefu asked.

Xia grunted. "Five of us, along with three from Justice for Iraq, two from Stop the War, seventeen from Campaign Against the Arms Trade – well done them – and one unaligned."

Cassie laughed. "That's the nice lady from Games Workshop who I talked into coming yesterday when I went to pick up my orks."

I saw Sefu blink. "You did what?"

"I know, I was surprised as well. But I put the action in her terms, right? I said, imagine the Space Marines wanted to go to war, but instead of going up against Chaos or someone, they decided to just bomb a load of Gretchin villages and destroy their squig farms."

"And that persuaded her?" Sefu sounded confused.

"Hey, that's the power of orks."

"If you say so."

"I do say so. You wouldn't catch any of those smelly Tau players getting anyone to come along to an action like this."

"Smelly what players?" asked Sefu.

"Space Stalinists," said Xia, "and I hate that I know that. You've broken me, Cassie. You're supposed to treat your elders better than this and not fill their heads with the grim darkness of the far future."

I smiled at this. Cassie was obsessed with a game that involved shoving orks and other painted models about on a table. She'd conned me into playing it a few times. It was fun enough, although it would have been nice to have some diplomacy mechanics.

A splash on my cheek indicated some ballistic spit had hit me. "Saboteurs! Saboteurs! Crush the saboteurs!" cried the mob past the cop line. I could hear Carling and bulldog tattoos in their chants. The mob was from Patriots

5

Unite – a right wing group who we'd got a bit previous with.

Another splash on my cheek, then another. I'd been wrong. It wasn't spit, it was rain. Well, maybe getting soaked would cool Patriots Unite off a bit. Rain wouldn't bother us; we were just lying here.

The left side of my face had gone numb from pressing into the stone step. The rain was making the right side feel pleasantly damp. I was tingling, partly from vodka, partly from adrenaline caused by being this close to Patriots Unite and partly from feeling helpless.

Five days ago, my country had lost its senses. Five days ago, on the 24th of June 2003, the referendum result had been announced. 52% of the voting public had answered the question 'Should the UK intervene in Iraq due to Saddam Hussein's refusal to disarm?' with a 'yes'. 48% had answered 'no'. The referendum question and its campaign had made it all sound painless and easy. Not a single mention of bombing villages, schools or hospitals.

We had been promised that the vote would be meaningful – the UK wouldn't intervene if the public voted 'no' – but the Americans hadn't wanted to wait. The US military had begun Operation Iraqi Freedom nearly two months before the vote, on the 2nd of April, bringing troops, armour and warplanes to Iraqi soil. As far as the 'yes' campaign – the pro-war campaign – was concerned, Saddam Hussein hadn't been found and neither had the weapons of mass destruction. So the job wasn't done, and we needed to wade in even deeper.

The big three political parties in the UK were all split. Only the smaller parties like the Greens and the SNP were able to maintain their coherence. The Labour Party was so split on the issue of war that it couldn't risk a vote in the House of

Commons. The referendum was simply a mechanism for the government to get what it wanted. It was never about taking it to the people. The 'yes' side was aided by an incompetent opposition and the press, who cared about helping their allies in the 'yes' camp, or staying doggedly neutral in the face of this looming catastrophe. This wasn't how our democracy was supposed to work.

The only voices of reason were coming from groups like ours who could see through the lies, and we were being largely ignored by the media. Patriots Unite and their brother organisations, by contrast, were being interviewed on BBC News, Question Time and a dozen radio shows to proselytise about the benefits of war. We had to fight to get our voices heard every day, despite the majority opinion clearly being that needlessly killing people was a bad thing. Patriots Unite had friends in high places, so its voice was the one the nation heard.

I'd spent the day after the vote wandering in a state of shock around the farm where I lived. We'd all worked so hard... and this was the result.

"So, Xia," Sefu said. "What do we want to do tomorrow?"

Xia put on an affected, scheming accent. "Same thing we do every night, Sefu. Try to take over the zeitgeist in order to counter the neo-liberal pro-war narrative."

"Have you been watching cartoons with your grandkids, Xia?" Cassie asked.

"Never you mind what I've been watching with my grandkids. Anyway, I'm being optimistic. If we get arrested properly, theoretically they can hold us for 24 hours without charge. That might stop us doing an action tomorrow."

The thought of another action tomorrow made me want

to sink into the stone steps and die. I was so tired. I hadn't slept properly in two weeks. I'd been suspended from work. My car was making a strange banging noise. There were probably other things I should be worrying about, but the world around me swirled subtly, and I found myself unable to focus.

"I was thinking we should take tomorrow off," Sefu said. "We've been on overdrive since the run up to the referendum. The Stop the War campaign can manage without us for a day."

Xia sighed. "The people of Iraq won't get a day off when we invade."

"That's true, but we can't help if we burn out." This was true, very true. I wanted to back Sefu up but didn't want to draw Xia's scorn, "Look, I didn't say anything during the referendum campaign – that was our raison d'être. We brought in Gus, Liam and Cassie so we could fight it. But we failed, and, I don't know about you, but some of us are feeling ragged and lost and scared... and it's not selfish to look after ourselves if it means we can campaign for longer as a result. It's strategic. Cassie, back me up here. What would your ork warboss do?"

"Send wave after wave of her greenskins at the enemy until they ran out of bullets, then use whatever soldiers she had left to crush her foes into submission."

"You ask a silly question," Xia said.

I heard footsteps approaching, several pairs. The police had probably returned to collect us. I wanted to get up and run, but I didn't want to let my friends down. The cops usually started by asking if we'd come with them quietly. With any luck they'd give up and not arrest us this time, not with Patriots Unite pushing ever closer.

Sefu shouted in pain. My head whipped round. One officer had her boot on Sefu's head, and another was clawing at his arms, trying to get them behind his back. This officer had cuffs in his hands. They were serious this time. A third officer was closing in on Sefu as well.

This was absurd – we weren't a threat. They knew that. They only needed two officers per protestor. The third officer grabbed one of Sefu's arms as a fourth approached. This was bad. Four white cops surrounding a young black man was how 'accidents' happened.

I leaped to my feet and staggered shakily, as my left leg had gone to sleep after lying on the stone steps for so long. Sefu cried out again, and I hurtled to his side. I couldn't push the cops off him – they had very liberal interpretations of assault – but I could try and draw some of them away from him. I got up in the face of the last cop to arrive and started yelling, "No blood for oil!" at the top of my lungs. It didn't really apply to the situation, but my panic had fought through the fog of alcohol and had a neat little grip on my heart.

Thankfully, the shouts and spittle caused the cop to turn, and she grabbed me by the arm. She spun me round, and I felt another pair of hands grab my free arm and haul it behind me. I struggled as much as I could, but they locked my arms up good and tight. I felt the cuffs go on, just as Sefu was hauled up next to me. He looked annoyed but unharmed, which loosened the anxious knot in my chest a little. The cops led us away, along with a good cluster of the other protestors.

This time, we were not de-arrested. The last thing I saw as the doors of the police van closed was Cassie, who had made it into the crowd, just another citizen. She waved to Sefu and me, and made a gesture of solidarity.

**The red campaign bus that the Yes Campaign
drove around England:**

× Chapter Two

They drove us to the police station, checked us in and separated us. They searched me and took my fingerprints, then asked a bunch of questions about my mental health. They took my phone, my shoelaces and my necktie. During this process it became pretty obvious that I'd been drinking, partly because I was unsteady on my feet, but mostly because of the booze in the pocket of my suit jacket. They gave me a plastic bottle of water and stuck me in a holding cell. It had white walls with a blue stripe at waist height. The mattress and pillow that occupied one end were also blue. There was a grill covering the light and a toilet behind a waist-high modesty barrier. A painted sign on the wall declared: 'Would you damage your own home? Damage the cell = a charge and a court visit!' I pondered this warning and decided not to damage the cell.

I sat on the mattress. It was a cheap foam thing covered with waterproof plastic. It reminded me of the bed I'd had when living in student halls during my first year of university. I breathed out, feeling the empty space surrounding me. "Well, this is less awful than I was expecting."

I lay back on the mattress, stared at the ceiling and started drinking my water. Slowly, ever so slowly, I sobered up.

I found my eyes darting from point to point in the cell. My gaze fell on the corners of the room and places where the blue stripe met the white wall. I was expecting, at any moment, to feel the familiar sensation of panic start crawling up from my feet to my chest to my neck to my head, but so far I wasn't feeling anything.

When I was young, I was force-fed a phantom snake. A terror python. It couldn't be seen on any x-ray, but its presence was as real to me as the sun. I first became aware of it when I was watching my sister Melissa in one of her fencing matches at school. I started wondering what would happen if my sister's opponent accidentally impaled her with her epée. I thought about how everyone would be really sad, but they'd worry about me. My teachers, my friends, maybe even my parents would feel they needed to really take care of me. I'd just lost my sister after all. I wondered how long I'd be able to string being traumatised by my sister's death out, so that everyone would keep being nice to me.

Melissa had won two matches and was well on her way to a third by the time I wondered if it was okay that I was casually fantasising about my sister's death. That was when I first felt the terror python stir in my guts. It slithered up my intestine, twisting me up as it went. I didn't understand what was happening, all I knew was that I was going to die and there was nothing I could do to stop it. I ran to the toilets and cried for ten minutes, then cleaned myself up and returned to the sports hall, where my parents were applauding Melissa's third victory.

Seventeen years later, the terror python was still with me. The possibility of removing it hadn't even occurred to me. It was just a fact of life, like taxes or disappointing second albums.

Occasionally it would take me over, swallow me whole. When it did, I couldn't leave the house, or if by some miracle I could, I then couldn't get into a car or walk past the end of the street. I couldn't focus to get any work done. Those were always bad, bad times. They'd pass in agonising seconds that felt like weeks.

Mostly I was just aware of the python. It reminded me to be careful, to not take any chances or do anything rash. It would always remind me when I was taking a step beyond what I was allowed to do. But as I lay on the squishy bed in my cell, I just felt surprisingly... kind of... normal. The air in the cell was cool but not cold. The mattress wasn't the height of luxury, but it was perfectly fine. If I was going to be stuck anywhere that wasn't home, I supposed it might as well be here. At that thought, I blinked, remembering high ceilings, expensive furnishings and cold expressions. There were much worse places I could be.

I wondered how Mel and Sefu were doing. And the others. They'd probably be fine, assuming Sefu hadn't had an 'accident'. Even if an 'accident' had happened to Sefu, there was nothing I could do about it from my cell.

Katie, my niece, had an afterschool play date, and the parents concerned were sympathetic to the cause. She'd be able to stay with them if Mel didn't get out in time, and the farm should be okay without any of us for a few hours. Besides, Sefu had said Paula had escaped capture, despite her banner escapades, and I'd seen Cassie was free and clear.

My sternum felt oddly light. The terror that had occupied the space between my throat and the base of my ribcage had almost entirely lifted. I wondered what I'd done to make this happen, but maybe it was the lack of anything I could do. I was alone in this cell. My fate, for the next few hours, was out of my hands.

I rested my head on the thin blue pillow, and finished

my water. I screwed the top back on and placed it delicately down on the floor of the cell. The hatch in my cell door opened and then, after a pause, it closed. My eyelids felt very heavy.

✕

I jerked awake at the sound of my cell door swinging open. I heard my name being called, although it was indistinct, as if I was under water. I rubbed at my eyes and heard the same voice tell me I was needed for an interview.

The Terror Python stayed away, lazily coiled, not even raising its head as I followed the police officer into a room that was only slightly more interesting than my cell. I sat on the chair presented to me and tried to avoid the gaze of the two officers sat opposite me. There wasn't a table between us, which was a surprise. I felt oddly exposed.

One of the officers looked uncannily like an oversized hamster that had been strategically shaved. She started a tape recorder and introduced herself as Sergeant Powell. She also introduced Constable Amid, who was a friendly looking cop in a headscarf. I didn't trust her – not because of the headscarf, but because she looked friendly. Nothing good could come of cops looking at you in a friendly manner.

Powell asked me to confirm my name.

"Lawyer," I said.

"Your name is Phoebe Green, correct?" Amid tried.

"Lawyer."

"How old are you, Phoebe?"

"Lawyer."

"Phoebe, I would like to give you two hundred pounds. All you have to do is reply with anything except the word 'Lawyer'," Amid said.

"Lawyer."

It was very important that you never say anything to the police without a lawyer present. These people liked to get you talking in the hope that you say something that lets them lock you up permanently. Just because I was less at risk of this than Sefu or Paula thanks to my skin colour, didn't mean it couldn't happen. Best to get the lawyer thing out of the way as early as possible.

"Is your lawyer's name Eryl Iwan, of Iwan & Iwan Associates?" Powell asked.

My eyes widened. They'd been spying on me! Or one of my friends had already asked for Ms Iwan.

Still, that put me in a bind. I couldn't answer with the word 'lawyer', as that would feel like a step backwards. I settled for a cautious nod of the head.

"Can you see if Ms Iwan is done with Melissa Green, please?" Powell said, turning towards Amid. Amid gave a smile, which briefly illuminated the room in a serene, amber light. She walked from the room, her steps sounding soft and soothing against even the hard stone of the interview room floor. I was left feeling deeply confused. Try as I might, I was finding it very difficult to dislike that cop. What was she doing working for their side? It was like finding a Disney princess working for the SAS.

Powell made the occasional attempt to get me talking whilst we waited for Eryl, but I refused to speak. Eventually, she gave up and started flicking through her notebook. Well, I could wait better than any cop. I stared at my fingernails for a bit. Then I started counting stains on the floor.

I'd never been arrested before. Given my reptilian companion, I'd expected to find this whole experience

15

terrifying. I didn't. The snake was still. I frowned as I counted stains and wondered how that could be true. Maybe, after years of fighting a losing battle against forces far larger than myself, it felt good to be locked in a room with people who wanted something from me, and all I had to do to beat them was keep my mouth shut. I could win this fight. The thought swept a smile across my face.

I heard the door open and turned to see Eryl Iwan Jr enter in Amid's wake. Eryl Iwan Sr had been helping us with legal matters for years now, as had her granddaughter, Eryl Iwan. Eryl Iwan was a delightful woman – funny and energetic with a formidable legal mind. Eryl Iwan Jr was similarly skilled, but she lacked her grandmother's kind character. I was used to seeing Eryl the Younger angry, furious, irritated, annoyed, cross, exasperated, frustrated, and, worst of all, professionally displeased. What I saw on her face at that moment chilled me to the bone. She looked tired.

"Hello, Phoebe," she said. She sat down on the chair next to mine. "Sorry to have kept you waiting. And my apologies to you, officers. I'm sure you can understand my client's hesitance to answer your questions. Please continue."

"Your name is Phoebe Green?" Amid asked.

I looked at Eryl, who nodded. "Yes," I said.

"You are twenty four?"

"Yes."

"Employed at EquiCare specialist rehabilitation facility in Kings Heath?"

"I'm training to be a social worker," I said, defensively.

"But you do work at EquiCare?"

"Sorry. Yes, I'm employed there. For now."

"Don't editorialise please, Phoebe," said Eryl.

Amid smiled at me beatifically. "Is there something we should know?"

×

Two weeks before, at the care home, I was already on edge as I entered the games room where the morning briefing was held. Action after action had left me feeling run down, with the start of a cold and the unpleasant edge of a hangover. Things got worse quickly. All the chairs around the table were full, meaning we already had the usual number of staff members present, but there was no room for me. Was I not supposed to be working? Had I got my shifts wrong again?

"Phoebe!" said Steph, the boss, who had apparently been waiting for me. "Please join me in my office."

She drifted upstairs and I followed, feeling like my feet were struggling to stay on the ground.

"So, Phoebe," Steph said. She took her glasses off and tapped them against the arm of her chair in a gesture probably designed to make her look approachable. "We have to talk about your attendance."

"Sure," I said, very much not liking where this was going.

"Over the past month, you have missed work seven times. That's eighty-four hours. I'm afraid company policy is clear on these matters."

The terror python didn't move in my guts. If anything, my guts felt entirely absent. It felt like I was a shell and there was nothing inside me except empty, white space.

"We're going to have to suspend you pending a review of your attendance."

My vision felt as if it was receding – as if the room around me was steadily growing, or maybe my eyes were retreating into my head.

"You will be contacted about the meeting by HR. Until then, your shifts will be covered by other staff members."

My boss sat back in her chair and placed her glasses back on her nose. I hesitated for a moment before I realised the meeting was over already. I wondered if I should mount some sort of defence, but I couldn't think of anything that would change Steph's mind. She was right. I'd missed the shifts. I'd known what I was doing. This was always a possibility.

I staggered to my feet and stumbled out of the door. I clattered down the stairs to the ground floor, to see the morning briefing had broken up and my colleagues were rushing about the place on errands. I focused on the front door, trying not to think about how I was letting everyone down by leaving. The impact of missing just one member of staff in this place couldn't be overestimated. If I stayed, we might have been able to complete our daily scheduled tasks, rather than struggle to keep our patients' heads above water.

Still, I felt bitter about my suspension. I was also more tired than I could remember being ever before. I slumped towards the front door, and had nearly reached it when I saw Sally, the supervisor for the day, packing up in the games room. "You heading off?" she asked.

"Uh-huh."

"Steph told us you were going to be suspended." Sally's voice usually sounded kind – a Wolverhampton accent will do that for you. She didn't sound kind in that moment.

I looked up from the carpet. "Mhm."

"Did they tell you it was because you kept missing shifts?"

"Yeah."

"It's not because you're missing shifts, Phoebe. It's because you're a traitor. Don't come back. Find another home to work at. We don't want you here."

I fled out the front door and into my car. I wasn't able to wait for my tears to dry before starting the engine and pulling out into the road.

✕

"Phoebe." I blinked. I looked up at the two cops who were interrogating me. Eryl had rested a hand gently on my shoulder. The gesture felt oddly alien from the lawyer. I wondered if she'd read about people doing such things but had never got around to trying them for herself. I looked up at her. "Phoebe, focus, please." Her expression looked sad.

"Sorry," I said, "there's nothing you need to know there."

"Phoebe, how well do you know Cassandra Samson?"

Cassie... why were they asking me about Cassie? Had she done something... adventurous after escaping the protest?

"Pretty well, although I haven't known her long. Why?"

"Phoebe..." Amid sat forward in her chair, her large eyes stared up at me, imploring. "Can you think of anyone who'd want to hurt Cassandra?"

Deep in my stomach, the terror python suddenly realised it was needed. It grabbed its hat and a cup of coffee and got to work, twisting my intestines into knots.

"No," I replied. "No one specific."

"Perhaps someone non-specific?" Powell suggested.

Eryl made an annoyed grumbling noise. That was more like the lawyer I was used to.

"I'll rephrase," Powell said. "Can you think of any person or persons who might wish Cassandra harm?"

"Well," I said, not really liking where this was going, "you might be aware that Patriots Unite aren't fans of us. They graffitied the exterior wall of our farm last week."

"What did the graffiti say?" Amid asked.

"Crush the saboteurs, along with some other, less coherent things."

"Did you report this vandalism?"

"No."

"Why not?"

I looked at Eryl. She shrugged at me. I stayed silent.

"Phoebe, I'm sorry to have to tell you this." Amid said, her face looking dreadfully sad. I wanted to take her hand and tell her everything was going to be okay. "Cassandra Samson was found dead in a pub in the Jewellery Quarter two hours ago."

What?

"We're making enquiries but as we had some of her friends with us in the station, we thought we'd ask if you knew anyone who might do such a thing?"

"No!" the word stumbled, strangled out of my throat. "No – there are people who have a political beef with us but no one who'd want to kill her. What happened?"

"There was a fight," Powell said. "It's unclear who started it. Cassandra was caught up in it."

Tears bloomed in my eyes. Next to me, Eryl wrapped an arm around my shoulder and pulled me into an anaemic hug, which was, for her, the equivalent of a clinging, tearful embrace.

Constable Amid leaned forward and took my hand. "I'm so sorry for your loss," she said.

The officers asked me a few more questions. Eryl didn't make any disapproving noises about them, so I answered to the best of my ability. I felt detached from the room I was in, from the questions, from Eryl and the officers. The terror snake had me thoroughly in its grip, but there was something inside me that was refusing to give into it. I tried to focus on it as I was led back to my cell. It felt as if a pearl was lodged in my gut – it was painful, but it brought relief at the same time. It was something to focus on, and the terror snake didn't seem to want to go near it.

The pearl was this: *why Cassie?*

Excerpt from interview with Alastair Campbell, press secretary to Tony Blair, 20 days before the Referendum Vote:

Campbell: I think the people in this country have had enough of experts, with organisations with acronyms, saying –

Interviewer: They've had enough of experts? The people have had enough of experts? What do you mean by that?

Campbell: People from organisations with acronyms saying that they know what is best and getting it consistently wrong. They thought Al Gore would win the last US election. They didn't see 9/11 coming.

Interviewer: The people of this country have had enough of people who know what they're talking about?

Campbell: Because these people are the same ones who got consistently wrong what was happening.

Interviewer: So who should we trust because experts have been unable to develop the ability to accurately predict the future? Who should we trust? People who don't know what they're talking about? If we're not trusting experts, what are we trusting? Ignorance?

Campbell: No, it's actually a faith in the –

Interviewer: It's people like you, isn't it?

Campbell: It's a faith in the British people to make the right decision.

× Chapter Three

I couldn't stay away from Cassie's funeral.

Everything rational told me that it was a terrible idea to go. Going to the funeral and seeing her lowered into the ground wouldn't make her any less dead. Paula and Mel had both argued that having Cassie's activist friends at the funeral might upset her mum. We were, after all, some of the people who had lured her away from her nice safe life in Liverpool. We hadn't been the first to light the fire in her heart – that honour belonged to the animal rights activists who'd protested at a nearby restaurant that served *fois gras*. Then she moved to Greenpeace, then to Amnesty International and then, when the referendum was called, to us.

Nonetheless, if Cassie hadn't come to us, there was a very real possibility that she wouldn't have died. No one would go so far as to say we were responsible for her death, but we definitely shared some of the blame – at least, that was how I saw it. The closer the funeral crept, the more certain I became that I needed to go. It was the scab I shouldn't pick at, and yet, I needed to see everyone Cassie had left behind, everyone who wouldn't be able to see her again, because of us.

Xia eventually tipped the scales for me. I'd barely seen her since we'd been released after the die-in, but she'd emerged the morning of the funeral looking sleep deprived and carrying a crocheted blanket. She had asked who was going to the funeral in a way which made it clear she hadn't considered the possibility that we'd skip it. I'd spoken up. Xia had pressed the blanket into my hands and then fled to her room. When I'd unfolded the blanket, I found a crocheted pattern of a greenskin cradling a fallen comrade. She must have spent the whole two weeks between the murder and the funeral working on it.

It was easy for me to get stuck in my own head, and I think part of the reason I ended up going to the funeral was because I was twisting myself into knots over the death of my friend. Justifiable knots, perfectly understandable knots, but knots nevertheless.

Vince had offered to give me a lift, which had been a surprise. He'd never really been close to Cassie, but I wasn't going to turn down backup. He drove me down, and together we sat at the back of the church during the ceremony, and then traipsed along to the Funky Ferret in Hunt's Cross, where the wake was held. The rain soaked us on the way, which I think Vince found helpful. He had been trying to hide his tears.

It was when I saw Cassie's mum at the wake that I finally managed to align what I was feeling with the world in which I was living. She was cold, but she still shook my hand on the way in. She was so distant you could have easily slipped a few continents between us, but she still thanked me for coming, and accepted Xia's blanket with a smile. Her eyes didn't call me a murderer; they said that this was the worst day of her life, and the real problem was there'd be another day along tomorrow just as bad.

Vince dodged the line of people shaking Cassie's mum's hand and linked up with me inside. There, he started doing what he always did, chatting to people and raising their spirits. For my part, I stood in the corner of a pub, snacking on some rather nice sausage rolls, watching the flow of people and trying to find comfort in the number who had come to celebrate Cassie's life.

Someone had left little green orks around the place. One of them was currently subjugating a stack of cheese sandwiches. It was nice to be around the little things. They'd been scattered around with care, and I found myself trying to image what sort of story Cassie would have told with them. This filled me with a warm glow of nostalgia for the girl I had known, along with terrible sadness.

Vince seemed to be coping better than I was. He was at the centre of a throng of people, telling grand stories of our actions: "So, Cassie says to me, she says 'you can't sling a banner between those lamp posts, you zogging grot! We're going to have to slip into the offices over the road and hang it from a couple of the windows. Come on, you be the executive, I'll be your secretary!' So before I know what I'm doing, I'm leading Cassie, who's rustled up a suit from goodness knows where, and I'm giving her all these made up instructions about quarterly VAT returns to try and pretend like we're supposed to be there, and we slip our way up to the sixth floor, and we're just hanging the banner when security shows up and asks us what we're doing. Cassie bears down on them like a tiger and starts telling them how we've been instructed to hang this here and why don't they take this up with – I can't even remember who she said – but it worked. They left us alone, we got the banner up. Cassie got the banner up."

A smile swept across the small group of people clustered around Vince. This warmth seemed to spread past me and across the room. Many of those he spoke to hadn't known about Cassie's activism and they seemed delighted to hear about it from Vince.

"Had you known Cassandra long?" asked Edith, one of the old women Vince was currently charming. They were standing near a low table, on which perched pictures of Cassie, along with maybe a dozen model orks.

Vince smiled, his face the picture of someone who was deeply sad but also determined to remember the vitality of Cassie. "Not long enough, definitely. But the time I spent with her left me so exhausted it feels like we spent a couple of lifetimes together!" Vince passed an arm across his brow and swooned playfully. His leg brushed the table and sent a squad of orks reeling.

A grin flashed across Edith's face. "That's lovely to hear. I'd only met her a few times myself, I'm here for her mum, you know?" She glanced down at a picture of Cassie in a school play. She was dressed as a pirate and waving a cutlass.

"I never met her mum," Vince said.

Edith looked from Vince to Cassie's mum. "Oh, I must introduce you!"

Vince glanced over to where Cassie's mum was propping up the bar. She was surrounded by figures in black and looked like she was holding herself together, but only just. At the sight, Vince took a look down at his watch and turned around to look for me. When he saw me, he took a reflexive step to the side so that he was closer to me, and Edith was in between him and the bar. A small, sickening crunch caused him to shift his foot slightly to a new spot. I saw the crushed form of a model ork where Vince's foot had been. He casually pushed it deeper under the table with the side of his shoe.

"That'd be wonderful!" he said. Edith started leading

him towards Cassie's mum. When he passed me, Vince shot me a grimace.

I also glanced at my watch and my eyes widened. Katie would be back from school in a few hours and Melissa was teaching tonight. If we wanted to be there to make sure she was doing okay in this chaos, we'd have to leave now.

"Vince!" I cried, "It's time we were leaving."

"Oh no!" Edith pouted.

"So sorry, I have to get this one home," Vince smiled sadly. He made his way to the exit and I followed in his wake. We slipped into his car and started off on the long road back to Birmingham.

I felt empty as we drew away from the mourners, but my thoughts seemed strangely sharp. Cassie was occupying most of them, and the questions surrounding her. The senseless tragedy of her death felt like it could never be put right, but it could be understood.

I rested my head against the passenger window. The glass was hot and it vibrated uncomfortably, but the slumped position felt comforting. The same question that had been rattling around in my head for two weeks was still there: *why Cassie?*

The question had been joined by other, more urgent questions. *If Cassie could be snuffed out like that, were any of us safe? Would Mel be next? Would Katie be safe? Who did this and would they come for the rest of us?*

My head buzzed with frenetic images of imminent catastrophes. They flashed through my vision, each more horrible than the last, but each moving so fast that I wasn't able to work through any one scenario. I was furious with myself. My head was filled with situations that were laughably unlikely, but not *so* unlikely that I was able to completely dismiss them: murderers coming for us in the night, the state breaking down our doors and hauling us off to secret courts, a deadly fire sweeping through our home killing everyone inside. The terror python was never short of ideas for me to get lost in.

My hands were shaking, my vision was spiking with strange pinpricks of darkness. My heartbeat and breathing were racing. I ended up bashing my head against the car window to try and jolt myself free.

"You alright, bab?" Vince asked, sounding slightly alarmed.

I couldn't answer.

"Is this about Cassie?"

I didn't know how to answer that. Yes, it was about Cassie, but it was also about everything else. I felt overwhelmed and helpless and completely lost and alone, as if I was always just one, tiny step away from catastrophe.

"You need to try to not think about it, Phoebe. Shut this stuff out. It's all in your head and it can't hurt you if you just push it away. Take a deep breath in." I latched on to the calm in his voice. I breathed in deeply. "Okay," he said. "Now hold it. In a moment, you're going to breathe out, and all of your worries are going to blow away with that air. Ready? Breathe out."

I exhaled, slowly. I tried to force all thoughts of the oncoming storm out along with the air. And again. In. Out. In. Out.

"Doesn't that feel better?" Vince asked.

"It does, yeah."

I felt slightly freer than I had. I'd been looking out the

window for well over an hour, but for the first time I actually saw where we were. We had just turned onto the long, winding road outside Birmingham where our farm was located.

Paula owned the farm, and she let us stay there for a percentage of our wages, which she put towards upkeep and improvements. In my case that was 5%, but that was because I only earned minimum wage. Care work does not pay well. Mel was a teacher, so she paid 10%.Vince earned decent money as a landscape gardener, so he paid 15%. The idea was everyone paid what they could so no one got left behind.

The farm had once been just that – a farm. A dairy farm, to be precise. It had been sold off in the '90s to a developer who had wanted to create a luxury country retreat sixteen miles from the middle of Birmingham. A stable had been converted into a secondary residence, whilst the farmhouse itself had been bulldozed in an act of prime vandalism. The developer had run out of money before he'd managed to knock down any more of the buildings. He'd left behind the converted stable and a few sheds surrounded by a two-metre wall. There were a few other buildings dotted about the land as well.

The next owner had used the place to store tractors that he then sold on. He'd left the stable and the lodgings above it pretty well alone, so it had decayed quite badly. When the property went up for sale again in 1998, Paula had snapped it up for a song because, it turned out, no one wanted a half-developed country retreat in the middle of nowhere, especially as the walls were all lined with barbed wire. The tractor owner hadn't liked the idea of his vehicles getting nicked.

Vince pulled off the road that ran past the farm and in through the gates. He then jumped on the brakes, causing my seatbelt to dig sharply into my sternum. The courtyard looked different from when we'd left it. Leaflets from our stable had been scattered all over the ground. Many had drifted into piles against Paula's Land Rover. Sefu, Mel, Paula and Gus were clustered into a tight knot in the centre of the courtyard, while Mel's daughter, Katie, was pushing a broom about the place enthusiastically but to no real effect. As we drew closer, I saw that Mel's white hatchback had been spattered with glittering crimson droplets. Even from here, it was clearly blood.

A series of statements said by key figures in the Conservative party from before & during the 2003 referendum:

"The intervention that we will have to do with Iraq should be one of the easiest in human history."
Liam Fox MP

"If a democracy cannot change its mind, it ceases to be a democracy."
David Davies MP

"The day after we vote to intervene in Iraq, we hold all the cards and we can choose any strategy we want"
Michael Gove MP

"I believe it is clearly in our national interest not to intervene in Iraq"
Theresa May MP

"There will be no downside to invading Iraq, only a considerable upside."
Boris Johnson MP

"There is no exit strategy, because we're going to invade so comprehensively we don't need one."
Boris Johnson MP

"We might have two referendums. As it happens, it might make more sense to have the second referendum after we have successfully changed the regime."
Jacob Rees-Mogg MP

"Absolutely nobody is talking about threatening to launch a full-scale invasion of Iraq."
Daniel Hannan MEP

"Only a madman would actually invade Iraq."
Owen Patterson MP

× Chapter Four

Vince parked at a rough angle in front of the other cars and leaped out. I disentangled myself from my seatbelt and followed. My heart had leapt into my throat at the sight of the blood but had settled down into a sprint, rather than a gallop, at the sight of my friends standing around, apparently not in any immediate danger.

"What happened?" Vince demanded, as our friends turned to look at us. "Anybody hurt?"

Sefu had two strips of medical tape binding a fresh cut at his temple, and in two strides I was at his side. "Are you okay?" I murmured, under Vince's alarmed half-shouts.

Sefu grinned at me as if I'd just met him on the way out of the cinema, but there was an edge there I might not have seen were it not for the cut on his face. "We had a little visit from the cops."

I looked from Sefu to the ruins of our courtyard and back. "How many?"

Sefu grinned again. It looked brittle. "Just two," he said.

The terror python, already uncoiled, was slithering delightedly from my head to my gut, unsure of where to start snacking first. "Two cops did this?"

Raised voices from behind me reminded I wasn't alone. I turned to see Mel, who looked shaken and lost. Katie came running up with her broom. "I swept the leaflets over there, Mummy!" she said, grinning and posing with her broom.

Mel's expression brightened as she saw her angel. "Good job, my love." She squatted down and high fived her daughter. "Do you want to do some more or take a rest for a bit?"

"Um," Katie looked up at the sky whild she thought about the question, "I want to sweep some more. Can I?"

Mel passed a hand over her face and smiled. "Of course, sweetie. Remind me later you've earned a treat for working so hard."

Katie's eyes widened. She gripped the broom tighter and flashed off and started thrusting the broom at the drifts of paper. The leaflets detailing the case for pacifism in the face of the United States' desire for oil didn't seem to notice the enthusiastic seven-year-old poking at them with a bristled instrument.

I looked back to Mel and saw her eyes were glistening. I rested an arm across her shoulders and she buried her face in my shoulder.

"So, what are we going to do?" Vince said.

"Do we call Eryl?" Gus said, his voice rasping in the clear air.

"About what?" Melissa said. "The cops show up and shake us down. What do we complain about?"

"Police harassment," Gus said, rolling his shoulders.

"What happened?" I asked.

Paula took a step forward. She held up a hand. Quiet descended like a blanket. She looked to each of us in turn with raised eyebrows. One by one, we all nodded. "A cop car came," she said, looking at me. "A male cop and a female cop. They got out and swaggered around the courtyard for a bit. I came down to see what they wanted. They yelled at me for a bit, before putting me in cuffs."

"Just like that?" I asked. This was all wrong. There were procedures for this sort of thing. They were supposed to tell us we were under arrest and what we were under arrest for. A democracy is built on protection from arbitrary police actions. "They didn't ask your name or anything?"

"No," Paula said. Her back was straight and her eyes were steel. "I don't think this was that sort of visit. Anyway, the male cop held me against their car whilst the female cop went into our stable and started destroying the place. You can see most of what happened. She got the stacks of leaflets we'd printed and started scattering them. She started laying into our banners a bit with her baton, but the noise drew Gus, Sefu and Mel. That was when things got ugly."

"The male cop abandoned Paula and got all up in my face," Gus said, his jaw tight. "I'm pretty sure he wanted me to swing for him, and... and I probably would have."

Gus and Sefu shared a glance. Sefu punched Gus lightly in the forearm. "I got you, mate," he said.

"What did you do?" I asked, warily.

"Sefu tried to talk the male cop down," Paula said, moving so that she was standing next to Sefu, "and the female cop took offense to this."

I looked at the cut on Sefu's head. I looked at the spatter of dark droplets that stippled Mel's hatchback. I looked at Sefu. I looked at his hands. They were down by his sides in a pose that was clearly supposed to be relaxed. I could see his fingers weren't moving. They weren't idle; he was holding himself still. I wanted to ask him again if he was okay, but he'd already told me he was. Asking him again in front of everyone wouldn't get a different answer, it would force him to double down on this one. I moved my eyes up and found them locking on to his. He smiled at me. I frowned. I needed to think about that smile.

"What happened next?" Vince asked. I turned to see he was shifting his weight quickly from foot to foot.

"The male cop seemed to think about what had just happened," Paula said, folding her arms. "He pulled the female cop off Sefu and they had a quick, quiet conversation. They uncuffed me, got in their car and drove off."

"Just like that?" I asked, the surprise obvious in my voice.

"Yup," Sefu said, shrugging. His casual air while blood still stained the medical tape across his wound made me shudder.

"They didn't arrest anyone?" I looked around, checking who was here. "Where are Liam and Xia?"

"They're at work, don't worry about them." Paula smiled. "Yes, the cops just upped and left. We're trying to puzzle out why."

Gus folded his arms. "I still think we should call Eryl."

Paula smiled at him, sadly. "I'd love to call her, but she has limited time. She is already charging us a... criminally low rate for her services?" she glanced about to see if we had appreciated her attempt to inject a bit of levity into the situation. I smiled half heartedly. "I don't want to risk exploiting her time when there's nothing much she can do about it."

"We can sue the police for harassment," Melissa said.

"We could try. The police would circle around their own, the cops who showed up would find a few colleagues to swear they were elsewhere when we were attacked, and that would be that." Paula shrugged. "I've tried following up on harassment through legal means a couple of times."

I frowned. "One car? Two cops? There weren't any others?"

Paula shook her head.

"And they didn't ask any questions or try to find anything out from you?"

Paula shrugged again. "No, I'm used to the cops showing up here unannounced because they think we've done something and they want to haul us in, or maybe goad us into saying something we shouldn't... This wasn't that. This was something new."

There was something wrong with the account. "They were in their uniforms, were they?" I asked.

There was a chorus of agreement.

"What's up, Phoebe?" Mel asked. She was looking at me with a puzzled wrinkle tweaking her forehead.

"There's something..." I said. "Were they carrying anything with them when they left their car?"

"Usual police kit," Paula said, she glanced about at the mess covering the courtyard and pinched the bridge of her nose.

"Did anyone see anything..." I paused and tried to put the thought I was having into a coherent shape. "Out of place? Cops usually do their best to not show what they're really thinking. It seems like these two weren't really thinking at all."

Gus pulled his lip back from his teeth whilst he stared blankly at the place where the cop car must have been. Paula cast her eyes towards the sky. Melissa tapped a finger against her teeth.

Sefu caught my eye. "There was a newspaper," he said. "The cop who hit me threw me up against her car and started

36

trying to cuff me. The male cop came over and stopped her, but while she held me there, I saw a newspaper in the back seat."

"Which newspaper?"

"The Daily Mail."

"Ah."

"It had a headline." Sefu was keeping his face carefully blank. "It said 'Crush The Saboteurs!'"

There it was.

"You're kidding," Gus growled.

Sefu shrugged at him.

"They came here and did this," Gus glanced at Katie, who was still diligently sweeping, "and they did this because…"

"We don't know why they did it," Paula said. She walked over to Katie, took the broom gently from her hands and murmured in the angel's ear. Paula started sweeping the courtyard herself, with less energy but much more effectiveness. "Dozens of cops must have read that paper this morning."

"Sure, but apparently these two particular cops decided that the headline was a directive," Gus said. He hadn't moved from where he stood. Mel looked from him to Paula. She shook herself and walked across to the stables – the ground floor of the building we lived in, which was protected from the elements by strips of thick plastic sheet. She emerged again a moment later with another broom and started working away at the other end of the courtyard from Paula.

"Aren't we going to do anything about this?" Gus demanded to Paula's back.

Vince put his arm around Gus's shoulder. "Come on, mate," he said, "let's chat about this." He led Gus away, leaving Sefu and me alone. I didn't ask 'are you sure you're okay?' and Sefu didn't reply with a stoic smile. I didn't hug him. I didn't hold onto the hug.

Instead, I tried to focus on what I should be doing. There was something I had forgotten to do, but it had...

Sefu slapped me playfully on the shoulder, and together we started helping Paula and Mel clean up the courtyard. We worked for over two hours as the sky changed from blue to grey. Mel approached me once we were done: "I have to get changed for work, love. Are you okay?"

I hesitated. "Vince gave me some advice on the way back from the funeral."

Mel narrowed her eyes. "What advice?"

"I'm trying to just push things a bit further away from me, trying to not let them get to me as much."

Mel winced. "You could do that, bab, you absolutely could. It's just... we all loved Cassie and it's natural to be really hurt by what happened, and because of our history, our reactions might be a little more extreme than some others."

I looked up at her, my eyes wide. It hadn't occurred to me that Mel would be having trouble as well.

"Hey, hey," Mel said, drawing me into a hug. Her head slipped neatly in under my chin. Hugging Mel felt like hugging a warm summer's day. "You need to give yourself time, love," she said, "but you need to accept what you're feeling. Don't lock it up inside you because that'll just cause it to burst out later. Let yourself feel it but try to not let yourself get overwhelmed. Balance, balance, everything in balance."

"I don't know how..."

"I know, love. I'm lucky, I've got Katie to look after. Look, to start, I haven't had a chance to hand the post out yet, what with the cops paying us a visit. I have to get changed for work. Can you pass the post out? I had a look earlier and couldn't see anything for you, but there was something for Paula, I think."

I felt a smile creep onto my face. Mel and I had been quite competitive over who got to hand the post out since we'd been living here. It was a game we'd used to play back home, and it was nice to play it in a safer, more homely place. To date, I'd managed to get to the post twelve times, meaning Mel was beating me by a factor of about a hundred. She was giving me an easy win. In other circumstances, I might have felt patronised.

"Of course," I said, after drying my eyes. Mel and I separated and she stroked my arm once before disappearing inside. I walked to the post box and opened it. Inside were two letters and a parcel the size of a couple of paperbacks. I reached in and grabbed them, surprised by how the world around me had taken a momentary break from spinning out of control.

I grinned at the sudden lightness in my chest and walked across the courtyard towards the house. The courtyard was one of the areas where the developer had put a serious amount of work in. His work was then mostly ruined by having tractors run all over the place, but it was still a pretty nice place, all things considered. The concrete wall that surrounded it was painted a pleasant shade of white and hadn't felt the brunt of our Midlands weather too badly. The gravel that lined the ground was made of small white and grey pebbles that gave the place a modern yet welcoming feeling. The clean white walls and ground served to accentuate the warm, rich red the house had been painted in, and the comforting natural brown of the sheds that lined the west wall reminded me of the farm's original purpose. I took in a deep breath. There was no pollution this far away from the city, and the lack of any actual farms nearby meant the place didn't smell of animal droppings either.

The house was a two-storey affair, although the ground floor was entirely occupied by the stables, protected only by thick plastic sheeting with occasional slits cut into it to allow us in and out. The first floor was where we lived. There were bedrooms, a kitchen, toilet, shower and utility room. The only way to get to the first floor was through a door at the south end of the stables, then up a staircase that ran most of the length of the west wall. At the landing at the top of the stairs, a window looked out over the courtyard, through which I could see Sefu. He grinned at me.

His grin gave me an idea for something that Mel would approve of, something that would keep me busy, make me smile and give me some space to think all in one go. Something I hadn't done for a while. Sefu, you see, was one of those guys who collected swords. I first encountered this type of guy when I went to university and I ended up sort of... collecting them. If you follow me. I... collected Sefu a while ago. We stopped having that sort of fun about six months ago, partly because it could get messy to do that when two people live under the same roof, and partly because I was pretty sure he could do better than me. We'd been pretty chill since then. I did, however, enjoy messing with him by moving his swords.

Sefu was the kind of sword guy who hid his Katanas in any room he was likely to be in. Just in case. 'In case of what?' was the natural follow-up question. 'Just in case,' was the only reason Sefu had. It was one of his little ways, and the rest of us had grown used to finding swords in the kitchen, toilet, bathroom, stables and sheds.

I poked around in the stable, looking for one of Sefu's swords. I searched behind palettes of leaflets, tables and our printing machinery. While I did this, I tried to relax and let my thoughts about Cassie and what her death might mean for the rest of us bubble away quietly in my head.

I felt tension return to my chest, but not in sudden spikes like I was used to. It felt like an old friend opening the door with a key I'd lent him. I kept up my search, checking in on my unwelcome houseguest every once in a while.

Eventually, I found a 60cm black sword propped up against one of the walls. I moved it to the other side of the stable, putting it behind a pallet of leaflets, but I was careful to leave a little of the handle poking out so as not to make things too difficult for Sefu.

The man in question was still smoking on the landing when I emerged from the stables. He shot me a questioning look through the window. My replying look was much more mischievous. He rolled his eyes and smiled back. Someone was about to spend five to fifteen minutes searching for a sword. I'd essentially just given him a quest.

I climbed the stairs up to the house's landing. Sefu finished his cigarette and slipped the butt into the jar. "Any clues for me?" he asked.

"It's an easy one today."

Sefu looked contemplative. I stepped aside and he strode down the stairs, humming to himself.

I giggled, surprising myself, then turned to my right and walked down a short corridor, past another window that looked out over the farm to the north. At the end of the corridor was the first of the house's bedrooms, the one that had belonged to Cassie. I turned right again once I reached that door. Ahead of me stretched a corridor. At the end, I could just see Liam emerging from the communal area at the far end. This was fortunate, as one of the letters was for him.

"Liam!" I called, but softly. The walls in the house were very thin and it didn't do to yell anything too loudly in case you annoyed someone. He saw me and strode to meet me. Liam was a thin, tattooed white man in his 30s. He kept his hair and beard well-trimmed nowadays, but he'd been an enthusiastic punk as a teen, and that ebullient spirit had never died. He was the tallest of our little group, and we're a tall bunch. Mostly. Mel and I are definitely on the shorter side.

"What's up?" he said, once he reached me. I handed him his letter, and he made a face when he saw the hand-addressed envelope. "One second..." he said. He opened the envelope and glanced at the single sheet of A4 inside. He inhaled sharply. "Thought so. Listen, Phoebe, there might be some drama incoming. You know how some of us have things in our pasts we're not exactly proud of? Someone might be raking stuff up."

"Can I do anything to help?"

He grimaced. "Nah. It's all ancient history, and I hope you know me well enough to know you're safe around me and everyone else who lives here, right?"

"Right."

"Some old stuff might be about to bubble to the surface like an unwanted fart."

"Really? Why?"

Liam waved his letter absently, then shrugged. "Never

mind, sorry. I've got to go see to some things." He shrugged and brushed past me. I heard him descending the stairs out of the house.

This left me alone in the corridor, outside Paula's room. The parcel was addressed to her, so I knocked on her door. It took a little while for her to answer, possibly because she was napping. She hadn't been sleeping well recently, what with the stress of our actions and the referendum.

The door opened and a bleary-eyed Paula stood there. She was an elegant woman with a long face, slightly taller than average, with hair that was moving from black to silver. She blinked at me.

"Post for you, Paula," I said. "Sorry to wake you."

She held out her hand wordlessly. I handed over the jiffy bag and she glanced at it. A look of hatred shot across her face. I'd only ever seen this look when she was confronting neo-Nazis. The expression was only there for a second. She looked up at me, and smiled in a way that was probably supposed to put me at my ease. "Thank you!" she said, before turning on her heel and shutting the door behind her.

Oh-kaaay. Was I just delivering evil mail today? I looked down at the last letter. It was addressed to me. I opened it and found I had been pre-selected for a new type of credit card. That settled it. It was definitely an evil mail day.

I slipped into my room and changed out of my funeral clothes. My room was my own little sanctuary. A lovely dark blue carpet lined the floor and, while the walls were painted a disappointing pale-yellow colour, I had decorated with Christmas lights and film posters. I rummaged through my wardrobe and selected a pinstripe suit with a red lining, and trousers with actual, honest-to-goodness pockets. I finished the ensemble with slipper socks because I was feeling fancy. I stepped out of my room and nearly ran into Katie, who was thundering down the corridor.

Katie was superficially like any other seven-year-old girl. Her mundane exterior disguised an angel whose existence would be proof of the divine in the face of all but the most devout atheist. She hugged me as soon as she saw me, because she liked to regularly demonstrate how adorable she was. Also, she knew I found her cute, and she could manipulate me into giving her chocolate.

I looked down at Katie. Her smile reminded me of Cassie's. Cassie... She'd been caught in a fight. Could Katie get caught up in something like that? What about Mel? Sefu?

Was Cassie just the first?

"Auntie Phoebe, are you crying?" Katie asked.

"No, no, sorry love. Have you done your homework?"

"Yes! I'm getting a biscuit."

"Good girl. Off you go then."

"Okay!"

Katie scampered around me, and I was left alone in the corridor. Alone, just like I would be when all my other friends were dead.

I closed my eyes and concentrated on my breathing. I needed to focus on something that wasn't death... No. Mel was right. That was the wrong way to look at it. It probably wasn't surprising that I'd been unable to escape thoughts of death since what had happened to Cassie. Maybe I needed to accept what I was feeling, but try to turn the feelings I couldn't shake into something useful. The Terror Python had been a companion to me for many years. I wondered if it could be a tool as well.

There was one thing that would let me continue thinking about my lost friend, but also keep me busy, not losing myself in despair curled up in bed. There was one task that I could throw myself into, all whilst not shutting the pain out.

I was going to find out. I was going to find out what happened to Cassie.

× Chapter Five

Cassie had died in a fight in a pub. On the face of it, her death appeared totally random – so was there any way I could find out if it was actually random, or if there was something lurking in the background that hinted at darker motives? Her room might contain some hint or other but the police had probably removed everything useful. A more likely source of information was our lawyer, Eryl Iwan Jr. She'd been following up with the police to see what progress had been made, and if any legal action could be taken.

I returned to my room and rooted out my phone. I didn't have Eryl's number stored in there, so I dug a bust card out of a drawer.

A bust card is an essential tool for activists. It lists your rights in case you get arrested, what you should say and what you shouldn't, things that might expedite your release, and, most crucially in this case, the phone number for Iwan and Iwan Associates.

I dialled the number and a crisp, professional voice answered. "Iwan and Iwan Associates. This is Jane speaking. How may I help you?"

"Jane, hi, it's Phoebe Green. Is Eryl Jr available?"

"I'm not sure if she's in, let me just see," Jane lied smoothly. She put me on hold. I started aggressively humming over the music to block it out.

Abruptly the music stopped. "What do you want, Phoebe?" Eryl Jr said.

"Ms Iwan! Sorry to bother you. I wondered if there had been any movement regarding Cassie's case? I'm wondering if there's anything I can do to help."

"Oh, that. Well, Phoebe, I won't lie to you on this one occasion. It's not going well. The police have questioned a lot of the usual people that they go to when something like this happens, but the investigation seems to have stalled. They have people working through the items they confiscated from young Cassandra's room, but otherwise they seem to be taking *Expecta Patienter Et Spera Ut Aliquis Vertat Se Ad Repente Confidendum*."

"I don't speak Latin, Ms Iwan."

"The 'Sit Tight and Hope Someone Randomly Decides to Confess' approach."

"Lawyers are weird," I muttered under my breath.

"There's not a whole lot I can do, you understand. I can get Granny to try talking to some of her friends higher up the chain, if you think it's worth it?"

"Do you think it's worth it?"

Eryl sighed down the phone. "Phoebe, in your interview just after you were arrested, you mentioned Patriots Unite had graffitied your wall."

"That's right."

"Did anything like that happen before the referendum?"

"No."

"Would it surprise you to learn that I've heard colleagues of mine report similar problems – vandalism, destruction of property, assault and now murder – and the police seem strangely hesitant to investigate the issues as soon as they learn Patriots Unite might be involved?"

"Honestly, I don't know. The police are just tools of their bosses, and their bosses are political appointments. I bet they'd be willing to look the other way about some right-wing thugs spray painting Telegraph headlines on our walls, but I don't think that would stretch to murder... would it?"

"Possibly not. We live in interesting times however, Ms Green. We both know, for example, that had a group with hard-line Islamic ideology committed exactly the same acts that Patriots Unite had, they would have been arrested, charged and tried by a secret court within a few days. In this instance, there may be something more sinister afoot. I noted, for example, that one of the investigating officers into Cassandra's case was Anthony Thompson."

"I don't know that one."

"There's no reason why you should. The only reason I bring him up is he was in the same school, in the same year and in a lot of the same classes as Edmund Tilbury-Minkton."

"Who?"

"Edmund currently goes by the name of Winston Stuart."

"No way!" Winston Stuart was the founder of Patriots Unite.

"Yes, in fact, way. So you see, this might all be nothing, or there might be something extremely fishy going on. It's hard to tell, and without anyone inside the investigation ready to blow the whistle, I doubt we'll be able to find out for certain one way or another. You know what, I think I will get Granny to have a word with one of her friends. I was teetering on the brink of doing so anyway when you called. Thank you. I'm sorry I snapped at you earlier, and I'm sorry I told Jane you were a time-wasting martyr with a tiresome sense of humour."

"Don't mention it."

"Good, I won't. Ever again. I'll be in touch."

Eryl hung up and I stared at my phone. I supposed we could be on to something. Or we could be on to nothing. Not for the first time, I found myself more confused after speaking to Eryl than I had been beforehand. Well, maybe there really was a point to my working through Cassandra's belongings. I might find something that would help.

I grabbed a cardboard box from my wardrobe, turned the DVDs out of it and set off for Cassie's room. I found Mel in the corridor; she had her hand on the handle of her door, but paused when she heard me emerge.

"Phoebe!" she said. "Hi, sorry I didn't get to talk to you more earlier. How was the funeral?"

"Better than I expected. Vince made a lot of new friends. I lurked in the shadows. I feel a bit better for going. Thank you for – wait. You said it was a bad idea. Never mind. You were wrong, I was right, I want a mark in my column please."

Mel picked up an imaginary piece of chalk and drew a neat check mark in the right-hand column of an imaginary chalkboard.

"Thank you. Anyway, I was going to gather up Cassie's stuff so we could return it to her mum. Or at least, ask her if she wants us to do anything with it, you know? How would you feel about helping me?"

Mel looked at her watch. "I've got to feed Katie in a bit, and I'm going to work in..." she paused and glanced up at me. Her expression softened. "Yes, I've got time. You want my help?"

"I'd appreciate your help. I'm sure I'd be fine if you don't have time. You don't have to."

She smiled at this. "No, it's fine. Many hands, light work, not enough cooks, not enough broth to go around, all that stuff. Come on, let's go. We need a box – oh, you've got a box. Well done."

Mel set off down the corridor towards Cassie's room. I followed.

My sister is four years older than me (twenty eight to my twenty four), as well as four inches shorter, which means she's four times cuter than I am. I wouldn't be surprised to learn she has 4% less body fat than I do, and her IQ is higher than mine by a factor of four – no, wait. That would mean it's impossibly high. Forget the IQ thing. My point is, for most of our formative years, I always saw Mel as someone to aspire to be. She was stronger than me, faster than me, smarter than me (although I was always the snappier dresser) and much funnier. It was no surprise that she attracted a lot of attention when she reached the age of sixteen.

This interest culminated in a night with Mel and a chap whose name was Tim or Tom or something. That was where Katie's story started. Thus, I was the golden child for six years. I went to a good university, read Philosophy and found myself at the end of my studies with a choice to make: do I return home, strike out on my own or take the third way?

I think I surprised everyone – myself included – by not returning to my parents' seven-bedroom house in Solihull. Instead, I visited Mel at the farm. I only meant to stay for a week, but I went along to a few actions and a week turned into a month, then three months. Three years later, I was still here.

Mel opened the door to Cassie's room and stepped inside, holding the door open for me to follow. I hadn't been into this room since Cassie's death, and I was shocked by the state of it.

Cassie hadn't been a neat person. She was always leaving glue and weirdly shaped bits of plastic around the place. Two shelves in her bookshelf were usually filled with green, angry-looking plastic orks. Her small desk was usually covered in modelling tools, books, random bits of paper or, more usually, a mix of all three. The police had taken this wonderful jumble of chaos and added their own unique spin.

Books lay in heaps on the floor, categorised by some system I could only guess at. Most of her papers were gone, as was her outdated computer. Her soft toys were still here, as were some of her orks. Her clothes had been removed from her wardrobe and piled onto the bed.

Without saying a word, Melissa started folding Cassie's clothing and loading it into my box. I felt a burst of something in my head – it might have been a snatch of a song that repeated and repeated until it started to spread and expand until I was losing who I was, losing myself in the thrashing, churning noise. My hands were shaking. Melissa had her back to me. She was working away. I needed to be more like her. I found a pen and paper and, being sure to not let my hands shake, I started noting down the titles and authors of Cassie's books.

I'd send the information across to Cassie's mum to see if she wanted them. I wrote down *Eye of Terror*. I wrote down *First and Only* and *Ghostmaker*. I wrote down *Inquisitor, Harlequin* and *Ghost Child*.

I felt Mel's hand on my shoulder. "How's it going, bab?"

I wiped the tears from my cheeks. "Cassie was such an unapologetic Goth."

"Do you need to take a break?"

I looked at the book in my hands. The title was *The Guns of Tanith.* I held it up. "Do you think Tanith is a person or a planet?"

Mel peered at the cover. "What I think is: why is title is about some guns when clearly the important thing is what's going on with that person's unbelievably pointy hat?"

I cackled and noted the title down on my list.

"Do you think Mum and Dad would want our stuff if what happened to Cassie happened to us?"

Mel blew a strand of hair out of her eye. "Hm. Probably not. They'd probably be appalled if Paula handed them a box containing everything one of us owned. Your DVDs and comics. My lesson plans, marking and French textbooks."

Noise sparked into my head – it felt like I was filling up with static. My thinking was fuzzy and I was having trouble concentrating, but I also felt it pinching at the nerves in my fingers and forearms. I tried to focus on Mel's face.

"We both have climbing gear," I pointed out. "They might approve of that."

"Hm," Melissa said again. Her back was towards me, and she sounded casual in a way that I knew was carefully calculated. "Are you worried we're going to go the way of Cassie?"

Had she asked me this just after Katie hugged me, I might have tried to lie. As it was, I was suspicious. I had a feeling that Melissa was trying to sound like Mel. My serious and stoic sister was trying to sound like the person I loved.

The terror python should have started thrashing about

when Melissa asked that question. Instead I felt... strange. Like I was in the calm space between the cops and the demonstration. The inhalation of breath. The moment of hope where everyone believes that our action might change the minds of those in power. "Yes," I said, "a bit. That's why I'm doing this – I want to take the noise in my head and point it in a useful direction. I'm also going to look into the circumstances behind Cassie's death."

Mel swivelled around to face me. She looked thoughtful. "What an interesting approach," she said. "It could well work... or it could make things worse. Would you be okay with talking to someone if you feel yourself getting worse? It doesn't have to be me; it could be Sefu or anyone really."

I shrugged. "Sure, but I honestly feel better for doing this already. I feel like I've got something that I can get my teeth into. You know, I love our actions but after doing so many and seeing no change of direction from Westminster, it can start to feel a bit futile, you know?"

"I know," Mel agreed. "Tell you what, if you want to get your teeth into something, try this: the demo at the train station? Do you remember a group there from Stop the War?"

"From Liverpool?"

"Yes. I know a couple of them, we've done a few bits of organising together. Anyway, one of them, her name's Ifza, said she recognised Vince."

"Okay," I said. I narrowed my eyes and waited to hear what was so remarkable about that. Everyone knew Vince. Even if they'd seen him from a distance, they'd remember him. Meanwhile, I can get up close and personal, and people struggle to recall me.

"Nothing special about that, I know. Vince knows a lot

of people. Still, Vince didn't seem keen on talking to Stop the War, and when I asked him about Ifza directly, he said he didn't know her."

"So Ifza's wrong."

"She's sure she isn't."

I shrugged. "Sure. Ifza probably threw a drink on him when he was being annoying at some party or something."

"Yeah. I just…" She trailed off.

"You just want to know whatever it is your partner doesn't want to talk about, without coming over as prying, so you're going to outsource it to me instead, and let me take the flak."

"No! Not entirely, anyway. I'm going to have a chat to him when he gets back from his work. But if you do happen to learn anything, I'd be grateful. I'm worried about him, you know." Her gaze darted around the room.

My immediate reaction was that I didn't have time for this… but Mel was hurting and I had a chance to make things hurt less. I gave her a reassuring smile and nodded. We went back to work.

Mel finished folding Cassie's clothes away and I stacked the books neatly before collecting everything else that still needed packing. Twenty minutes later, we were more or less finished when we heard footsteps outside the room, and the sound of Vince talking to Liam.

Mel and I shared a glance. It was around four in the afternoon. It was a bit early for Vince to be back from his landscaping gig. Mel shrugged and slipped out of the room. I heard her ask Vince why he was back, and he said the work had to be delayed until tomorrow.

Their chat dropped below my hearing as I poked about the room, seeing if there was anything I'd missed. I got down on my hands and knees and peered under the bed. Besides dust bunnies the size of orks, not a lot there. I was pretty sure I'd gotten everything when I spied the tip of a piece of paper sticking out from underneath the wardrobe. I tugged at it gently, having too little of a grip and not wanting to tear it. It didn't move.

I stood up and rocked the wardrobe to get it to move. Now that it was empty, it was easier to shift backwards and to the side. Easier, certainly but still not easy. I rammed my shoulder into it and my feet scrabbled against the floor. I heaved and with a grunt of effort, I managed to expose more of the paper. I bent down and snatched up a printed A4 sheet.

The paper contained a sheet of a single name and list of addresses. It was clearly output from some database or other, possibly from the internet. There was no printer in Cassie's room, so she'd probably done it at the library. The addresses were all different but the name, repeated over and over again, was Richard Lampart.

Who on earth was Richard Lampart and what had Cassie wanted with him?

Mel came back into the room, looking exasperated. "Vince totally shut me down about Stop the War," she said. "So I twisted his arm into coming to Xia's climbing trip tomorrow. Katie's really excited about it, so I have to be there. If you come too, you can take the chance to pump him for information."

A spark of jealousy flared within me. "Why wasn't I invited climbing earlier?"

Mel rolled her eyes. "You were. Xia asked you ten days ago. You mumbled something about work and stumbled off. I think she was a bit annoyed off at you. Anyway, the climbing is before his landscaping gig, and I already told him I was worried about you and wanted him to have a word, so now you have to come."

I sighed. I hadn't been climbing in quite a while and had no real desire to get back into it. Then I had a thought. "The pub where Cassie died is near the climbing centre, isn't it?"

"Practically round the corner."

"Fine. I'll come and see if I can find anything out. It'll give me the chance to drop in at that pub afterwards and ask a few questions." I paused. "I'll even pretend to be appreciative of Vince's gleaming pearls of wisdom. But you owe me, and more so if I actually get the dirt for you."

Mel thanked me and checked her watch. "Gotta run," she said. "Work beckons. Thanks again, little muffin." She smiled warmly and left the room. I put the last of Cassie's items into the box and slipped it into the wardrobe. I thought about calling Cassie's mum then and there but reasoned the afternoon after the funeral would be a terrible time to reach out.

I took in the rest of the room. I thought something, and then had an urge to say it aloud.

"I'll find who did this to you, Cassie."

Speech by Deborah Frances-White on *The Guilty Feminist Radio Show*, Episode titled Anger, broadcast on Radio 4, 4th July 2003:

I am angry about the invasion of Iraq. I am angry that entitled, smug, privileged, powerful men got in a big red bus and told poor people lies so that they could have even more entitled, smug, privileged power even though they knew it would cause poor people in a country far away to die so that we could take their oil.

I am angry at those men. I am angry at myself, that I was complacent. That I knew that the inequality in wealth and property and opportunity was getting worse and that this was making people scared. Scared of another terrorist attack. Scared of WMD. And I didn't do anything about it.

I am angry at myself that in truth my own immediate and fearful reaction is 'what does this mean for me?' What if some poor desperate people decide to take revenge for the invasion and bring terrorism to British shores? Will there still be fun and high paid work for me in Europe, knowing that my country chose to do this?

I am angry that most of my middle-class friends are angry with the poor disenfranchised people who were told lies. I am angry that British citizens and residents are being shouted at on buses because they look and sound different.

I am angry that racism and fear of human beings who are from somewhere else is the outlet for those who have been fed on a diet of Rupert Murdoch's poison for too long.

I am angry at Rupert Murdoch who knew he would have more influence on Number 10 Downing Street if the UK was isolated by this war, and so incited racial hatred in his tabloids to split us up.

I am angry that today I watched the president of the European Commission in the European Parliament shout at Labour MEP Glenys Kinnock 'Why are you here? Why are you not waiting for a UN resolution? Why are you so determined to go to war?' in exactly the same way people are shouting at women in headscarves at British bus stops. I am angry not because the president was shouting at Kinnock, but because it was virtually the first time in my life I felt unwelcome somewhere because of my nationality. It made me realise I may not be welcome in Europe for a while because of my accent.

I am angry that it has taken feeling like this for us to do more than write letters to The Guardian. I am angry that most of us will just continue to write letters to The Guardian.

I am angry that there is not more room for women in our society. That diversity of thought and emotional intelligence in bio-chemistry is not deemed necessary or in some cases even desirable because women are deemed an unknown quantity in leadership... and that we continue to trust straight white men with almost all of the difficult decisions and influence even though they have shown us time and time again that as a homogenised, unsupervised group they make terrible, unsustainable decisions which tank the economy and the environment and everything for everyone.

I am angry.

I am angry.

And if I feel this anger and bring it out into the light maybe I can turn it into action and hope and power.

Chapter Six

I was clinging to a wall, and it wasn't even nine a.m. My fingers ached and my feet were screaming at me. Around my waist, a harness cut into my flesh. I had apparently put on a little weight since I'd last gone climbing. A rope ran from a knot at the front of the harness, level with my belly button, up to the top of the wall and then back down again to where Xia was gripping the other end in a piece of safety equipment called a belay device.

The drive to the climbing centre had been tiresome. Vince obviously had not been in a climbing mood, but he'd dutifully come along. Somehow, despite him taking his car so he could go on to his gig, and Mel taking hers because I was going to investigate afterwards, I was the one who ended up with Xia as a passenger.

I liked Xia, I really did. She was a fantastic friend to have in your corner, and she was absolutely fearless. But she'd been relentless since the start of the referendum campaign. When I'd first gone to live with her, Paula, Sefu and Mel, she'd been more relaxed. We spent most of our time printing leaflets and banners for marches while Sefu and Mel tried to place interviews with local news to further the cause. The referendum had awakened something in Xia that couldn't have been seen since Desert Storm.

"I know you're sad and tired, Phoebe," she'd said, as I'd manoeuvred towards a parking space. "But our mistakes aren't tribal anymore. When we mess up, it's not one small group of people who'll suffer. For the first time, our conflicts put the whole planet at risk. Everyone and everything you love, evaporated in an instant. We've been handed the spoils that colonialism stole from the less fortunate. We have power – they don't. We're the front line. If we falter, there's no one left to change things."

I'd mumbled an agreement and turned off the engine. I agreed with Xia. The problem was that I had two imperatives: stopping a war for the good of everyone, and finding out what happened to Cassie. I also had to hold myself together until I'd completed these goals. So make that three imperatives. My problem – the real problem – was I wasn't sure I could focus my attention on all three of those goals. I'd chosen to focus on the reason I'd come out today – to interrogate Vince. I tried to chat with him as we paid our entry fees. He was open and charming as usual. My attempts to uncover anything sinister in his past seemed ridiculous.

I hadn't been in the climbing centre for maybe three months, and I'd forgot just how alive the place made me feel. It smelled of chalk and sweat – jagged slashes of paint charged across the walls, punctuated by luridly coloured plastic handholds. The floor was lined with thick black matting, which bounced under climbers' shoes. The dark floor could have muted the effect of the colourful walls a little, but instead it seemed to emphasise them. It gave the ground a reassuring feeling – solid, yes, and not something to fall onto from a great height, but a cushion between us and concrete.

The plastic rocks I was clinging to scraped at my fingers. It felt like I was clutching at fine sandpaper. This felt unpleasant, but it meant that I had a great grip on the wall.

The harder routes in the centre had much smoother rocks – holds that hands and feet could easily slip off without the strongest grip and perfect technique.

Below me, Vince had joined Xia, and they were doing their best to intrude on my glorious little moment. They stood shoulder to shoulder as their conversation floated up to me, borne on an ill wind.

"Paula was saying we should have a meeting about what to do next," Xia said. "I'm going to recommend we fold our group into Stop the War. Our purpose was to fight the referendum and we lost that one, but we can still help."

"I don't know," Vince said. "Stop the War already has a lot of resources and they were slow to move. A quick responsive organisation like ours, prepared for direct action, is needed."

I tried to tune them out. I tried to focus on the holds on the wall. My hands were sweating, and the holds at this point in the route were small and technical. I paused and rested my hands.

"I think we should focus on actions where we can really make a difference, rather than focusing on the war." Vince was still talking. "There are still causes that need us. I know it's not why this group was formed, but I saw one of the big department stores in town was selling fur coats. That's something we can stop here and now."

"That's a great idea. Plan an action to deal with the fur coats, and I'll support it, but I'm not taking my eyes off this war."

"People voted for the war, Xia."

"People voted for Thatcher. People voted for Bush."

"Most of them didn't vote for Bush. And Thatcher didn't always get a majority."

Xia sighed at him. "If 52% of our country voted for us to drink poison, it wouldn't be the right thing to do. There is no excuse."

"That would never happen."

"Vince, it just happened."

The conversation was threatening to bring my mood crashing back to earth. I could have put a stop to it, entertainingly enough, by crashing back to earth, albeit in a safe and secure manner. I concentrated on the route ahead of me instead, springing my left foot up onto a tiny hold and using it to propel my body upwards. I slipped my right hand off a tiny hold and shot it upwards towards the next plastic rock. I was worried that I would fall short, and then fall as far as the rope at my waist would allow, but my hand grasped the hold easily. My weight tugged at my grip, but it held. I found a new foothold for my left foot, stood up onto it and reached up with my left hand. I tapped the pulley at the top of the route, the one which my safety rope ran through. It made a cheerful clanking sound, which got Xia and Vince to stop bickering about The Topic. I waved at Xia, who grinned at me and started lowering me to the ground.

I untied the rope from my harness as soon as I landed and, not wanting Xia and Vince to get started on The Topic again, I said the first thing that came into my head. "So, Xia, you want to get us to join Stop the War?"

She beamed at me. "See, I knew you got it. Yes, but not necessarily Stop the War. I've been talking to various groups, including some people that Melissa's friend, Ifza, has put us in contact with."

"Oh?" Vince took the rope from me and started tying himself in.

Sadness flickered across Xia's face and was gone. "I haven't got that far with it. Planning things since Cassie... you know. Several of us have been a bit overwhelmed. But she knew what was at stake. It's vital we don't slow down, particularly now. I've been reaching out as much as I can, but I could really use help. This is such an important time. Lots of people are preparing actions every day, and they all need help."

Vince's eyes lit up. "Yeah?"

Xia looked around cautiously. "The American B-52s have landed back at RAF Fairford. A bunch of people are going to travel down there and sabotage them. We can stop some of the bombing. We could use you."

"That's hard core," I said.

"Yes, but these are literal flying death machines that are going to be used to commit absolute carnage, and we have a chance to actually do something about it. It will do actual, definite, measurable good. We'll be saving lives. It's something we have to do."

"It's something that might get us actual, definite, measurable prison time," I said.

"I'd rather be in prison than have my whole world obliterated by flying death machines."

"Fair point."

Vince gave Xia a grim nod and started his climb up the wall. As she braced the rope to belay him, I wandered over to the café, where Mel was sipping at a mug, watching Katie spider around on the children's wall.

I sat down next to her and watched the spider-angel for a moment. "Vince and I had a bit of heart-to-heart before my climb, but I didn't manage to steer the conversation anywhere useful. Later, Xia actually mentioned Ifza for me afterwards.

Not a flicker. Sorry."

Mel shrugged. "It was worth a try. Thanks."

"So what's your plan now?" I asked.

"I asked him flat-out about what Ifza said again, a few minutes ago," Mel said. "He said he had no idea what she was talking about. I think I believe him, but... I don't know, I've got this bad feeling and, even though he's being perfectly normal and reasonable, I can't help thinking that there's something off. Maybe I'm just all twisted up by what happened with Cassie and it's coming out this way. I'm turning on Vince."

"Seems like you should have some me time instead."

"I will. But first, I'm going to follow him when we leave the climbing centre."

"You're following him to *work* because he might know someone from *Liverpool*? That doesn't strike you as an overreaction?"

Her eyes narrowed, and her voice crisped up. "He said his project was just near here. The Jewellery Quarter isn't exactly known for lavish gardens. Can you think of anywhere around here that could require a landscape artist?"

I searched my memory.

"It's all flats," Melissa said firmly. "There's something else going on. I think he might be having an affair."

"No! Really? Vince?"

"If this was the 1950s, Phoebe, I'd hire a private investigator. Instead, I'll have to settle for some sleuthing of my own. I will get to the bottom of this."

"Wait a sec, Mel. First the problem was that he couldn't remember someone from Liverpool. Now the problem's that he's got a landscaping project in the wrong part of town."

Mel fixed her eyes on me. I stared back. I took her unspoken point on board. I was hardly the model of reasonableness myself, fixating on the answers to impossible questions. Mel was obsessing over Vince's not-very-weird behaviour. "Trying to understand Cassie's death feels less bad than lying in my bed feeling like I'm being slowly crushed by everything around me."

Mel rested her head on my shoulder. "I'm glad you've found something that helps you," she said. "Just be braced for failure, that's all. It might well be impossible to work out what happened to poor Cassie."

"I know, it's just… What do you think our parents would say if they knew I was investigating Cassie's death?"

"Putting yourself in danger to try to get justice for a working-class teenager from a single-parent family? I imagine they'd be pretty furious."

"Right. I'm using that as motivation for when I worry I won't be able to work out what happened."

"If you want, I can go and tell them, and try to get a picture of their faces for you to put on your wall."

"Please don't, you might give one of them a heart attack." I grinned and strolled back over to Vince and Xia.

Twenty minutes later, my hands ached and my feet were objecting strongly to being squeezed into climbing shoes. Xia was meeting up with someone from another group soon, and Vince was due at his landscaping gig, so we decided to call it a day. I gave Katie and Mel long hugs as we were leaving. I whispered, "Good luck" to my sister, and then she was gone, along with her possibly-unfaithful-but-probably-not partner.

I found The Jeweller's Sword free house – 'IPA our speciality' – on the corner of one road occupied by massive decaying megaliths that had once been factories, and another that was occupied almost exclusively by gravel parking lots. I parked in one of these and attached the lock to my steering wheel before getting out.

It was just after ten on a Saturday, and the pub was already open. I went inside and found a pretty typical English pub. Dark wood and burgundy carpets failed to hide stains and decay. Several fossils were slowly making their way through pints in the darkest corners they could find. Taps of Stella, Carling and Carlsberg occupied the ignominious end of the bar, while pumps containing beers named by people who could never get enough puns occupied the rest.

There were two people working the bar, a crusty man who probably owned the joint, and a young woman who couldn't have been much older than Cassie had been. I'd have to ask my questions quickly, before the staff got so busy they'd have no time for me. I approached the barmaid and asked for an interesting beer and a packet of crisps. When she returned with my prizes, I did my best to subtly engage her in conversation.

"Hi," I said. A strong start. They don't call me a conversational genius for nothing.

"Do you want something else?" There was a hint of Eastern Europe in her accent.

"Yes, actually. I wondered if you were here when the woman was killed a couple of weeks ago." The words clattered out of my mouth like marbles.

She stiffened and drew her arms up, folding them across her chest. "Why?"

"Why what?"

"Why do you want to know? I talked to the police. I am not going to tell just anyone who wanders in."

"The girl who died, Cassie, was my friend."

"I have already told everything to the police."

"The police are stalling. Our lawyer is trying to find out why, but in the meantime, I'd appreciate it if I could ask you some questions."

She rocked slightly from the balls of her feet to her heels and back. Her jaw tightened and jutted forward. Then she strode to the crusty man leaning on the bar, and had a whispered conversation with him. The man glanced up at me, and I nodded politely to him.

The barmaid returned and smiled grimly at me. "What do you want to know?"

"What's your name?"

"Izabella."

"Hi, Izabella, I'm Phoebe. Was Cassie here with anyone?"

"No. She came in looking tired. I pulled her a pint of Tempting Badger. She stood at the bar to drink it. It was quiet so she chatted to me. She said she'd been at a protest and came in for a celebratory drink. She said she came in on a whim."

"The police told me there was a fight. Did she start it?"

Izabella shook her head. "It was not a fight. I *told* them. I..." Her voice tightened. "Four men came in and attacked her."

I took a step back. "They just walked through the door and started attacking her? They didn't, I don't know, say something first?"

"One moment I am talking to her about the referendum and some people with green skin, the next some thug is hitting her, and his mates are closing in on either side."

"What did you do?"

"I hid under the bar and called the police."

"Thank you. Did anyone try to help Cassie?"

Izabella shook her head, unhappy. "Who? It was just me and a few old men, and there were four of them, big men."

"What did they look like?"

Izabella shrugged.

"What were they wearing?"

Izabella looked up at the ceiling and chewed her lip. "I don't remember. Nothing jumped out at me. T-shirts mostly, I think. One wore a white shirt. They had short hair. One was bald."

"Any tattoos? Distinguishing features?"

Izabella shook her head.

"Once they were finished, what did they do?"

"They left."

"Just like that? They came in, they attacked Cassie, they left. They didn't say anything at all?"

She sighed heavily. "That's right."

"That doesn't sound like a fight. It sounds like a hit."

"So," she said, not looking at me. I saw wetness at the corners of her eyes. "Do you have any more questions? I would like to get back to work."

I didn't have any way of adequately thanking her, other than to get out of her pub as quickly as possible and with a minimum of fuss. "No," I said. "Thank you for helping me. I really appreciate it."

Izabella swiped a cloth across the bar without looking at me. I took my crisps, and left the pub and my untouched pint. I don't know exactly what I had expected from talking to her. Maybe a few more pieces of a puzzle, maybe proof that the attack on Cassie had been random. I hadn't been expecting confirmation of a targeted attack.

Interview with Sarah Prendeghast in June 2004:

Sarah Prendeghast: Blair, Campbell, Blunket, Prescott, they all made promises in the run up to the referendum and didn't keep any of them. That's your fault.

Interviewer: How is that our fault?

Sarah Prendeghast: Think back to 1997 – Tony Blair promised a referendum on the voting system. He didn't keep his promise. So every time you interviewed him for the referendum you could have said, "Mr Blair, you promised the nation voting reform. You broke that promise. Why should anyone trust what you say now?"

Interviewer: All politicians make promises they don't go on to keep.

Sarah Prendeghast: I'm sorry, could you say that again? I don't think I heard you correctly.

Interviewer: Politicians not sticking to their manifesto promises is not a new thing.

Sarah Prendeghast: Do you hear what you're saying? "Politicians have lied to the nation about what they'll do in the past so we should expect them to not keep their promises"? This is your job! We don't have access to the people in power. You do. Every time you talk about Tony Blair and don't remind the public that he broke the promises he made to the nation, you're failing us.

Interviewer: We have impartiality guidelines to consider.

Sarah Prendeghast: Tony Blair breaks promises is a statement of fact. It sounds partisan but unless you can say something that's fundamentally true, and crucial, you act as if lies don't matter. If you don't call this stuff out, you say to these people that they can say and do whatever they want to get elected, or win a referendum, and what they then do once they've won power doesn't matter. For decades, now, politicians have treated the public with contempt, and that's because you refuse to consistently hold their lies and broken promises to account. You need to remind the public that they lied and broke their promises every time you talk about them. "Tony Blair, who lied to the nation about reforming the voting system and the house of lords in order to get elected, opened a new shopping centre today". If you did that every single time, they'd start taking their promises to the people much more seriously.

× Chapter Seven

I tried to pay attention to the road as I drove back to the farm, but the image of Cassie being beaten to death kept invading. The men must have come to the pub specifically to attack her. So, they'd known she was in that pub, but how had they known that ahead of time? She hadn't told us she was planning to go anywhere after the protest. My mind bounced around trying to make sense of it all. It was the only way to keep the horror at bay.

It didn't sound like Cassie had been there to meet anyone. Maybe she'd just wanted to get some distance from the protest, so she couldn't be identified as an activist by Patriots Unite – or a dozen other groups like them. These groups have a history of attacking lone activists. A couple of years ago, one group caught the head of the local trade union by herself after a protest, and put her in hospital.

The men came to attack her specifically. Maybe they'd intended to murder her, and it had been an actual assassination. Or maybe they'd just gone too far. Hard to say. But why her? Why, very specifically, Cassie? She'd been sweet.

Once I found out the answer to that question, all the other answers would probably slip into place. I parked my Almera in its usual spot and saw Sefu emerging from the house. He looked worried – his face usually had a small smile or stayed carefully neutral if he was engaging in a debate. Now, he was frowning. His expression cleared as he saw me.

"Hi Phoebe! Did you see anyone as you came in?"

I shrugged. "Nope."

"Hm. I heard an engine and looked out over the courtyard, but didn't see anyone pulling in. Then I thought I saw someone by the sheds past the wall, but I wasn't certain. After the last few days..." His voice trailed off. "You sure you didn't see anyone?"

I pulled at my earlobe. "I mean, I wasn't fully concentrating on the drive. At points, there could probably have been a military band marching past on the other side of the road, and I wouldn't have noticed."

"Lost in something, were you?" Sefu grinned.

I liked this particular grin. Sefu had a range of grins and used them like punctuation. Some of them, like this one, made me feel warm and safe whenever I saw them. Others, I didn't like to think about too much because I couldn't be sure if they were genuine or something Sefu was doing specifically to put me at ease around him.

"I was thinking about things," I admitted.

"In that case, I might have a bit of a poke about the farm, just in case someone's messing about."

"May I accompany you on your search for miscreants? I could go and get snacks..."

"Great! Two heads are better than one, snacks are better than no snacks and, most of the time, one Phoebe is better than no Phoebes."

I chuckled and scampered into the house. I found a bag of nuts and raisins in the communal snack cupboard, and returned to Sefu's side, proudly bearing my bounty aloft. "Did you find your sword, by the way?" I asked, as we turned right out of the entrance to the courtyard and followed the track that led towards the outbuildings to the north.

"Yeah. You weren't particularly devious with that one."

"I felt you wouldn't appreciate anything particularly complex."

Our shoes crunched on the gravel track that led up to the barns, where Sefu had thought he'd seen someone. In the near distance, a rumble obliterated the crunching for a few seconds. I looked up at clouds that had long passed angry and were well on their way to furious. "We'd better get a move on," I said. "Looks like a storm's coming."

We picked up our pace, passing the snack bag back and forth as we power-walked. I cast my gaze across the overgrown fields and out-of-control bramble patches in the distance to see if I could spot anyone lurking about.

"I don't see anybody," I said, as we approached one of the barns. This was one of the ones we didn't use, faded with age, with its door hanging open. Sefu stuck his head inside. I followed his lead. Rusting machinery lay here and there, and a few half-broken stalls lined the northwest wall. There were dozens of places to hide, but nothing seemed disturbed. The place looked like a tomb for a disorganised farmer.

"See anything?" I asked.

"I thought... No." Sefu shook his head. "I'm just on edge. Come on, let's check the other barn."

The door to the second barn was closed, which was slightly interesting. I hadn't been in this barn for a while, but I couldn't think of a reason for the door to be shut. Sefu and I swung it open together, although I admit that Sefu did most of the actual work. Inside, things looked much the same as the last barn, except for the motorbike.

The bike had seen better days. It looked like an old

Triumph, although I wasn't sure. Cars and bikes were only sporadically my kind of thing.

"Is this new?" Sefu asked.

"Definitely not."

It was extremely old, but well cared for. The chrome bodywork had been polished, and the leather seat had been patched multiple times.

"But I've never seen it before," I added.

"Maybe one of our people is restoring it?"

"Maybe. Stashing it out here does make some sense. It's not in the way, like it would be if it was in the sheds."

"Could someone else have driven it out here?" Sefu asked, looking around the barn.

"They could have done. I don't know why they would have..."

I checked the tyres, and they were clean. The roads to get here from the city are all tarmac so this didn't tell me much, but if they had been caked in mud we'd have known they were local. There were mud tracks all around the farm that led to old homesteads, forests and the like.

A crack of thunder sounded nearby. Rain started to patter on the roof. "We should go," Sefu said. "The rain is only going to get worse. We can ask at the house if the bike belongs to one of us."

Sefu stepped outside and I followed him. He held up a warning hand, but I had already stopped.

"Wait," he said.

And – "Over there!" I said.

We looked at each other, confused. He had been looking to the east. I had been looking west, back towards the first barn. The rain pattered down on us.

"What did you see?" I asked.

"People. I'm not sure how many. Two or three. They were heading towards the old silo by the ruined tractor sheds. What did you see?"

"Someone stuck their head out of the barn we were just in. They ducked back as soon as they saw me. I couldn't tell who it was."

The rain falling on our heads was quickly turning into a torrent. Lightning flashed, and a crash of thunder swept over us. I was freezing.

"Which one should we check out?"

"It's probably nothing," I said, "and they're inside and we're out here. Let's go back to the house and see if anyone knows about the bike."

I thought Sefu might be about to argue, but the rain increased in intensity by another couple of notches. He looked down at his soaked shirt and shivered. "Okay," he said. "Okay, let's go."

We ran back down the track towards the courtyard and, while we were completely soaked by the time we got inside, we didn't actually drown. We retired to our rooms to dry off. I changed my clothes, and emerged to find Sefu walking down the hallways, knocking on doors. No one answered except Katie, who had been in her room.

"Hi Katie," said Sefu. "What are you doing?"

"Playing The Sims," Katie replied. "I'm making Ethel the Vampire and Erica the Ballerina study science so they can invent laser guns."

"What will they do with the laser guns?"

Katie paused and stared up at the ceiling for a moment. "Nothing?" she suggested hopefully.

Not for the first time, I was regretting installing those Sims mods on Mel's computer. "We should worry about that later. Katie, is your mum back?

"No."

"Katie, do you know if anyone's in?" Sefu asked.

Katie shook her head.

"Okay, thanks," I said.

Katie turned on her heel and went back to planning the glorious revolution with lasers. I walked to Paula's door and was about to knock, loudly, when I heard an engine. Sefu heard the same thing and joined me as I walked to the window that looked out over the courtyard.

Vince was pulling up in his car. He got out and put up an umbrella with his free hand. He was on his mobile phone. He looked like whatever he was discussing was very important, but the rain washed the words away before they could reach us. Vince bumped his car door closed with his bum and walked to the middle of the courtyard, where he stopped.

"What's he doing?" Sefu asked. "Why not come inside?"

I frowned, but I wasn't really paying much attention – there was something moving by the courtyard entrance. It was hard to make out in the grey and the rain. "Sefu, is someone moving around by the gate?"

He peered forward. "Er... yes. I think so. They look like they're trying to stay hidden, or maybe they're sheltering under the wall's overhang."

Vince was pacing in short, quick circles. Beside me, Sefu gasped. I looked up and saw that two figures had broken away from the gate and were rushing Vince. They wore grey jogging trousers and hoodies with the hoods up, drawstrings tight to keep the rain out.

I hauled at the sash of the window to try and yell a warning, but it was jammed shut. Sefu ran to the window next to us, in the north wall, and yelled out it. "Vince! Look behind you!"

I saw Vince turn as one of the figures approached him. The other was heading towards the cars along the north wall of the courtyard.

"What do we do?" Sefu asked.

"Do we call someone?"

Vince took a step back as the attacker raised an arm. I saw the flash of metal, grey and glinting. The attacker held a knife.

× Chapter Eight

Vince swung up both his arms to block the knife. His umbrella spun off in one direction and his phone in another. I felt the terror python laughing at me as I stood there, unable to move, watching my friend fight for his life. *Not again. I couldn't let another of my friends die.* I tried to breathe out. I couldn't afford to do this! I couldn't be Phoebe right now. Phoebe couldn't help here! Who could help? Sefu was paralysed next to me. Who else was there?

Melissa.

Melissa wouldn't get stuck in her head. Melissa would act. I spun myself around and hurled myself down the stairs. Behind me, I heard Sefu, his footsteps hammering the old wood as we ran down the stairs. I burst out into the open and charged towards the fight.

My friend was no longer fighting. Instead, Vince was slumped in his attacker's arms. I yelled as I charged, a desperate wordless cry. I saw the grey figure turn towards me. I caught a decent glimpse of their face.

It was a face I knew, one I'd seen before, at maybe a dozen protests now. A line of cops had always separated us before. It was a face I was used to seeing twisted into a rictus of hatred, screaming at me for being a saboteur and a traitor. It was a face that read The Sun and wouldn't let his kids watch Doctor Who because it was too sissy. It was the face from Patriots Unite. I'd long ago named this particular man. In my head, he was Racist Carl.

Racist Carl saw me charging at him, looked down at Vince slumped in his arms and turned to run. He was stumbling away as Vince collapsed to his knees. Vince fell on to his face, his arms splaying forward at unhealthy angles. Would my inner Melissa charge after Racist Carl or stop to help Vince? I didn't know. I dithered as I reached Vince's still form and, in that moment of hesitation, I realised I had lost the essence of my sister. I was back to being me. Well, Phoebe would always check on her friends before pursuing justice.

I heaved at Vince's shoulder, trying to roll him onto his back. Sefu reached me and rolled Vince's hips. Between us, we were able to get him face up. Rain drummed down on us. Vince's eyes were closed. There was a cut on his cheek. "Vince?" I called.

The rain suddenly stopped. I looked up in surprise and saw that Sefu had grabbed Vince's umbrella and was holding it over us. "Is he okay?" Sefu asked. "We need some help out here!" he called at the top of his voice. "NOW!"

He hadn't moved since I'd reached him. I felt at his neck for a pulse, but couldn't find one. I held my wet hand over his nose and mouth. I couldn't feel any breathing. I rested my hand on his chest, around where his heart should be. I had to move it about a couple of times to be sure, but after a minute or two, I knew for sure that his heart had stopped.

I looked up at Sefu, tears running down my face. "I think... I think he's dead."

It had happened again.

I looked down at my hands. They were stained red. I checked Vince and saw a wound in his chest, just to the right of his sternum.

I heard feet blundering down the house stairs. I stared down at my hands. The sticky mess clung there, I felt hands on my shoulders, easing me to my feet. I took a step away from the body, and then two.

It happened again. It happened again. It happened again. It happened again.

The terror python was wrapped tighter around my chest than ever before, crushing the life from me. I tried to retreat up to the safety of my own head, where nothing bad ever happened, where I had never been neglected, where it was safe and rational and not messy and emotional. I did my best to shut everything out, the blood on my hands, my friends clustered around the body. I couldn't shut out the thought that it had happened again. Again. Again. Again.

And it would yet happen again.

It would happen again and again and again, until we were all... I stumbled back until my back hit the concrete wall of the courtyard. The breath was driven from my lungs. I stared at the shapes of my friends, made hazy by the lashing rainstorm. The python crushed the air out of my lungs. It sang over my teeth and out into the air as a desperate, thin howl of despair.

I felt hands take mine and lead me inside. I was eased into the house. My shoes were taken from my feet. I was led up the stairs and into the bathroom. Someone stared pulling at my clothes. This, by some ancient, terrible instinct, caused me to focus a little. I saw that I was alone in a room with Paula.

"It's okay, bab," she said. "We just have to get you out of those wet clothes is all. I'll just hang your jacket up."

I let her take the suit jacket from me. She hung it from a hook on the back of the door. I wanted to put it back on. That jacket was mine, it was my favourite. It was the first suit

I'd bought with my own money – a swishy grey two-button number from ASOS. Besides, it wasn't that wet. I went to recover it, but at that moment, someone knocked on the door. I shrank back. Who had come for us? Were they here for Paula? Could I protect her? I'd failed to protect Cassie and Vince.

Paula slipped past me. I squeaked in alarm as she opened the door a crack. A hand reached through – Sefu's. He was holding a neatly stacked pile of my clothes. Paula took the clothes.

"Mel just got back," Sefu murmured.

Paula nodded. "Thanks, mate." She closed the door softly. She eased me out of my clothes, talking to me all the time as if I was some small, terrified animal that might bolt at any moment. She hung my wet clothes from the shower curtain rail, and she dried me off.

Feeling dry and safe in the room with Paula, who was drenched herself, finally made me emerge from myself, just a tiny bit. I was able to help get myself dressed in simple cotton trousers, along with a black shirt and tie. I volunteered to go and get Paula a housecoat or something. Paula smiled sadly, and said that, actually, I was needed elsewhere.

"Where?" I asked, confused.

"Mel needs you, bab," Paula said, sadly. "Sefu said she just got back. She needs to process this. Can you go and tell Katie to come to us in the kitchen? We'll look after her."

"Won't you all need looking after?" I asked.

"In time. We're going to have a space where people can mourn in their own ways, but we need to establish something first. It's very important."

"What's that?"

"We need to know if we're calling the police."

"Oh." I tried to focus. "All right."

"Gus will want to. Liam might. Otherwise, I don't know. What do you think?"

I shook my head, attempting to clear it. The police? The police didn't care about us. Given their lies about their Cass investigation... their Cassvestigation? Given their lies about their Cassvestigation, they'd just ignore that I'd seen Racist Carl. They'd probably just lock me and Sefu up. Scratch that. They'd just lock Sefu up. Maybe Paula as well, depending on how many copies of the Daily Mail they'd been reading. That said, Paula had been in front of a court before on spurious charges. You wouldn't believe how positively the jury reacts to the terms 'Quaker', 'grandmother', and 'collector of novelty trivets'.

"We shouldn't call the cops," I said. "We should sort this out ourselves." I looked up at Paula. "I can sort this out."

Paula's face was carefully neutral. "You?"

"Me and Sefu."

She nodded. "Check with Sefu before you volunteer him, eh bab? Look, we'll have to talk about it. We'll see what everyone else thinks. Are you okay to go and look after your sister now?"

No?

"Yes." I strode to the door, where my jacket was hanging. I took it from its hook.

"What are you doing, love?" Paula asked. "Don't put that back on, it's soaked."

"I need it," I said. I turned to look at her, and I knew my eyes were shiny with tears. "It's mine."

Suddenly, I was eight years old again, trying to find some

comfort in that dark, empty house. Paula didn't argue. "At least let's wring it out over the bath, eh?"

She took my grey woollen relic from me and got as much water out as she could. She tutted as the water turned crimson but handed the jacket back to me without arguing. I shivered as I slipped it back on, but felt better nonetheless.

Paula gave me a cold embrace, although the chilliness was down to the damp jacket rather than the woman who had taken me in without asking any questions and sheltered me for three years. She left the bathroom ahead of me, crossed the corridor and went into the kitchen area, where I could see Sefu, Xia, Liam and Gus.

I turned right and walked the long, long distance towards Mel's room. Behind me, I heard Paula starting the discussion about calling the police.

My hand hovered over Mel's door handle as I heard Gus speak up.

"I think we should call the cops and come clean," he said. "They know we had nothing to do with Cassie's death. They might think someone is targeting us. Hell, someone *is* targeting us."

"The problem is," said Liam, "if we call the cops, they'll come here blaring blues and twos. The murderers will hear them and leg it. They'll never catch them. We should go after them right now. They won't be able to get far in this rain."

"Does anyone own a 1960s Triumph motorbike?" Sefu asked. It must have sounded like a total non sequitur. There was a chorus of denials. "Phoebe and I found one in the northmost barn," he continued. "They must have come in on that. It'd be a nightmare trying to get that antique up the track and out of here in this storm. They've probably gone to ground. Phoebe and I will go find them."

"You realise you just volunteered Phoebe to go looking for murderers, right?" Xia asked, which caused Paula to chuckle.

"She needs this."

Xia said. "We need to get down to Fairford and stop the B52s in the next twenty-four hours. We have to prioritise that."

This declaration jolted me. Paula and Xia were great believers in consensus decision-making. This meant a commitment to finding solutions that everyone actively supported, or at least could live with. It was unusual to hear Xia try to steamroll the discussion like she just had. Still, I was willing to bet none of us were really feeling normal in that moment.

"I think we're getting distracted here," Liam said.

"No," Xia insisted. "It's you that's getting distracted. If we don't manage to sabotage those planes, thousands will die. Vince was all-in for this. He knew how important it was. He wouldn't want his death to get in the way. Sefu can play Matrix some other time."

You couldn't fault Xia on her ability to focus. She had a goal and she was going to go for it, no matter what. I shivered and knocked on Mel's door. Little feet pattered on the other side of the door, which swung open. Katie stood in the doorway. There was chocolate around her mouth.

"Katie, can you go and play your Nintendo in your room please? Or go sit with Sefu and everyone in the kitchen? I need to have a chat with your mum."

"Okay," said the angel, before scampering off.

I stepped into Mel's room and closed the door. One side was gloriously messy, as always. Crisp packets and students'

French worksheets littered the floor, along with toys, items of clothing, and part-read books. There was a locked box with a six-digit combination in which Katie's chocolate was kept. Things took a turn for the worse on the other side of the room, where Mel made way for Melissa. Melissa's side of the room was terrifying. Everything was folded, stacked, and rigorously organised. The desk was divided into sections according to her calendar, showing her shifts, her pens (sorted by colour, naturally) and her professional documents. Study materials and training materials occupied drawers one through three, carefully stratified by ability level. Her anti-anxiety drugs and gin were kept in the secure bottom drawer.

Mel was sitting on the edge of her bed, leaning forwards so her arms rested on her thighs. She looked blank. She looked absent. She looked like she needed a hug.

"How are you doing, mate?" I asked.

Sefu's voice floated in through the wall. "This has nothing to do with vengeance." The thin plaster struggled to keep sound out at the best of times, and it couldn't stand up to heated conversation.

I crossed to Mel's CD player and pressed play – Nick Cave started groaning out of the speakers. My jacket was starting to feel heavy and stiff. I closed my eyes and tried to breathe. I was safe here. Sefu with his swords and Gus with his army training were just in the kitchen. I was here with Mel. I had always been safe with Mel. This room was bright, it was warm, I could stand to take my jacket off. I stripped the plate armour from my shoulders and hung it from a hook on the back of Mel's door. I whipped my tie from my collar and slipped it into the jacket's outer pocket.

I sat next to my sister on the bed and wrapped an arm

around her slumped shoulders. I pulled her towards me and she melted into my arms. I felt her start to sob, then cry, then howl. Her grief flooded into mine.

After maybe ten minutes, we separated. I eased Mel down onto her bed and I took her shoes off. I then lay down on the bed with her, wrapped my arms around her and tried to take her away from everything she was feeling right now, just as I had so often wished she'd done for me when we were growing up.

I needed to look after Mel, and I needed to do it right. In her last year living with us, I was having some argument with Mum about... something. I can't remember what it was. If I had to guess, I'd say that I wanted to do something and she didn't want me to do that thing. It's the sort of thing that happened every day, hundreds of thousands of times. I don't know. Maybe I was weak for letting these arguments get to me. Maybe I was a bad person for feeling so crushed by them, for feeling as if the world was closing in around me as I stood there while Mum shouted.

I'd cried a lot as a child, far more than was usual. Other times, I would be almost deliriously happy. Throughout it all, I began to suspect that my parents didn't actually like me that much. I was sure they loved me, but it was distant and undefined. They were always there when society said it counted. They never missed a school play or a sports day. But for much of the time, they were off doing poorly-defined things. In their place, there was a succession of nannies and au pairs and minders, never there long enough to ever really become people to me. When my parents were actually present, there was this distance between us that only shrank when the shouting started. I sometimes felt like I was living in a house belonging to two strangers – like I'd been taken from my real mum and dad to live with these two people who seemed perfectly nice most of the time… but they weren't mine. And it was surprisingly easy to make them furious with me.

For most of my childhood, Mel had been absent as well. She'd kept to herself, or she'd been at some sporting event, or, when she was older, at an endless cavalcade of parties. When we were in the same place at the same time, we ground against each other like ill-fitting gears. It had taken years for us to be able to talk about the dark years, in that house of endless beauty and sudden anger. I'd thought Mel was living the perfect life, but she'd been suffering as much as me. Over time, she'd become hard, like a diamond. She started to run away. She got involved with things and people that she shouldn't.

That one time, out of thousands that Mum was shouting at me, Mel had stuck her head round the door and said to me, "Come on, we're leaving." In that moment, I think I would have gone with Jason Vorhees if he'd offered me an out. We went straight to the house of one of her friends whose parents were away. The three of us ate frozen pizza and rented The Fifth Element, watching it in the dark. I slept over, and Mel drove me home the next day. I slept hard and deep. It was the safest I'd felt in years. Years later, The Fifth Element was still one of my favourite films, which was embarrassing because it wasn't very good.

My point is that Mel had always been there for me when it really counted, even if Melissa hadn't. Now I had the opportunity to pay her back. I was quiet as she cried. There was nothing I could say, certainly not 'It's going to be okay.' I was just there to be whatever she needed.

She cried in my arms for a timeless age. At some point, she must have fallen asleep. I eased off the bed but the movement caused Mel to stir. She rolled over to face me and I saw that she didn't look so dreadfully empty any more. I smiled at her. "Go back to sleep," I said. "I'm going to see what the others are up to."

I straightened my shirt, put my tie back on and re-donned my jacket. I turned to say goodbye to Mel. A look of horror contorted her face.

"What? What is it?"

She didn't say anything – her mouth opened by no sound came out. She pointed. I slipped the jacket off and inspected it. When I turned it around, I saw what had caused her reaction. A large smear of blood had soaked into the back of my jacket, staining the sodden grey with a sickly stain of burgundy.

× Chapter Nine

I slipped out of Mel's room, keeping my back to her so she wouldn't have to look at the blood. I didn't want to upset her any more than I already had. I went to my room and slipped my jacket off again so I could examine the bloodstain. It was still wet, thanks to the soaking Paula had given it, and it had very definitely not been there before... what had happened to Vince. It was about the size of one of those small bowls we used to eat puddings out of – a ramekin, I think they're called. It looked like it had originally had some shape to it, but it was now just a damp, fading blob.

I must have picked it up when I was rolling Vince over or something... but the stain was on my back. I never had my back to Vince, had I? I'd run down the stairs. I'd run at the attacker. I'd knelt down by Vince. I'd rolled him over. I'd checked his pulse –

A flash of memory stopped my attempt at dispassionate recollection. I saw Vince lying there, blood pooling underneath him. I saw his face as I rolled him over. His eyes stared up at me while his mouth formed a question.

'Why weren't you faster?'

My hands spasmed into fists. I realised I was now pacing about my room, clutching at my head, trying to make the memories vanish. I found myself making a groaning, keening sort of noise, and clapped my hands over my mouth. It wasn't my first time making a noise like that – I got moments when

I felt like I was going to die and I'd have to get up and pace and sometimes I'd end up hitting myself and just have to scream or make this guttural 'arg' noise. I always tried not to. I knew the walls here were thin. I knew I was annoying the people I lived with – the people who took me in and cared for me because it was the right thing to do. They'd told me it wasn't my fault, that it didn't bother them, but I knew I could stop it if I tried hard enough. I just hadn't been able to yet.

I lay on the floor, leaving my jacket where it was, and felt the panic begin to fade from me. *Forget the bloodstain.* Focusing on the bloodstain wouldn't help. What could help with this? What could help?

Nothing.

Nothing would help. I would always feel like this. Nothing. My life was nothing. I was good for nothing. I was nothing.

The government had lied and lied and lied, and apparently no one cared. What had all my truths done? Nothing. The referendum had been completely crooked, a deception at every level, and I'd spent so long fighting it in order to achieve – nothing. We were trying to show people how bad the war was, and the British people couldn't even agree if the referendum had been democratic or not. Did the vague question mean the government couldn't act? Did the fact that it had actually been a plebiscite mean the results could be nullified once the electoral irregularities were found? Who knew. But this much I did know: our whole group was just nothing. Less than nothing. And now we were being picked off one by one.

If I was next, a month down the line, would anyone even miss me?

An angelic little face swam into my mind's eye, and I clutched at it. Yes, Katie would miss me. I needed to keep her safe from our enemies.

There were several groups who considered us foes, but Patriots Unite, in particular, knew us, hated us and had now started coming here to attack us. An enemy meant you had power, even if you didn't see it yourself. No one bothered counter-protesting someone meaningless. Even a pack of radicalised thugs understood that we were a threat to their goals, to the point that they were killing us. It was the ultimate compliment, if you thought about it.

So, okay. I wasn't actually nothing. Maybe I wasn't doing anything particularly useful, but it was enough to scare a pack of racists.

But actually that wasn't entirely fair either, was it? Just a few hours ago, I'd discovered a tiny truth about Cassie's death. I was clearly the only deliverer of justice who was going to step up for Cassie. My Cassvestigation was worth pursuing, and I needed to just stop spiralling out of control.

So.

I forced myself to get to my feet. I stripped down and put on clean underwear, a blue shirt and a black single button suit with aggressive pinstripes. This one had cost me four months of pay. This was the suit I'd solve Cassandra and Vince's murders in.

I stared at myself in my bedroom mirror. I looked scared. I couldn't be scared, not in this moment. I needed to focus. I glared at myself, willing myself to leave the fear behind. Then my phone rang, which broke my concentration completely. I scrambled around in my discarded clothing to find it.

"Hello?"

"We're suing the police," said Eryl Jr. She was crunching some sort of biscuit. I started pacing around my room.

"What?"

"You heard me."

"Why are we suing the police?"

"There's something really fishy going on, Ms Green. You remember I was going to get Granny – sorry, Eryl Iwan Senior to have a word with her mates in the high echelons of policing? So she did. The answer came back loud and clear: stonewall. Nothing doing. Whatever you want, we can't help you."

"Is that unusual?"

"Granny has worked with a lot of people in her time. She knows where a lot of bodies are buried. Metaphorically as well as literally. She's terrifying, but a very good lawyer. If she's being stonewalled, it's because something seriously fishy is going on. Remember Anthony Thompson, the cop who was at school with the head of Patriots Unite? It seems he's one of a little clutch of cops who share a similar sort of ideology. 'Some of those that work forces,' and all that stuff. Anyway, Granny and I have noticed a pattern. Over the last six months, a lot of these cops have been deployed to investigate Patriots Unite and groups like it. You'll be amazed to learn that these investigations haven't led to anyone being arrested, let alone charged."

"They're shielding far right groups?" I felt a knot twist inside myself. We couldn't call the police about Vince's murder. They'd actively shield Patriots Unite and use us as the fall guy.

"That's what I thought, but Granny doesn't think so. They'd be making more trouble for themselves in the long run because it'd be a serious scandal if it came out. They must be doing something very specific which involves these groups, something they don't want other people finding out about. So we, along with Cassandra's family, are suing the police."

"What for?"

"Oh, a whole number of things. Partly we just want to light a fire under them and see what happens. Terrible legal practice but, as Granny said, they're being terrible police right now so if we can drag some of it into the light, we'll have done well."

"Okay. Listen, Ms Iwan, we've had a spot of trouble at the farm."

"How bad?"

"Pretty bad."

"Is it related to the Cassandra situation?"

"Some of the same people are, yeah."

"Want me to come out? I'm in meetings for a few hours but I can come out after that?"

Previously, Eryl had only come out to the farm if we threatened to actually pay her. Usually, her granny paid her a reduced wage to work for us because Eryl Sr. and Paula go way back. "That would be wonderful, thank you Ms Iwan."

"I don't like filing frivolous lawsuits, no matter how good the justification. If it helps with the Cassandra matter, I'll come out. You think it will help?"

"It might make it a lot more complicated."

"Whoopee." Eryl's voice was flat. She crunched down on another biscuit. "Then I'll be with you in a couple of hours. Whatever the situation is, don't let it get any worse until I arrive, okay?"

"Okay. Thank you, Ms Iwan."

"See you around five when I'm off the clock. About three hours. I'll update you if I'm going to be late." Eryl hung up.

I dropped the phone to my side. I allowed myself a second to process what Eryl had said. I was still determined to solve Cassie and Vince's murders, but now I was on the clock. I couldn't afford to panic any more. I needed to track down the Patriots Unite guy who murdered Vince and hand him over to Eryl Jr when she showed up. Otherwise, we'd go down as his murderers. Eryl, I trusted. The other institutions of our government, not so much. And with that done, I'd be able to focus on my Cassvestigation. But I couldn't track and contain Vince's murderer alone. I needed help. I needed Sefu.

"The question the referendum asked was about 'intervening' in Iraq," Liam was saying as I entered the kitchen. His fingers were drumming a complex beat on the table, a sure sign he was wound up. "Plenty of ministers and MPs insisted invasion wasn't even being contemplated. We didn't vote to invade."

"That's my entire point," Xia nodded. "Vince was insistent that we had to respect the referendum, but that's never been the issue. It's got nothing to do with it, in fact. He was dragging us down." Xia's expression was rigid. Her eyes spoke of some personal nightmare she was living in.

"No," Gus insisted. "Vince understood that it didn't matter if the people were misled. Even if they based their votes on bad info, that didn't matter because it was still what they wanted. They still made their choice. It was the authorities that were in the wrong. The people who set the vote up with an open question, and then lied repeatedly to the press about the facts. The people who chose to leap straight from the referendum's result into an invasion. And that's even before we get further down the food chain. The police attacked us just yesterday. You want to give them an excuse? They'll fit us all up for Vince's murder."

Xia shook her head. "They won't. Those rogues yesterday were acting on their own. If we call them in for something like this, they'll have to go by the book. We can't let Vince hold us back now that he's dead. We have to hand him over to them, let them do their police thing, and – stop – those – flying – death – machines."

Sefu looked up at Xia. "What if we call the cops, and we get the two from yesterday? They must be locals or they wouldn't know about our compound specifically." Sefu tapped the medical tape at his temple. "I got this because I tried to calm them down. What might they do to me if they find me near a dead body?"

Xia started to reply, and then paused, clearly searching for something to say. I seized the opportunity to jump in, trying to reclaim some of the momentum I'd lost by hovering in the doorway as The Topic dragged me down

"I just spoke to Eryl Jr," I said. "She is of the opinion that Patriots Unite are being shielded in some way. They have friends in the police. She's named names."

"You're kidding," Liam said.

I shrugged. "That's what she said."

"Then we can't go to the police," Liam concluded.

Silence shrouded the room. One by one, my friends nodded. We had been fighting to prevent a war. We were under attack by both the police and fascist groups. We had to sort this out ourselves, and soon, before Eryl showed up.

We needed Eryl Jr and Snr. We needed some legal shelter. But it had to be from people who were genuinely fighting for what was right, who would hear our side of the story and help to protect us from the forces so committed to crushing us. We needed her badly.

Handing this whole mess over to her was a possibility, but she was constrained by the laws. Her profession was bounded, so I had to give her something to work on, an explanation for who and what killed whom and why. It made her job a lot easier. Making Eryl's job easier made her more effective, and also less likely to yell at us.

I broke the silence. "I need Sefu's help."

Stunned expressions stared back at me. Xia recovered first. "For your killer hunt? Absolutely not."

"We need to find Vince's murderer, and we can't rely on the police," I said, as calmly as possible.

"We need to stop the planes at Fairford from slaughtering hundreds of Iraqis." Xia's voice was cold and definitive. "Your ego needs to let to go of heroics. You can't find the murderer, you're a care worker." She looked down at her hands. "Cassie would want us to do this. Stop making this all about you."

I had been wavering. Xia was right about stopping the B52s, just as Sefu was right about needing to be a long way away if the police showed up. Still, when she accidentally echoed the words my mum used to say before social events, I felt myself dig in and harden up, just as I had before I'd left that huge, thunderous house.

"Xia, I love you, but this is something I have to do. Which reminds me, actually, as you're all here, I picked up a bloodstain on the back of my jacket somehow. The thing is, I'm absolutely sure I never had my back to Vince's corpse. Anyone got any ideas what that could be about?"

Xia shuddered and looked down, her face turning a shade of grey. Everyone else shook their heads solemnly. *At least I stopped the argument.*

As rain was still drumming against the windows, they had resorted to electric light, which looked brash and unnatural at this time of day. I missed the smells of the room, Katie in her spot doing her homework, Sefu and I spending hours on the bench dissecting The Lord of the Rings, the whole pack of us sitting around the table discussing our action plans. It all seemed fractured and sharp now, and I didn't want to stay here any longer than I had to.

Sefu looked up at me and grinned his agreement. *Thank you, Sefu*, I thought. *Thank you for always being there when I need you.*

"Look, if anyone goes killer hunting, it's me. I'm the one with army training and I'm the one skilled in combat." Gus was right but he was also, well, Gus. Unpredictable.

"That's why you're needed here," Mel said softly, laying a hand on his arm. "We need you to protect Katie and the rest of us." I watched Gus hesitate, torn between competing needs. Then he too nodded. I turned away, in case the relief showed on my face.

I heard footsteps behind me and I turned to find Sefu had joined me in the corridor.

I looked up at him. "Are you happy for us to go and see if we can find Vince's murderer? I might be being unbelievably stupid, but Vince's attacker struck when he was distracted. They didn't seem like the Michael Myers type."

"We don't have to confront them if we find them. If we know where they are, that'll be something."

"Great. What weapons are we taking?"

Sefu held up a finger. He disappeared into his room before emerging holding a five-foot-wooden staff, which he handed to me. He'd wound a belt around his waist, which contained a training weapon and a massive sword I'd never seen before.

"Why do you need both of those?" I asked.

"The bokken is if I actually need to hit someone. The ōdachi is to intimidate them."

I thought about the sanctity of life and the importance of non-violence in all but the most pressing of circumstances. "Fair enough," I grumbled. I wasn't sure how I'd feel if we actually found the people who'd murdered Vince. Hopefully I'd be able to stick to this high principle.

We pulled on raincoats. Sefu handed me an umbrella. He held his own umbrella in his right hand and his enormous ōdachi in his left.

We clomped down the stairs and out into the courtyard. I'd expected the wind to immediately snatch the umbrella from my hand, but I barely felt a tug – the rain was the thick, fat kind that fell straight down.

I nodded. "Should we check the sheds out? It would be pretty bad if Patriots Unite were hiding out this close to our house."

Sefu nodded. We opened the first shed, which was mostly used for storage. Shelves lined the walls and there was conspicuously nowhere for any number of fascists to hide. Unless they were only a few centimetres tall. Ten-centimetre fascists, what a horrible thought.

The second shed was much the same, except this was the one that contained Vince's body. Sefu hesitated on the doorstep, which surprised me. I remembered something I'd thought earlier and was about to volunteer to check the shed out without him, when he took a step forward and the moment was lost.

There was no one hiding behind the door. There was no one behind the two crates filled with packing foam and tools. There was the body of one of our friends. We both tried to ignore this, which only struck me as disrespectful after we'd left.

It felt like I should gasp as soon as I was back out in the rain – make some big gesture to show I'd crossed a threshold. I was away from death and back in the real world. I spent too long thinking about it, however. Just as I felt like I might be on track to coming up with something which would truly underline the difference between the world out here, and the underworld in there, Sefu interrupted. "Okay, shall we check around the compound wall now?"

"What?" I asked. "Yes. Yes, I remember what we were doing."

The rain drummed rat-a-tata-tat-a-ta-tat on my umbrella. Next to me, Sefu's umbrella accompanied mine. We turned out of the courtyard gates and followed the west wall northwards up the track, just as we had a few hours earlier. I was concentrating on where I was – I was in the farm where I had made my new life. I was with my truest friend who I could talk to for hours, whose depth and breadth of knowledge dwarfed mine. I was snug and warm, protected from the rain twice over. I was doing good work, making sure my friends were safe from my prey.

The area around the track was pretty empty. There were some areas of slight discolouration that I didn't remember from previously, but I had to admit I rarely memorised the precise dappling of every piece of terrain I traversed. We turned right off the track when we reached the corner of the courtyard and started picking our way along the north wall. Knots of bushes lined the area next to the wall, so I checked to make sure they looked undisturbed. Sefu kept his eyes to the north to see if he could spot anyone skulking in the open terrain, or near any of the barns to the north.

Somewhere in the distance, an engine roared into life, harsh and throaty. Not a vehicle I recognised. A motorbike? It was coming from somewhere to the north, but it was hard to say exactly from where. Even with the rain and the trees, it didn't sound distant enough to be coming from the road...

Sefu and I spun around but couldn't see any lights through the rain. The engine noise was definitely somewhere close by. It wasn't constant though, it was fading in and out, flaring and then dying back. Revving.

Then I heard the motor roar, and a short grating of movement. The engine surged. It sounded like whatever it was had just started moving at speed. I turned on the spot, trying to pinpoint the source of the noise. There – from the track leading up to the barns. I looked up at Sefu, who had just realised the same thing.

"Should – " I began. I was interrupted by the sound of a huge crash, metal howling against metal, punctuated with deep, thudding noises. The distant engine faltered and died.

National newspaper coverage on the subject of House of Lords reform:

2001:

"The House of Lords needs reforming, but abolishing it is not the answer"
The Guardian

"House of Lords reform 'will cost taxpayers £500 million"
The Telegraph

2002:

"House of Lords fails to represent much of UK"
The Guardian

"As part of their cynical manoeuvring to rig the British constitution, Labour are threatening to block long-overdue changes unless their self-serving proposals for Lords reform are forced through Parliament."
The Daily Mail

2003, just after the House of Lords amended several bills to ensure scrutiny on the Iraq war:

"The Lords are playing outrageous games over Iraq"
The Telegraph

"House of unelected wreckers"
The Daily Mail

"The House of Lords is a cancer eating away at democracy"
The Sun

× Chapter Ten

We dropped our umbrellas and started running. The area of the crash became less murky as we approached. The motorbike we'd last seen skulking in our barn was lying near the gravel path, at the base of a rotting stump of a tree. A deep gouge in the grass slashed towards the gravel path, showing where the rider had lost control. The bike's wheel had bent, the light on the front had smashed and the rider, judging by the scraped mud beyond the tree stump, had gone over the handlebars.

We were near the west barn, the one we'd poked our heads into before Vince's murder. Sefu was looking around the area to see if he could find any tracks. I looked at the barn. Could it be that easy?

"Sefu, where would you go if you'd crashed your bike and needed to hide quickly? Would you pick anywhere except the west barn?"

"Probably not. Let's check it out. Carefully."

We stalked towards the barn. I held my staff at the ready. Sefu still gripped his sheathed sword. It was strange to be visiting the barns twice in one day, when usually I never thought about the things. I was sure the developer had some grand plans for the things but we hardly used them.

"You're not going to get your sword ready?"

Sefu shook his head. "Unsheathing it is quite intimidating, it might be enough to get our fascists talking."

We reached the barn and saw no signs of enemies lurking

anywhere. Just inside the doorway, we paused and scanned our surroundings. Like the other barn, the place was littered with rusting machinery with semi-intact stalls lining the northwest wall. There was also a half-disintegrated platform running along the southwest wall. Sefu turned to me and put his finger to his lips, then his ear. I listened for signs of life in the barn, but didn't hear anything other than those that we were making. Together, we walked into the barn.

There were few places to hide, so I checked the stalls as we moved. The first stall had been swept out an indeterminate amount of time ago, leaving a bare concrete floor. The next stall contained coils of old leather. The next stall...

The next stall had a woollen blanket lining the floor. Unlit candles lined the edge of the stall in saucers of water. All the straw had been swept clear of the area. A small wicker basket sat in a corner, and next to that was a small set of speakers with a trailing wire, which could plug into a portable CD player. A rolled-up yoga mat was propped against one wall.

Sefu and I stared at the scene. I felt like I'd just stumbled into the preliminaries of a picnic. I glanced at Sefu, who was clearly as surprised as I was. I stepped forward, trying not to stand on the blanket, which was clean and clearly cared for. I reached for the wicker basket but had to kneel on the blanket to reach it. I had expected to feel the hard concrete of the barn floor under my knees, but the floor felt soft and forgiving. I flicked up a corner of the blanket and saw that the stall had been lined with those jigsaw mats you find in gyms.

Sefu joined me on the blanket. He picked up something I couldn't see and stepped back. I opened the wicker basket. Inside was a bottle of wine and two glasses. I closed the lid, feeling like I was invading someone's space. As I stood up,

Sefu handed me a bottle about the size of a shot glass. It was coloured black and had 'SILVER HAZE room odorisor' written on the side. What on earth? I spread my hands in confusion at Sefu, who shrugged in reply. I slipped the bottle into my pocket.

This left one single stall for us to search. If the Patriots Unite person was anywhere, he'd be there. I shifted my grip on the staff, realising I had been holding it so tightly my fingers ached. I was keeping my breath shallow and slow, but the effort to not hyperventilate was exhausting. I didn't want to take the next two steps to see if our prey was in the last stall. What would I say? What would I do? They were dangerous, we knew that. Would they go for Sefu? Would he be safe? I couldn't lose another friend today. I'd rather put myself in harm's way, but then... I couldn't do that to Mel. I couldn't take away her partner and sister in the space of a few hours.

I needed to stop and properly build up to this. I needed to close my eyes and just...

I stopped, closed my eyes.

My eyes popped open and I saw that Sefu had continued walking while I'd had my little quiet panic. I had to move. I charged round the wooden barrier, brandishing my staff. A snarl died on my lips as I saw concrete, rotten straw and plastic tubing. But no fascist. I grunted in surprise and shock.

"You okay?" Sefu whispered in my ear.

I whirled to look at him. He looked concerned and I did my best to calm down. I nodded. I looked theatrically around the barn, before looking back at him. He pointed up, above our heads, to the platform that lined the southwest wall.

I looked up at it, doubtfully. The barn was in a poor repair, but that platform was even worse. It was near collapse. There was a metal ladder leaning up against the wall of the barn that allowed access, but I wouldn't like to trust even my weight to that platform.

If the Patriots Unite people were up there, how could we snare them? Climbing the ladder would put our heads in range of a weapon or a boot. I looked from Sefu to the ladder and back.

Sefu beckoned me towards him. We were already standing quite close to each other. I took a step towards him. He motioned again. I blushed and took another step, so that we were standing toe to toe. This was the closest I had been to him for about six months. My heart was thumping in my chest harder than it had when I'd charged into the final stall. Still, I felt safer than I had for hours.

Sefu leaned down. Was... was he going to kiss me? Now? Was this a way of calming me down? Because it would work, it was that brilliant an idea. I couldn't believe I hadn't thought of it earlier.

Sefu's lips didn't touch mine. Instead, he leaned past me, so that his lips were next to my ear, and my lips were next to his. I drew in a surprised breath. "I thought this would be a good way to talk to each other without the fascists hearing us."

"Y-yeah," I whispered. "Good thought." I swallowed.

"Phoebe Anne Elizabeth Katherine Roughbone Wellforth Trombone Green, did you think I was putting the moves on you?" I could hear the amusement in Sefu's whisper.

"Yes," I hissed. "No. Shut up." My cheeks were burning. "And only three of those are my real middle names." Silence hung in the tiny amount of air between us for a long moment. I could feel his heart beating. I mentally slapped myself.

"How can we tell if there's a fascist above us without putting ourselves in danger?"

"We could just call out?"

"But that would show that we don't know they're there."

"Yeah. Okay. We could pretend to leave the barn and try to spy on the platform to see if they move."

"If there's no one up there we could be waiting a long time."

"It feels like you're shooting down all my ideas, Phoebe."

"Sorry, yes, I am. How about this, I give the underside of the platform a forceful poke with the staff. That might well provoke a reaction. If it doesn't, we can try your spying plan?"

"Sounds good," Sefu whispered. "Go for it."

He took a step back, and I felt suddenly chilly. I shook myself and gripped the staff. I crept so that I was standing as close to the centre of the underside of the platform as I could. I cast my gaze up and did my best to examine the structure. It wasn't especially easy. Light filtered in through the barn windows, but there wasn't much, thanks to the storm.

After a couple of moments, I had a good idea of the construction. The platform was supported by bars attached to the walls of the barn. Two cross beams ran between the walls, supporting the centre of the platform in an X shape. They looked like they'd shrug off a poke from the staff. The platform itself looked like it might not weather a poke quite so well.

I aimed the staff carefully so that it was targeting the mid-point halfway along a floorboard, far enough away from the cross bracing that I should be able to make a nice, alarming noise. I breathed in, then out, then struck the staff straight up. I felt the power run from my knees, to my hips, to my shoulders, to my arms, to my hands, to the staff, just as Sefu had taught me. The staff struck the board and snapped it into two rotten halves.

A strangled cry sounded from the platform, very close to where I'd stuck.

My heart suddenly ran into overdrive. We'd located our prey, but that meant we were also in a crumbling barn with a right-wing extremist, probably armed and definitely dangerous, and who'd very much like to see Sefu, as well as me, come to serious harm.

If I was going to go back to my room to hide and cry, now would be the time to go. The thought was appealing, but I couldn't face the idea of letting Vince's killer escape justice. I struck the platform again. I nearly jarred the staff out of my hands, but another board crumbled under the strike.

Above us, I heard a scrambling sound move away from where I was.

"We know you're up there," said Sefu, his voice coldly authoritative. "Come down!"

"No way!" said the voice. It was male and sounded like it belonged to a weasel. I imagined greasy hair and a perpetually outraged expression.

"Hit the platform again, P," said Sefu. He'd never called me 'P' before in his life. He was probably keeping my gender a secret from the fascist. Smart man.

I struck up at the platform at about the point where I'd heard his voice. This time, I was rewarded with a cry of pain as my staff struck something fleshy. I decided to call this man Cowardly Winston. He scrambled about on the platform again, causing it to creak alarmingly. I shifted out from under the thing, just in case it collapsed.

"If the platform collapses, you'll fall twenty-five feet to land on concrete and steel. And then the rest of the platform will collapse on you with its nails and broken boards. It'll be easy to get you then. Or what's left of you."

"Okay, okay!" cried Cowardly Winston. "Look, what do you want?"

"For you to come down," said Sefu. "We have things to discuss."

"I can discuss from up here."

"Hit him again," said Sefu.

"Wait!" squeaked Cowardly Winston. "Wait, look, I'll tell you whatever you want, all I want is to get out of here. Please."

Sefu and I looked at each other. This was going differently from what I'd expected.

"Are you alone up there?" Sefu asked.

"Yes! Yes, I don't know where my mate is and I crashed his bike and I just want to go back home."

"You haven't phoned for help?"

"I can't get a signal out here, man!"

"You're from Patriots Unite?"

"How do you know that?"

"We recognised one of you. Not sure if it was you or your mate."

"Right." Pause. "Can I go now?"

"No. Why did you come here?"

"We just came to say hi, you know."

Sefu couldn't answer this for a good few seconds. "One of you attacked my friend with a knife. Do you want to try answering that question again?"

"Look, it was nothing like that, we were just playing around, we weren't going to hurt anyone. It's just, you're lefties, right, we just came round to play a bit of a joke on you."

"What sort of joke?"

"Nothing! Nothing, don't worry about it. We weren't going to hurt anyone."

"Your friend attacked my friend. With a knife. And you weren't going to hurt anyone?"

"Yeah! Yeah, he wouldn't hurt your mate, he's not like that."

I was losing patience with this lying coward and struck up at where he was speaking. This floorboard didn't shatter, but the platform groaned, threateningly. Cowardly Winston yelped, but stayed where he was. "Hey!" he cried "Why do you keep attacking me?"

"Can you describe what you saw when your friend was playing his little joke with his knife on my friend?" Sefu asked, wisely deciding not to rise to that particular piece of bait.

"If I do that, will you let me down?"

"We'll certainly think about it."

Cowardly Winston didn't respond to that. Sefu turned to me. "Could you motivate him a little please, P?"

I strode to near where his voice had last been heard, which prompted Cowardly Winston a little. "Okay, okay," he said, "it's like this. My mate went to say hi to your mate, when suddenly this crazy guy lunges out of the shadows and attacks your fella with a sword! A sword! Come on! Who does that? I was watching from stage two of the prank: I saw him run away from your mate and climb up a drainpipe that was in the corner of your courtyard, by your little den of saboteurs. He disappeared along the top of the wall."

"You," said Sefu, "are lying. We were watching from the window. We would have seen that."

He was right. We couldn't have seen the drainpipe that ran up the wall from our window, but we would have seen someone attacking... unless they struck when we were running down the stairs...

"I'm not lying! I'm not!" Cowardly Winston whined. "Look, he was like a ninja, okay? He sheathed the sword he had and held it from a string in his teeth! When he was at the top of the wall, he took off his shirt and threw it away."

"What? Why did he take his shirt off?"

Cowardly Winston allowed a note of sarcasm to creep into his voice. "Oh, I don't know, maybe because stabbing your mate in the back caused some blood to get on his shirt? You know? Blood tends to get about a bit when attacking people with swords."

"Vince was stabbed in the front," Sefu said.

"Look, I'm just telling you what I saw, man."

"We need to check some of this out. Stay here."

"What? No! I'm out of here!"

"Hm. Did you hurt yourself when you crashed your motorbike?" Sefu asked.

"A bit, yeah."

"Are you going to die if we leave you up there?"

"You can't keep me up here!"

"Is that a no?"

"Let me down!"

"Take his ladder away, P."

I did as Sefu instructed. Cowardly Winston howled.

"We're going to check on what you told us," Sefu said. "If we find you've been telling the truth, we'll let you go, although you probably won't be able to get anywhere in this storm."

"Yeah, about that," said Cowardly Winston. "Some of your cars might not be working too well."

Sefu sighed. "What did you do?"

"Nothing! It was just a prank! We just spiked some of your tires, that's all!"

Sefu groaned.

I stepped to his side and whispered, "Where's his friend?" into Sefu's ear.

"Thanks, P," said Sefu. "You up there! Where's your mate? Should we be keeping an eye out for him?"

"I've got no idea, man! I ran after I saw that ninja. I don't know who else is in this crazy terrorist farm."

"Terrorist?" Sefu asked, bemused.

"Yeah, you lot are terrorists, you keep trying to intimidate people into rolling back the referendum. Why can't you people just accept that you lost?"

"I get you think that, but... terrorists?"

"Some of your people attacked one of my mates!"

"What with?"

"Eggs! That's an attempt to cause a change in political behaviour through causing fear! That's terrorism."

"That reminds me," I said. "Did some of your people... pull a prank on a woman in the Jeweller's Sword pub a few weeks ago?"

"Is that a woman down there?" Cowardly Winston said, sounding suddenly confident, like he could smell blood in the air.

"No," I said, lowering my voice a couple of octaves. I smacked the platform with my staff to punctuate the point.

"Sorry mate, sorry!" Cowardly Winston said, sounding this time like a cheeky, racist weasel. "The Jeweller's Sword? I did hear some of the lads talking about that. We got told by our boss that someone needed to be taught a lesson. They'd been sniffing around somewhere they weren't supposed to or something."

"You weren't involved?" Sefu asked.

"Nah, not me, they don't send me on stuff like that, I'm nobody, me."

"Mhm," I grunted.

"Let's check his story out," Sefu said. He took me by the hand and led me out of the barn. We walked back down the track, past Cowardly Winston's crashed motorbike, and retrieved our umbrellas from where we'd discarded them earlier.

"They did it!" I cried, once we were safely out of earshot. "I knew there was something more to Cassie's murder!"

"What, though?" Sefu asked. "It's all so strange. What could Cassie have found?"

"No idea," I said. "Are we alright to leave that guy in the barn? He's got a mate around somewhere. If they find each other, his mate could put the ladder back and they'll be out of here."

Sefu thought about this. "We can send Gus and Liam to watch him if we want, but I'd rather not. It's not safe; they might get jumped if they're just hanging around there. Likely his mate is around and watching us through all this rain. He's going to see us gone, and then slip in, stick up the ladder, help his mate and then get out. There's not a lot we can do about that. I need to check on Vince's body first."

"What? Why?"

"We saw the wound in his chest, but I want to know is that the only wound there? If he has a wound in his back as well, that guy –"

"His name's Cowardly Winston."

Sefu decided not to fight me on this one. "If he has a wound in his back, then Cowardly Winston might be telling the truth."

Sefu and I walked into the courtyard, and from there into the shed where we had stored Vince's body. At the far end of the shed, Vince lay, face up. His head had rolled to face towards us. The rain drummed a constant tattle-tattle-tattle on the metal roof of the shed.

I felt my hand take Sefu's. Together, we took one step, then two towards the body. It felt like we hadn't walked any distance at all. The shed should have only been a couple of metres across but it suddenly felt about the size of a hockey field.

"Zombies aren't real, right Phoebe?" Sefu asked. The tone of his voice suggested he was joking to try and lighten the mood. The slight tremor that crept in near the end of his question hinted that he was completely serious.

I squeezed his hand. "Zombies, very definitely, are not real."

We reached the body of our friend without screaming, crying or being sick, which was a minor miracle in itself. Sefu took a deep breath and bent down to take a closer look. I followed him, reasoning that being closer to Sefu was safer than standing straight up, where anything could just suddenly grab me.

I tried to clear my mind. I found the terror python was strangely absent, although there was definitely something stirring down there. Still, I decided to take advantage of this.

I examined Vince. A long, thin cut ran across most of his left cheek.

"Okay," Sefu said "we need to... roll him over."

"You're kidding." My voice sounded flat and lifeless.

"I can go and get someone else if it's too much for you?" He sounded kind, like he was trying to take care of me. I always liked that side of him. Sometimes, it could be a little patronising, but not now. Now, I was happy to be patronised. Still... I let go of his hand and together, we took hold of a part of Vince's left side.

Sefu counted down from three and when he reached 'one' I heaved. Unfortunately, it seemed that Sefu had meant for us to go on 'go' as in 'three, two, one, go', so I'd started hauling early. This meant Vince flopped over rather unevenly but, trying not to think about what we were doing, we sorted him out.

"Okay," Sefu said, "okay, now, what's here... oh no... there is a wound on his back."

Sefu drew out a pen from one of his pockets and poked gently at the wound with the blunt end. "What knife did the Patriots Unite guy have?" he asked.

I had to think back for a moment. "One of those big knives poachers have in the films. Crocodile Dundee had one."

Sefu nodded. He held his breath and slowly, delicately, inserted the pen into the wound in Vince's back.

"Okay," said Sefu, eventually. "Now I need to go outside again. Quite quickly, if you don't mind."

I was only too happy to oblige. What can I say, sometimes we're just in sync. I held an umbrella in one hand and rubbed Sefu's back with the other as he bent over and spat dejectedly on the ground.

"Okay," he said, straightening up. "I have an idea, but I need to test it. How would you feel about hugging me whilst I try and get at your back?"

"I feel you should take me out to dinner first."

"I'll buy you dinner once we've sorted this out."

Sefu walked into the other shed, the one that didn't currently contain the last earthly remains of our friend and raised his arms. Still not quite sure what this was about, I encircled his waist with my arms. I looked up into his eyes. He looked down into mine. Something smiled in the air between us.

"This," said Sefu, "isn't quite what I meant." I started to release him. "I didn't say I was complaining." I smiled.

"When we're both not living in the same extremely small, extremely public building," I said, "let's have a bit of a chat about this."

"Assuming we're not both murdered before then."

Silence.

"I get the feeling you thought that would be funny," I said.

"Yeah, as soon as I heard myself say it I knew where I'd gone wrong."

"Okay," I said, releasing Sefu, "how do you want me to hug you?"

"Like you're trying to grapple me. Like how Vince grappled the Patriots Unite guy."

"I'm not... sure..." I thought about this, then shrugged and gave an approximation of how I'd seen Vince after I'd run down the stairs.

"Okay," said Sefu, rather muffled. "Now, I'm going to poke your back, okay?"

"What with?"

"My pen."

"What *that* pen?"

"It'll just be a tiny poke, and you're wearing an overcoat. It'll wash off."

"...Go on then."

I was then treated to the feeling of an attractive, lithe man flailing in my arms. I tried to restrain him and he... tried to poke me in the back with a pen. I somehow managed to keep a straight face throughout.

"Okay," said Sefu, once he had done whatever it was he had been trying to do. "You can let me go now."

I let the poor duck go.

"Okay," he said, straightening up and stretching. "So, there's bad news and bad news."

"Give me the bad news first."

"Cowardly Winston was right. His mate didn't kill Vince. The wound in his back is too small. If a bowie knife had made it, it would be a good five centimetres wider. Plus, the wound on his back is lower than the wound on his front. It looks like he was stabbed with something that went all the way through him. That's the bad news."

"And the bad news?"

"If we decide we believe Cowardly Winston when he said a ninja used a sword to run Vince through, we either have to believe someone came here carrying a sword, or someone stole one of mine."

"Let's say for the moment someone came here with a sword. Where is he now? Where did he go? We were watching. Ninjas only vanish in martial arts films."

"If we were ninjas in a martial arts film, where would we go, besides a clump of bamboo, which we don't have."

Sefu's voice trailed off as he made a slow turn around the courtyard.

I was trying to hold it in my head, the picture of Vince grappling, the knife, the stabbing, the amount of time anyone had to get anywhere. Cowardly Winston said he'd climbed up a drainpipe in the corner of the courtyard and disappeared along the top of the wall.

I turned to look at the drainpipe. "A stranger wouldn't know to do that, would they?"

"You're saying he's lying?"

"Of course I am. Wouldn't you in his situation. We ran down into the courtyard while the attack was happening. I didn't see anyone in the courtyard other than Racist Carl and Vince. Did you?"

"No."

"And I didn't hear any vehicles leaving the courtyard, did you?"

"No."

"Okay. With that in mind, where could the killer have gone if they didn't climb up the drainpipe?"

"They could have hid in one of the sheds, or behind the cars where Cowardly Winston was hiding."

"Maybe, yes. Okay, that's good. Let's eliminate our friends from the enquiry quickly and then we can focus on working out where the attacker went. If there was an attacker. I still think that he was lying. But let's go through the motions. You happy to check on your swords?"

Sefu nodded. I felt him hesitate before leaving. Something was tugging at my mind. A memory that had been half erased by the events of the day. I watched Sefu as he disappeared back into the house. I cast my eyes over the house and saw the pipe that our ninja supposedly used. I frowned at this, before moving my eyes on. There was something else...

The courtyard wall... the concrete I had backed into when I had been pulled away from Vince's body. The bloodstain I had picked up from somewhere. I went over my actions after Vince's murder a couple of times but couldn't think of any other time I would have picked up the blood stain. I stepped back out into the rain, putting my umbrella back up as I did so. I walked over to the wall and stared at it.

The rain was still falling pretty much straight down. The overhang from the tiles at the top of the wall prevented most of the rain from reaching the painted concrete of the wall itself. Only a small area near the ground was wet, having been splashed by rain landing on the gravel. Some parts had been sprayed by rain caught by the odd gust of wind, but it was mostly dry. If this was where I had picked up the bloodstain, it should still be here.

It wasn't.

What was here instead, was a large, oddly shaped patch of discoloured concrete. I moved my staff over to the hand that held my umbrella, reached up with my newly free hand, and touched the concrete. It felt damp. I moved my hand a meter to the left. The concrete there felt mostly dry.

I traced the discolouration with my hand. There was no doubt about it, there was a large, unexplained, damp patch on the wall, about where I thought a blood stain should have been, and none of the rest of the wall was damp in the same way.

That was really not good.

Footsteps approached behind me. I sent my umbrella whirling off into the rain and spun, lashing out with my staff at my attacker. The figure dodged away from my staff. I snarled and stepped forward, only to look into the eyes of Sefu. I shuddered, shocked, and slammed the staff to the floor. "I'm sorry!" I cried, clutching at the back of my hair and trying to use the sharp feeling in my scalp to focus me in the moment. "Sorry, it's just, I've found something. I'm really sorry!"

"It's okay, Phoebe, it's okay. I should have called out to you. What have you found?"

"What did you find?" I asked, not wanting to say it out loud.

"There was blood on the sword under my bed. Someone had tried to clean it but they clearly did a rush job. They hadn't managed to get all the blood out of the hand guard. It's got to be the murder weapon."

"Did you get your fingerprints on the sword?"

"It's my sword. This is my home. My fingerprints are everywhere."

"Okay," I said, "Okay." The terror python surged within me as I unsteadily told him about the concrete.

"You know what this means?"

"It means," I said, "that Vince's murderer stabbed him from behind with a sword stolen from a non-obvious place in your room. The killer then smeared blood on the wall here. That means they were over in this corner of the courtyard, which means it's likely they *did* climb the drainpipe to get away, just like Cowardly Winston said. At some point in the last few hours, the killer cleaned the sword and put it back in its usual place in your room, and also came back down here to carefully wash the blood off the wall."

He looked at me with a nervous, incredulous smile. I really didn't want to say the next words, but Sefu kept on looking at me, and I broke.

"It was one of our friends."

My voice was barely a whisper, the best I could manage with the terror crushing my throat. "One of us murdered Vince."

Use of the term 'Will of the people' on websites hosted in the UK, 2001-2004

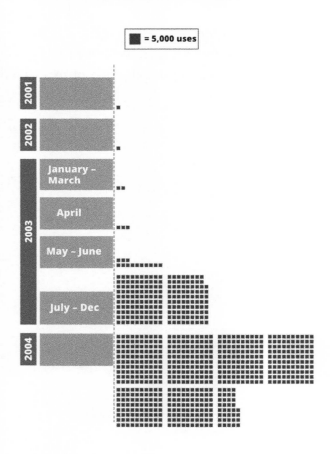

= 5,000 uses

2001

2002

2003
January – March
April
May – June
July – Dec

2004

× Chapter Eleven

We returned to the house, leaving our umbrellas and raincoats in the entranceway.

"Let's get warmed up," Sefu said. I could hear my friends still talking in the kitchen. They seemed to be stuck discussing The Topic in the same way we'd been stuck in one way or another since the referendum result. I didn't want to slip into that swamp, so slipped quietly into Sefu's room.

It felt like stepping into a sauna. I wanted to take off my clothes and lounge about in a towel. A cyberpunk-looking sound system stood on a shelf against one wall. This was always turned down to only output about 5% of its potential volume, so as not to annoy our friends. Stacks upon stacks of CDs were piled next to it. These ranged from classics of the new wave of British heavy metal, through to a clutch of CDs Sefu had received as gifts from his sister, Akina. I checked the stack and the most recently played artists were Rish, Dove Slimme and Crystal Axis. Most of these hadn't had an official release anywhere, let alone in Europe. Akina had sourced most of them from a holiday to Nairobi. I liked listening to Sefu talk about these albums, because I felt as if I was missing a good chunk of the context of the music whenever I borrowed them.

The first time I'd spent any real time in Sefu's room while I hadn't been distracted by other matters, I'd been surprised by the lack of mementos from his family or life before he came to us. I didn't have any either, but then I had Mel. Sefu was third generation British. His grandparents had come over in 1960, just after Kenyan independence. His parents had been treated pretty roughly, in a way that was completely unsurprising. It should have been a source of national shame, but somehow it continued to be waved away by most people. The struggles his parents had to go through meant they were determined for Sefu and his older sister to have the life they'd wanted for themselves. Sefu and Akina had lacked for nothing. They'd gone to good schools and good universities, on the road to getting the great careers their parents wanted for them. Akina was currently working as a specialist registrar, which was a fancy term for a junior doctor.

Sefu had read law at university. The problem was, the more he learned about the law, and how it treated anyone who wasn't the archetypal straight, white, non-disabled Brit, the more disillusioned he got. The way he told it, he was faced with a choice: do the right thing for himself or the right thing for everyone. I was extremely glad to have never been faced with that choice. I didn't like the idea that I'd fail in the face of something that important.

Sefu's parents had not agreed with his decision – the latest in a line of disagreements within the family. Sefu's parents were religious; he was not. They regularly took him back to Nairobi so he could see the place where his grandparents came from. Sefu had mixed feelings about that, but he said he always felt a wave of relief upon landing back at Birmingham Airport. Britain was his home, no matter how badly it treated him. He wanted to fight to make it better, and if his parents disapproved of his decision, well, hopefully they'd change their minds eventually.

I walked over to his sound system and pressed 'play' on the CD player. The opening track from the new A Perfect Circle album filled the room, shutting out the sounds of The Topic from the kitchen.

If I spoke so that Sefu could hear me over the music, our friends would hear me too. I thought back to the barn with Cowardly Winston in it, and sat down next to Sefu, who was towelling himself off on the edge of his bed. He turned to look at me, and I moved in close, so that our lips were next to each other's ears, much like they had been in the barn. Only this was a different situation entirely. "Are you okay with me being this close, Sefu?" I whispered.

He chuckled under his breath. "Yes, I'm happy being close to you, Phoebe. Emotionally and literally. I'm not fifteen – I don't think that by being this close we are teasing each other with… possibilities. Am I wrong?"

"No."

"We had a good time, but you were right about *us*. I didn't think you were at the time but now I agree. It would have been a bad idea for us to date in this environment where privacy is all but impossible."

I nodded, which was wasted on Sefu as he couldn't see my face and was instead staring at a Scarface poster.

"The thing is, Phoebe, I'm not sure you believe your own logic. I'm worried you didn't want to be with me because you don't think one of us was worthy of being the other's partner."

I blushed. "Is this really now the time to be talking about this?"

"Two of our friends are dead, Phoebe. If we don't do it now, we may never get another chance."

I thought about this for a moment. Was I trying to shut this down because I wanted to focus on finding out which of my friends... had...

Or was I trying to shut him down because I was running away? "No, sorry, please carry on," I said.

"So, here's my question: In your head, am I unworthy of you, or are you unworthy of me?"

"It's me," I said, the realisation clanging out of my mouth like a caltrop.

Sefu reached up and pulled me into a hug.

"I put up barriers between us right from the start," I said. "We had the Relationship Conversation early on, remember? You wanted us to date, I wanted us to stay casual. You were great about that, but it also meant neither of us got invested... and even though we were both not getting invested, I convinced myself that you didn't really care that much. Which is just stupid for so many reasons and I really don't want you to think I'm blaming you – I just got torn up and curled up in my own head and I'm really sorry and I know you don't need me to be sorry."

"No, I don't need you to be sorry."

Silence hummed in the wake of Sefu's statement. I could feel the weight of the words he wasn't saying. Sefu shifted uncomfortably, but I left the space for him to talk.

"Do you want me to be honest?" he asked, eventually.

"All day, every day."

"I worry that you were scared of getting hurt, so you pushed me away. I think being in control like that made you feel safe, but if you're regretting it now, that sense of control only meant you were sabotaging yourself. You wanted to be with me, but also you wanted to not run the risk of being hurt.

You couldn't sacrifice either of those impulses. That's just something to think about."

"Thank you," I said, so quietly it was barely a whisper. "I don't deserve you."

Sefu was silent for just a moment too long before he spoke next. "I wasn't going to say anything, because... well. Look, there's... look, I enjoyed being with you but if we're talking about things I deserve, I think I deserve to be with someone who doesn't hurt me."

Oh no... Sefu must have felt me freeze in his arms, because his embrace softened. I bit my lip hard in an effort to focus myself and dislodge that horrible snake. It and my insecurity were the enemy here. I had to not make this about myself. "Please tell me," I said.

"When we were together," Sefu said, "you said a few things that were painful, but the one that sticks in my mind was – we were holding hands and you looked down at our intertwined fingers and you said something about how much you loved the contrast between our skin – and you said it with this reverential tone... You seemed very impressed with yourself... impressed that you had a black boyfriend. And that really hurt, Phoebe. In that moment, you weren't seeing me, you were trying to achieve some kind of aesthetic. You were just another white girl fetishising about being with a black man."

I felt like I'd been slapped but I fought to get past it. *Focus, focus, focus.* "I understand," I said. "I'll do better – I'll work on that. I'm sorry for hurting you."

"Good," he said. He released me from the hug and gave my arm a soft stroke. I smiled at him and tried to concentrate.

"Thank you," I said. He smiled at me. We moved into

our lips-to-ear position once again so we could talk without shouting over the music.

I felt him nod. "Okay. So, our investigation. We don't have a massive amount of time before Eryl gets here."

"Where do we start?"

"Can we rule anyone out of our suspect pool? Other than us, of course. We were together at the time."

"I'm relieved it wasn't us," I said. "That leaves Paula, Gus, Liam, Xia, and Mel."

"It's a small suspect pool."

"Yes. Okay, let's start by finding out where they all were when the deed was done. If four of them have alibis that would make our job a lot easier. Can we talk to Mel first?"

"She didn't get home until we were all in the courtyard."

I thought back and remembered her pulling in, and feeling the desperate need to save her from having to see the body. "I'd forgotten," I said. I felt the tension drain out of my shoulders.

"You really suspected her?" Sefu sounded a little surprised.

I shrugged. "No, not really. I was scared it might be her, though. She's tougher than she looks."

"But it wasn't, so that leaves our mother hen, Paula. Our ideologue, Xia. Our ex-warrior Gus, who has occasionally been known to revert to warrior status. And Liam, who is very clever, very good, but also kind of lazy. Who should we tackle first?"

I thought for a moment. "Xia."

"You want to get her alibi first?"

"Yup. She's the best climber of the lot of us, and she's

been very… keen to get us focussing on Fairford and not the murder."

I felt him shrug. "She's also completely against violence."

"In theory, absolutely," I said. "But maybe she was pushed over the edge. Everyone has their limit."

"Do you really believe that?" He sounded a little sad.

"Almost everyone, then. Are you really telling me you think it's unimaginable that it's her?"

There was a long pause. Finally, he shook his head reluctantly. "No."

"Right then." I drew away from Sefu, slapped my knees and stood up. "Let's go talk to her."

Sefu agreed, and we made our way to the kitchen, where Paula, Gus, and Liam were still at it.

"You see this? This is the problem," Paula said. "It's taken people who should be on the same side and turned them against each other. No one benefits from this except the people at the top of the pyramid: arms manufacturers, BP and Shell, and the media corps, which feeds off people's anxiety. To me, it's obvious that this referendum was really just a means to consolidate power."

Liam nodded, and Gus shrugged noncommittally, but all three of them looked tired and sad, rather than angry.

Gus opened his mouth, but before he could speak, I leaped in. "Has anyone seen Xia?"

All three looked round at us.

"Have you found the Patriots Unite people?" Paula asked.

"One of them, yes," Sefu said. "He's stuck where he is for the moment." We neglected to tell them that his mate was probably in the process of rescuing him. At the moment, our problem was not with Patriots Unite but with us.

"We just need to check something with Xia," I said.

"She went to do more planning for Fairford," Paula said. "She's probably in her room."

"Actually, I heard her go downstairs," Gus said. "I haven't heard her come back up yet."

I managed a smile for them. "Thanks."

Gus nodded, and started in on another explanation of how no one would be divided if everyone just accepted the referendum result and moved past it. We left them to it and descended out of the house and towards the stable.

It was less obviously trashed than it had been after the cop raid. Yesterday morning? How was that only yesterday morning? It felt like months ago. The place looked deserted from the courtyard, but as I stuck my head through the plastic sheeting, I spotted Xia at one of the large trestle tables, poring over an Ordnance Survey map.

"Hey, Xia," I said.

She looked up, her gaze flicking between the two of us. Her expression tightened. "I'm busy. With actual useful work that will save lives. So if you're still playing cops and robbers..."

"We found some lummock from Patriots Unite," Sefu said. "He's hiding in a barn."

"So call the police," Xia said.

"No hurry, we've got him stranded," Sefu said. "He's admitted that he's got a mate here."

A flash of worry passed over Xia's face before she looked down at her map again and focused. "And?"

I stayed quiet, curious to see where Sefu was going with this.

"And we want to at least find where he's hiding. Did you see or hear anything? Everyone else is upstairs."

Xia shook her head and threw her hands up so they trembled by her temples. Her eyes didn't move from her map. "No," she said. "Look, I'm a little busy."

"Great, that lets us rule out wherever you were when he went to ground. You know, after Vince... Where were you?"

"I was doing Pilates in one of the old barns. Liam was there, actually. Then Vince was attacked." Her voice was getting steadily more irritated. "Then we came back, and we were in the kitchen for a while, but they wouldn't stop talking about the stupid Topic, and we've got so much planning to do if we're going to do this right, so I came down here. I need you all here on this. The people of Iraq need you on this. I understand Mel collapsing, but none of this is helping anything or anyone." Her voice was grating against her gritted teeth and tears hovered in the corners of her eyes. "Do you really think Vince would want to you to be running around chasing stupid little lummocks in his memory, or sitting up in the kitchen grinding over the same tedious arguments for the thousandth time?"

"Look, Xia," I began.

"Are you going to help me work out how we can assist in the Fairford action?" Xia asked, without looking up.

"Not yet."

The tension in Xia's voice sang like an angle grinder. "Then please let me get on with it."

"Of course," Sefu said. He gestured me towards the stairs, and I followed him numbly.

I felt shocked by the strength of Xia's reaction. I looked to Sefu, who looked placid. He looked at my expression and smiled, sadly. "You know that it's quite common for people to respond to grief by lashing out, right?"

"Yes," I said. "But…"

"But nothing. Try to cut Xia some slack. You saw how she was with Cassie, and then Vince. She's not herself right now. She's trying to hold herself together, and it looks like she's doing that by trying to establish some control over her life."

"She's supposed to be committed to consensus decision-making."

"She is, she's just not at her best right now. Two of her friends have died."

"You're sure it's that? You're sure she doesn't want us to stop investigating for some other reason?"

Sefu shook his head. "Don't start thinking about that just yet. First, we need to confirm her alibi."

The python retreated a little, letting me breathe a bit. I nodded, even though I wasn't convinced.

"Besides, that went perfectly."

I blinked at him. "It did?"

"Do you think Xia would have told us anything if we'd admitted we were after an alibi for her?"

I thought about it. "No. She'd have been hurt by the suggestion and gone on the defensive. More on the defensive."

"Right. We have an alibi for her that we can confirm with someone else, and she still thinks that the thugs killed Vince."

"About that. She said she was doing Pilates. Did that stall seem like the sort of place you'd do Pilates in?"

"There was an exercise mat."

"Yes, but it didn't feel like a spot to do stretchy exercise in, it looked like a sanctuary."

"We didn't ask what the space was, we asked what she was doing. Maybe it is her sanctuary. We all have ways of coping with living in a place like this, where we're all on top of each other all the time."

"There were wine glasses."

"Xia and Liam get on. Liam might have been trying to take Xia's mind off Cassie with a little Merlot."

"Okay, okay. What if Liam doesn't confirm her story?"

"I'm sure he will," he said. "But if he doesn't, then you're right, we should give some serious thought into why she's trying to shut us down."

"Right," I said. "So let's confirm Xia's story with Liam, then talk to the others."

"Yeah. But we need to not let on about the murderer. Xia isn't the only one who might call the police."

"We might need to tell them something. They might not buy vagueness a second time."

Sefu nodded. We walked back into the house and towards to the kitchen, where the interminable discussion of The Topic was continuing.

"I don't understand why people didn't just defer to the UN," Liam said. "They said there wasn't enough evidence of WMD. And, lo, none has been found."

"Yes, well, people have had enough of experts, apparently," said Gus. "I'm starting to think maybe listening to that big red bus instead of the UN weapons inspectors wasn't the best idea our country's ever had."

Paula looked up and saw us approaching. "Did you find her?" she asked.

"Yes, thanks," Sefu said. "I wonder if we could have a word with Liam outside?"

Liam raised his eyebrows. He turned to look at Sefu as if he was being worked by an arthritic puppeteer. "Why?" he asked.

"We just have a question we wanted to ask you about something Xia said, it's nothing to worry about."

"What's going on, Sefu?" Gus's voice sounded diamond hard.

"We're trying to work out some stuff involving the Patriot Unite thugs. We can't explain right now, but it's going to be much more reliable if we speak to you all individually. Memory is really easy to muddle, particularly when it's just a fleeting impression."

The air hardened between all of us. I decided to give them a little poke. "That's one reason. Another is because people are getting murdered and we'd like to keep the numbers low."

The air hardened for just a second before Liam broke into a laugh that hovered between 'I'm glad you broke the tension' and 'I'm on the edge of crying'. He got to his feet and traipsed out into the corridor. We led him down the corridor and the stairs. I'd been expecting to have to hold our discussion in the entranceway, but, to my surprise, I found the rain had stopped. The air was drying outside, although there were still angry-looking clouds overhead.

We stepped outside and breathed in the cool, fresh air.

"So, what's this about?" Liam asked.

"We're trying to get some clues on where the second thug is hiding. So it's really useful to know whether or not anyone saw anything, and where they were. So," Sefu said, "where were you when Vince was attacked, and then afterwards?"

Liam shifted from foot to foot for a while before muttering, "In one of the old barns."

"With Xia?" I asked. "She *was* there too?"

"Yup."

Sefu nodded. "Did you see anyone else?"

"... I saw Gus walking past the barn, northwards. I didn't see him again until we met up in the courtyard after your shout. We've been in the kitchen since."

"Okay, thanks, Liam, that's super helpful," I said. "Is there anything else you can think that'd help us?"

"I don't know if it had to do with Vince or Cassie, but Gus has been saying that something weird has been going on with the maintenance on the farm. I don't know what, though."

Sefu perked up. "The maintenance? How was it odd?"

Liam smiled, and in that smile I saw crow's feet at the corners of his eyes. "If you reflect back on what I just said, you'll remember I said that I don't know what was odd about it, mate."

"Okay, sorry," Sefu said. "That's it, questions over. I hope that wasn't too painful."

Liam smiled thinly and headed back inside.

"Could you ask Gus to come and join us?" I called after him. He nodded.

Gus joined us after a couple of minutes, clearly still reluctant. Sefu opened in the same way, explaining some not entirely untrue context, and asking where he'd been.

"I'm not happy with this, friends," he said, glancing at the both of us.

Sefu nodded. "I understand. Please believe that we wouldn't be asking about this if it wasn't important."

"Fine," Gus said, although it clearly wasn't. "I was out past the barns, checking them for damage. I heard the yelling and came back. Since then, I've been in the kitchen."

"Did you see any sign of our fascists? Movement, disturbed places, anything?" asked Sefu.

"No. Nothing."

"Okay," I said. "We heard that there's something weird about the maintenance on the farm. What's up with that?"

Gus pursed his lips. "It's not weird, necessarily, I just... There hasn't been any work done for a while. That's weird. The boiler needs servicing, the water tank should have been checked, stuff like that. I haven't wanted to bring it up with Paula because it sounds like I don't trust her. Maybe I'm getting the wrong end of the stick."

"Mm," I said. "Thanks. Can you think of anything else that might help us?"

He shook his head.

"Okay, thanks," I said. "We're done."

"You want me to send Paula down?" he asked.

"If you could, that'd be great."

Gus disappeared into the house. I turned to Sefu. "What do you think?"

"Well, Liam's out. He and Xia alibi each other... Unless you think they're in it together?"

I shook my head. "Not likely."

"So it's Gus. Or Paula. One or the other."

"It's probably Gus – *if* we trust everything Cowardly Winston said, which I don't." I sighed. "Paula isn't a good fit. We should talk to her so we've got as much information as possible, but we should also test to see if it's even possible to do what our ninja supposedly did. Even then, I'd want to know why Gus did it."

Slow footsteps alerted us to Paula's arrival. She emerged from the house looking more tired than I'd ever seen her. It was a shock to see her looking quite this bad. Paula was the person who'd taken all of us in. She was like a mother to some of us, but not in the awful way that phrase implies. She was like a mother in the unrealistic way films and TV portray them.

"Sorry for dragging you down here, Paula," Sefu said. If I'd noticed how Paula looked, there was no doubt Sefu was well aware too. "We'll be quick. Could you tell us where you were when Vince was attacked?"

"I was alone in my room," Paula said. "I was working on the accounts, then I heard Sefu shouting."

I wanted to give her a hug, but I didn't want to draw this out for her. "Thanks, Paula. Can you think of anything that might help us work out what happened?"

Paula shook her head. I wondered if I should ask her about the maintenance, but she swayed slightly on her feet, and I realised I'd waited too long.

"Thanks, Paula," Sefu said. "Sorry again."

Paula waved this away in a small motion that seemed to drain her yet further. She turned and walked into the house. Sefu and I looked at each other. He raised his eyebrows. I grimaced. We listened to the fading sounds of Paula climbing the steps up to the first floor. Once we were sure we weren't going to be overheard, I said: "It's not an alibi."

"No, it's not. I wish she'd seen or heard something that would let us rule her out. Poor Paula."

I nodded. "Okay, so, let's find out if it would be possible for a ninja to kill someone, climb up a pipe, shimmy along a wall, and disappear, all without any of us seeing them."

Voter representation for the 2003 referendum

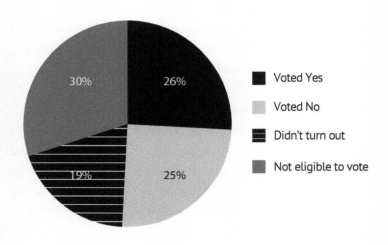

Legend:
- Voted Yes
- Voted No
- Didn't turn out
- Not eligible to vote

× Chapter Twelve

The exterior wall of the courtyard was two, maybe two and a half meters tall. I couldn't touch the top, but Sefu could if he jumped. On nice days, it shone in the sun, but even under today's grey sky, it looked like home.

Sefu peered up at the wall. "The boys from Yamakasi could have climbed this easily," he said. Yamakasi was a French parkour film Sefu had imported earlier this year. We'd watched it in his room along with a space cake apiece. It'd have been a cakewalk for them, so to speak.

He wrinkled his nose. "The thing is, barbed wire is strung across the top of this wall. Even if someone got up there, they'd have to stand on the barbed wire. Cirque du Soleil does something like that. But let's say the murderer is not an internationally renowned gymnast. Let's say that instead, they try to stand on the wall-top with both feet on one side of the barbed wire and try to not get their knees shredded. Or maybe they stand with one foot on each side of the wire, straddling it, standing just on the very edges of the wall."

Cirque du Soleil was looking like the more likely option. I decided to ignore the problem. "If they did manage to move along the top of the wall somehow, they could climb into the house through that window on the north wall. The window at ninety degrees to the one overlooking the courtyard"

"Yeah, but the barbed wire would have stopped them. How about this: Cowardly Winston is correct. They climbed the pipe, and then if they had an old carpet or something, they could have got past a few feet of the wire, like in Fight Club. Then it's easy to get into the house." He walked over to the corner of the house and inspected the drainpipe that ran up to the roof.

"That's no good," I said, "you can't climb drainpipes. Cowardly Winston is wrong or lying."

"Why not?" Sefu asked.

"Most drainpipes are light, hollow and plastic," I said. "The bolts that secure them to a wall aren't designed to support a person. If someone tried it, the pipe would either snap or pull away from the wall."

"Hm," said Sefu. "There's just one thing." He knocked on the pipe with his knuckles. "This pipe is metal."

My eyebrows shot up. "Well, that's different." And I joined Sefu in staring at the pipe. I looked up the length of the pipe to where it reached the top of the wall.

"I don't think this is a drainpipe," I said. "Look up there. I think it connects to the water tank in the attic, or some other system."

"Do you think one of us could climb it?" Sefu asked.

"Of course. Xia, Vince and I could, for sure." I shuddered. "You know what I mean. Gus, Mel and Paula might be able to. Maybe even Liam if he was desperate."

He stared at me for a moment. "Paula? She's about ninety!"

"Paula is in her mid-sixties, and you'd be amazed at the ages of people we get at the climbing centre. Paula is wiry. She's in a decent state. If she was determined, she might well be able to climb this. She's not the most likely candidate, but it's premature to rule her out."

Sefu nodded. "Okay, let's check the window and see if it's possible for someone to get in."

We went back up to the first floor, and Sefu opened the suspicious window. He peered out. "I'm not sure," he said. "Take a look."

I swapped places with him and leaned out of the window to look down at the wall. It was maybe half a metre below the window. It would have been an easy climb, if not for the barbed wire – past its best, but still not the sort of thing you wanted to be messing about with.

The wall was around fifteen or twenty centimetres deep so the barbed wire didn't cover all of it. Nonetheless, it would be a stretch for someone to climb the water pipe, edge along the wall without losing their balance, open the window and climb in through without shredding themselves on the wire at the same time. I cast my gaze meticulously across the zone where our climber might have traversed. I was looking for some sign that the wire had been disturbed or moved in any way. I didn't find one, but I found something quite a bit better.

"Sefu, come look at this," I said. I pointed at an area of the wire near to where the water pipe was.

"What am I looking for?" Sefu stuck his head out of the window next to mine.

"Can you see something clinging to the barbed wire by the water pipe?" I asked.

"Yes, I can..." Sefu said, "I just can't see what it is."

"We're going to have to get out there and take a look," I said. "Do you know where there's a spare bit of old carpet?"

"There's an old rug in the bedroom no one's using. We could use that?"

"Okay, but can you feel that? A breeze has picked up. If

I'm going out there, I need my gloves. One second."

I grabbed my winter gloves from my room and then snatched the rug from the spare bedroom. I folded the carpet over itself lengthwise and returned to Sefu's side, where I flung the carpet as neatly as I could over the barbed wire.

"You want to be the one to climb out?" Sefu asked. "I'm not one of nature's climbers."

I nodded and climbed up onto the windowsill, holding onto it with both hands. Gingerly, I lowered myself so that my feet were resting on the very edge of the concrete wall, then I turned so that my hands were resting on the carpet. The barbed wire gave alarmingly when I rested my weight on it, but I got used to the way it sprung and swayed after moving my weight across it a few times.

I wasn't particularly steady or comfortable, but I could move safely. I sidestepped away from the window, towards the courtyard. I felt chilly and exposed up here. The wind was tugging at my clothing. I also felt dreadfully visible. Just to check, I turned to look at where Sefu was standing, on the other side of the window, and gave him a little wave. He waved back. That settled it. This was far too conspicuous to try when someone was standing at that window. I looked down at the courtyard. I was definitely visible from there as well.

This put a pretty big hole in Cowardly Winston's testimony. If our ninja had climbed up the pipe and then in through the window I'd just climbed out of, they'd have had to choose their moment carefully. Any mistiming would have meant they'd be spotted either by me down in the courtyard or by Paula rushing down the stairs to help Vince. Surely the ninja wouldn't have had time to climb the drainpipe, sidle across the wall and come in through the window, all without being seen?

I looked down at the wire, past the end of our carpet. The thing we'd seen was a scrap of damp, reddish fabric, clinging to one of the barbs. I plucked it off and pocketed it. Then I sidled back along the wall to Sefu.

"What's up?" he asked.

I passed him the piece of fabric to look at and explained the visibility issue while he studied it.

He nodded, stuffing the bit of fabric into a pocket. "You're right, our ninja would have had to be very careful to not be seen climbing in the window. Tell you what, duck down as far as you can and I'll walk about a bit, see how obvious you are."

I tried to duck down so I was facing the window, but this didn't work as my bum always just hit the barbed wire. I ended up turning so I was at ninety degrees to the window, balancing precariously. I had both feet on the wall, one in front of the other, one hand resting against the building and one on the carpet.

I saw Sefu's head periodically pop into view as he moved about. It was pretty uncomfortable, so I was relieved when Sefu stuck his head out of the window, took one look at me and ushered me inside.

"I could always see you," he said. "Obviously you were better hidden when I was standing in some places than others but when it's a matter of getting away with murder, I wouldn't have thought our culprit would have wanted to risk any of them."

I stretched. "There was some space on the other side of the window, towards the east wall. We should try that one as well."

I started opening the window when Sefu stopped me. "I'll take this one. You look like you've got a cramp."

I wanted to argue, but I was cold and uncomfortable. I whipped off my damp gloves as he started to climb out of the window and held them out. Sefu put them on, gratefully, and nearly fell as he struggled to find a purchase for his toes on the concrete wall.

"Your shoes are too big," I said, conversationally.

"What?"

"If your toes are slipping it's probably because there's too much room in your shoes for your toes. Next time you need shoes, we should shop for some smaller ones."

Sefu stared up at me from where he was clinging to the carpet that was wrapped over the barbed wire. "Yeah, sounds good."

"Tell you what, while you're finding your feet down there, I'm going to wander up and down the corridor and you can tell me if you hear me. That way we'll know if our culprit could have lurked out of sight for the coast to clear."

I stomped up the corridor theatrically, then started wandering back down, pausing to check on Mel as I did so. It looked like she'd gone to sleep, which was a relief.

When I reached the window, I couldn't see Sefu. He'd either managed to hide, or he'd fallen off the wall. Or he'd got fed up and had come in. "Sefu?" I said, quietly.

"WoooOOOoooo, I'm a ghost," said a ghost. Sefu stuck his head around the right-hand edge of the window and waved.

"Sefu," I said, my voice expressionless. "Look out, there's a ghost out there." I moved to block the window entrance.

"Yup," he said. "Can you move so I can get in?"

"Not on your life, I've got to keep the ghost out."

"It's okay, it's gone now. Besides, we don't have that much time to mess about, we've only got two and a half hours before Eryl gets here."

I thought about this for a second and then moved out of the way.

Sefu climbed in and shut the window. "Okay," he said. "It's possible to hide round there, and I could hear you moving around. We're making progress."

"The last piece of the puzzle is whether it's actually possible to climb that pipe."

Sefu nodded. We descended back down to the courtyard and approached the pipe. I wrapped my right hand around it and gave it an experimental tug. It didn't budge or shift in the way a plastic drainpipe would have. That was the good news. The bad news was that the pipe was still wet from the storm. I'd have to do this quickly and safely.

The quickest way to climb a pipe or a bar next to a wall is to hold onto the pipe and place your feet on the wall. Push out with your feet for traction and hold onto the pipe for all you're worth. Then, simply walk your feet up the wall.

That wasn't going to happen, not in these conditions. I couldn't trust my hands were going to make it all the way up, not on wet metal. I was going to have to do something safer, but far less dignified. I tucked the pipe between my legs as if I was climbing the world's thickest and stiffest rope, and reached up and grabbed the pipe with both hands. Then I hauled myself up with my arms and gripped the pipe again with my legs.

I wouldn't be able to do this over any great distance. It required upper body strength I didn't have. It was only a short way up, though. The only tricky bit was when I accidentally grabbed a bracket that held the pipe to the wall and put my full weight on it. The sudden shock of angled metal biting into my hands made me wince. More than that, it nearly made me fall off the pipe. I gritted my teeth and made a complaining 'arrrggg' noise, while I wrapped my legs around my pipe and frantically repositioned my hands.

After a deeply unpleasant minute, I reached the point where I could step onto the wall. I reached out with my left foot and found a purchase. I shifted my weight before moving my right foot, then I moved my hands from the pipe to the wall of the house. I was safe.

"You all right?" Sefu said from below me.

I held out a thumbs up. I looked down at the pipe. "We've also just obliterated a load of forensic evidence."

Sefu threw up jazz hands. "Oh no, how will the cops tirelessly pursue justice now?"

My bark of laughter was cut short by the sight of the medical tape at Sefu's temple. Best not to think about Sefu's rhetorical question too hard.

Okay, so our theory was technically possible. It didn't seem especially likely, given how fiddly it was, but it was an option. We couldn't rule out Cowardly Winston as a liar. I climbed back inside and hauled the carpet in after me. It snagged on a piece of the wire and I had to tug it free. Once I'd managed to get it inside, I saw a decent sized hole near one of the edges. A large piece of the carpet had been left behind. I wasn't going to go fetch it.

I returned the carpet to the empty room, wondering if the murderer had done this exact thing only a matter of hours ago. The floor around the carpet looked darker than the rest of the boards. Also, now my hands weren't in gloves, I could feel the carpet was soaked through. Either someone had recently thrown a bucket of water over it for reasons unknown, or it had been out in the rain less than an hour ago.

When I returned to the courtyard, I found Sefu waiting for me. "I've been thinking. We should also have a look about for Vince's mobile phone. He was talking on that when he got attacked by the Patriots Unite guy, right?"

"That's right, I wonder where that got to…"

"Right? I also want to go through his pockets. I don't think anyone's done that yet."

"I'm not super keen to go through the pockets of a dead man."

"Neither am I."

"Shall we rock-paper-scissors? The loser goes through Vince's pockets and the winner gets to search for a mobile phone in the nice, open, non-haunted air."

"Do you have a thing about ghosts, Phoebe?"

"I'm open to the idea."

"Fair enough."

We held up a clenched fist each over the palms of our left hands.

"One, two, three." Sefu showed rock and I showed paper.

He shot an apprehensive look through the window at the shed where the last earthly remains of Vince were lying. "Best two out of three?" I asked.

"Thanks, but I've got this."

I went and stood close to where I'd seen Vince get attacked and turned slowly on the spot, looking around at ground level. This didn't reveal anything, certainly not a swishy silver Nokia. Vince had grabbed the arm of his attacker – the arm holding the knife. He must have dropped the phone to do that. It should be where I was standing, but it wasn't. Maybe someone else had picked it up, or maybe it had been kicked in the struggle.

It could have been kicked just about anywhere. The good news was that it would have skittered along at roughly ground level. Wherever it wound up, it must be on the ground. Hopefully it had been kicked somewhere out of the rain. I squatted down, and started looking around the courtyard, trying to ignore the cold dampness clawing at me. There was a deep shadow under one of the cars, which looked odd but not like a phone. I made a mental note to come back to that later. I swivelled and directed my gaze towards the north side of the courtyard. There – in a gap between the perimeter wall and the entrance to the house, something sat, squat and ugly. Again, it looked interesting but it wasn't a phone. I swivelled again.

There. In the stable, underneath a palette of leaflets detailing the case for non-interventionism, lay a small, dark rectangular object that shouldn't have been there. I scuttled over and reached under the palette to fish the object out. I drew it out into the light and, yes, it was Vince's phone. I stepped back into the courtyard and reached into the gap between the stable and the perimeter wall. My hand came up holding a wicked-looking bowie knife.

The weapon Racist Carl had attacked Vince with. I hadn't even thought to wonder about where that had wound up. The blade was long, wide and thin – it looked about right for the cut on Vince's cheek. Sefu had said that a bowie knife like this couldn't have made the wound in Vince's chest. Looking at the knife, I knew Sefu was right. It was much wider than the hole in Vince's chest...

I shook myself, trying to shake off images of my friend's eyes staring up at me. I turned my attention to Vince's phone. I pressed a button, hoping to access his messages and find something along the lines of 'Vince! You have crossed me for the last time, I shall kill you tonight by means unknown! – signed' and then there'd just be the name of our murderer. Such a text might well have been on the phone. I couldn't tell, because it was PIN locked.

"Found it?" Sefu asked from behind me.

I turned around to see Sefu emerging from the shed at the other side of the courtyard, looking a little grey. My concern must have shown on my face, because he smiled wanly at me. "I hope I never get used to seeing... that," he said, "but at the same time, it would be nice to be able to look at Vince and not want to immediately run away, cry or vomit. What's that knife?"

"It's Racist Carl's."

Sefu's eyebrows shot up. "The guy that attacked Vince? Good find, Phoebe. Mind if I take a look?"

I handed the knife over silently and smiled as Sefu began a minute inspection of the blade.

"There are some flecks of blood but nothing else. Where did you find it?"

I pointed to the spot, which was sheltered by the roof of the house. Sefu nodded. "Okay, I'll stick this with Vince's body for now. We can come back to it if we think of anything. Sound good?"

I nodded, absently. My attention kept getting dragged back to Vince's locked phone. I tried typing in Vince's birth year – 1967 – as Sefu's footsteps crunched towards the shed. Vince's phone beeped at me and I was met with the

147

unwelcome information that I only had two attempts to enter the correct PIN remaining.

"Okay," said Sefu, emerging from the shed again. Did you get anything off the phone?"

"It's locked."

"Urg. Did you try his birth year?"

"Yep. Didn't work."

"How about Mel's birth year?"

I tried 1975 but the phone didn't unlock.

"The most common PIN in the world is 1234," Sefu said. "I don't know if you want to give that a try?"

"We'd better not. Only one try left. Did Agatha Christie have anything to say about codes?"

"All sorts of things, but I can't remember anything relevant to the 21st century."

"Let's see if he kept the PIN written down or something. Did you find anything on his body?"

"Receipts. Some cash. Nothing particularly interesting."

"Okay," I clapped my hands. I felt like I had some momentum. We were finding things out, we were making progress. The terror python was... active but untroublesome. I should keep it that way. What would be good to do now? Ah, yes. "I want to wake Mel up and ask her about Vince. She followed him somewhere yesterday. I want to know what she found out."

"But Mel wasn't here."

"No, but we still might learn something about Vince that would shed some light on why someone might have killed him."

"Okay, but just for speculation's sake, who do you think is more likely to be the murderer, Gus or Xia?"

That caused me to stop in the middle of our courtyard. "Well, neither."

"Say what?"

"I don't think either of them could have killed Vince."

"You're saying we've made a mistake somewhere and we should consider Liam and Paula?"

I pinched the bridge of my nose. "No, no. Sorry. I'm really tired. I mean… It suddenly hit me that we're talking about one of our friends murdering another of our friends."

"That's what we've been doing this whole time, Phoebe."

"Yes, I know, I'm sorry, I always explain myself so poorly. I mean… Up until you said that, I think I'd been treating this whole thing as an Agatha Christie. As a puzzle, not something that would have real impact on anything. I think I'm still expecting Vince to stick his head out of that shed and say this has all been a misunderstanding."

Sefu steepled his fingers against his lips. "I think, under normal circumstances, that sort of displacement is unhealthy, but given we have to get to the bottom of this mess sooner rather than later, we should possibly lean into it."

"By 'it' you mean the puzzle nature of this situation."

"Yes. I shall start by calling you Miss Marple."

I touched a finger to Sefu's chest and put on a starchy accent. "Call me whatever you like, but don't call me late for tea."

"If that's what you're going to be like then I'd rather not call you Miss Marple, if it's all the same to you."

"Sorry, yes, that was a poor attempt at humour. Are there other women detectives?"

"Jessica Fletcher?"

"English detectives, please, I can't do an American

accent. Plus, the Americans got us into this Iraq Referendum in the first place because a bunch of people from Saudi Arabia committed a terrorist attack."

"I think some were also from the UAE, Egypt and Lebanon."

"But not Iraq."

"No, not Iraq. Don't look for logic with American wars... DCI Jane Tennison?"

"I can live with Helen Mirren, if you can."

"Sure. Now, are there any black English detectives?"

We thought about this for a few minutes.

"I can think of a few American ones..." I said.

Sefu nodded. "Mostly from The Wire."

"Its actors were English."

"Yes, but not the characters."

"Er..." I stalled.

"I can't think of any at all. How about you?"

"There has to be one, surely."

Sefu shot me a look that was half amused, but mostly dreadfully sad.

"Maybe let's drop the whole detective thing," I said.

He grinned. "We're making progress!"

We climbed the stairs up to the first floor. Things had fallen silent in the kitchen. Thankfully. I stuck my head in and saw that everyone had gone to their rooms. That was probably wise. I returned to my room and put my slippers on. I wasn't going outside again for a while if I could help it.

Sefu joined me after a short while. "I'm going to have a poke about in Vince's room and see if I can find the PIN for his phone, or anything else useful."

I nodded. "I want to check on Mel, see if I can establish

where she was when the murder happened. We know she wasn't here, but we don't know where exactly."

Sefu and I parted ways. I walked to Mel's room and knocked softly. No one responded from inside, so I eased the door open and stuck my head through. Mel was still lying in bed. I couldn't hear any sounds of crying.

I crept inside and loomed over her like the interrogating sword of Damocles. I had a quick peek around to see if I could see anything that would help from where I was standing but, unsurprisingly, nothing jumped out at me.

"Mel," I hissed, kneeling down.

"Mm?"

"Mel?"

"What?"

"We're trying to establish where everyone was around the time of the tragedy. Where were you?"

"Driving. I'd dropped Katie back after climbing, then I had a tutoring gig to go do." She waved a weary arm up at her wall. In the twilight, I could see the colour coded wall planner she used to keep track of her tutoring. I walked over to the planner and squinted at it before returning to my sister's side.

"Great, thanks. Sorry to bother you with this. How are you feeling?"

"Terrible."

"Of course. One last thing. You followed Vince, right? What did you find?"

"I thought he might have been having an affair," Melissa said. "But I followed him and he wasn't, it was just a work thing." Her voice sounded a little too deep. A little too controlled. Too Melissa-y.

"A work thing? Where was it?"

"Some house in the Jewellery Quarter."

"Where in the Jewellery Quarter?" If we could trace the house, we might be able to find out if it really was a landscaping gig or if something else had been going on.

"I don't know, Phoebe, it was near St Paul's church."

I suddenly felt very cold. "Great, thanks!" I chirped, before backing out of the room and sprinting away.

My sister had just lied to me.

× Chapter Thirteen

I stuck my head into Vince's room. Sefu jumped and spun to look at me. He looked cornered. He looked ready to attack. The drawer he'd been rooting through stood open.

I took a step back, my breath catching in my throat.

Sefu reeled himself back in. He moved his feet so that they were next to each other. He hunched his shoulders and smiled, charmingly. He held his left arm loosely at his side but moved his right behind his back. I saw the hand clenching into a fist just before it disappeared.

"What's up, Phoebe?" he whispered.

No.

Oh no, no, no, no, no. I had been an idiot again. I had been a selfish, selfish – no. I stopped that line of thought right there. I concentrated. I remembered Sefu – all the times tonight he had been hesitant or withdrawn. I knew what I needed to do.

I slipped inside, grabbed him and dragged him into his bedroom. I swapped another CD into his sound system, because I'd had enough of A Perfect Circle last time and pressed play. Pearl Jam oozed out of the speakers and I immediately regretted my decision. I started to go back before I shook myself. This was too important to keep my ears free from Pearl Jam. I'd just have to be quick.

There was this mantra that Mum used to get me to say out loud before every party I went to, before every school play, before every family event. I fell out of the habit when I went to university, but I felt it applied now.

I will not make this about myself. I thought. *I will be like Melissa. Melissa wouldn't mess this up. I will be like Melissa. I will not make this about myself.*

I bore down on Sefu, who clearly had no idea what was going on. I leaned forward so my lips were next to his ear as before. "Sefu," I said, "I'm sorry."

"What?" he said "What for?"

"You've been taking care of me today, a lot. A lot a lot. And – when I think about how we talk to each other, I've got a nasty feeling that you're always the one that supports me. Have I ever been there for you when you needed to cry or needed to hit a pillow or something?"

A dreadful pause followed before Sefu said, "I don't think so."

I wanted to rest my head on his shoulder and cry. I hated that some part of me was trying to make this moment about me.

"I might be pretty bad at it," I said. "For example, I'm really sorry for how I, just now… I looked at you like you were a threat. And I'm sorry for that. It's just, I'd love for you to feel comfortable enough around me to tell me when I hurt you. If you can't, or don't want to put yourself in that position I'll understand. I'll absolutely understand. You shouldn't have to sacrifice your mental health in order to help me. It's not your job to correct my every mistake. But if you're holding yourself back – if you're stopping yourself from showing anger around me because you're scared of how I'd react then I understand. I do, but if you were willing to be patient with me, to give me a chance to get past this bullshit in my head, then I'd love to be there for you in the way you're always there for me."

Sefu was still next to me.

"I'm angry about what happened to Vince," Sefu said, after a long moment. "I'm angry about what happened to Cassie. I'm angry about how you looked at me just now. I'm scared about what this means for our group. I'm feeling so, so sorry for Mel."

I embraced him lightly, wanting him to feel like he could break away if he wanted. He stayed motionless in my arms, and then, after a moment, he did move away. I stayed where I was, while Sefu moved to the bed. He sat there and I saw his cheeks were glistening.

He looked up at me and opened his mouth. No sound came out.

"Whatever you need," I said, "I'm here."

He fidgeted. He seemed torn between a couple of courses of action. I'd possibly made a mistake by bringing this up.

"Would you like some space?" I asked.

He smiled at this and patted the bed next to him. "I think you were right just now," he said. "I think I could use a hug."

I sat next to him and embraced him. I felt him shudder in my arms. Then a sound burst out of him. He sobbed. He hugged me back, and we stayed like that for what seemed like a long time.

Eventually he pulled back, and I stretched. "So," he said.

I felt an urge to babble apologies, to reel off excuses. I just couldn't think of any. "Sefu, I..."

He gave me a slightly tight smile. "What did you want when you interrupted my search of Vince's room?" He leaned in close, so we could talk without being overheard, just not as close as I was used to.

I had to think before I remembered the answer. "Mel knows something about the murder."

Sefu jolted as if I'd just electrocuted him. "What? What does she know?"

"I don't know, she didn't tell me."

"Why don't you start again, Phoebe?"

"Good idea. So, I asked Mel about her alibi. She said she was tutoring some kid. I got the name from her wall planner, so I'll try to find a way to check on that. Anyway, then I asked her about Vince. She was going to follow him after climbing. She said she followed him to a work thing by St Paul's church."

Sefu nodded. "Okay, so?"

"Sefu, I've driven around there after climbing. I've gone out for drinks there. The pub where Cassie died is near that church. There are absolutely no private gardens of any size down there. The only green spaces are cemeteries, those communal gardens blocks of flats have and public land."

"Vince could have been working on one of those?"

"Mel said she followed him to a house. Not an office. Not a council building to have a meeting about landscaping public land. Specifically, a house. She lied to me. She's hiding something."

"But what could Mel be hiding?"

"I don't know. Something about following Vince."

"How can we find out what it is?"

"Now *that* I don't know. I never worked out how to get Melissa to do something she didn't want to do." For that matter, no one else ever had either.

"You've always seemed super close. You can't appeal to her better nature or something?"

I grimaced. "We're close, but it's hard to let old habits go.

We were at each other's throats for most of our time growing up. Before I hit about fifteen, I spent most of my time annoying her until she yelled at me or punched me. I wanted attention, any attention, and she wanted to drive people away because that way they couldn't reject her first."

"That's messed up."

"Yes, well, she did okay out of it. She got a kid, and later a partner in Vince, and I grew up. What were we talking about before I got distracted?"

"You get distracted a lot, I'm noticing," Sefu said.

"Ssh," I said. "Don't do it again."

I opened my mouth to object before realising that I was doing exactly what Sefu had warned me not to do. Smart man, that one.

Behind us, the music abruptly cut off mid song.

"What are you two doing? Is that a special hug?" said the voice of a seven-year-old girl.

Sefu and I leaped apart, and I spun around to face Katie. In the face of her curious stare, I was suddenly transported back to being fifteen and trying to sneak people up to my bedroom.

"We were just talking!" I said.

Katie stared at me. Sefu leaned into my eyeline and gave me the sort of look that potential significant others aren't supposed to give each other.

"Your music was loud," said Katie. "Why?"

"We're sleuthing," Sefu said.

"Being detectives," I clarified.

Katie nodded, wisely. "I was a detective once. Do you need any help? I can help."

I thought of the body in the shed. The barbed wire. The

potentially bone shattering climb up the water pipe. I opened my mouth to say 'No thanks, love' but then I shut it again. I had the seed of an idea, but I needed it to germinate.

Sefu took a couple of steps towards Katie and knelt so that he was at Katie's eye-level. "Have you noticed anything strange around here recently, Katie?"

Katie thought about this. "You were hugging Aunt Phoebe."

"That's not strange, pet, that's awesome."

"Oh, okay. Paula seems grumpy about something."

Sefu looked over his shoulder and up at me.

"Do you know what she was grumpy about, kitten?" I asked.

Katie shrugged, looking at the floor. "She comes out of her room looking grumpy," she said. "She goes in fine and comes out as Mrs GrumpyBoots."

"Really? Thank you, that's actually super helpful with our detecting." Sefu held up his hand for a high five and Katie obliged, after a second's hesitation.

"Katie," I said, my idea having flowered rather nicely. "I need something from your mum's room, but I don't know where she keeps it. Her phone. Would you be able to fetch it for me?" Katie looked hesitant. "I'll give you an apple," I suggested, because bribery is an extremely effective force, no matter the age of the subject.

She thought about this. "I would like chocolate, please," she said, politely staking out her counteroffer.

"How much chocolate have you had today?" I asked.

Katie held up two fingers.

I rolled my eyes. "Okay. A bar of Dairy Milk."

She opened her mouth.

"And not a crumb more!" I said in my authoritative voice.

She nodded and slipped out of the room. I crept through to the kitchen and located the locked box where one of the chocolate stashes was kept. I retrieved the key from under the box of washing powder and obtained my niece's bribe. I sneaked back to Sefu's room and found Katie had just returned.

"Where did you go?" Katie asked, staring at the chocolate.

"Nowhere," I said, reflexively.

"You went nowhere and came back with chocolate. Where was nowhere?"

"Look, do you want this chocolate or not?"

Katie nodded. She held up a mobile telephone that was unmistakably Mel's. I held up the bar of chocolate. We traded one for the other, in the manner of guards at the Korean border exchanging prisoners.

"Thanks, love," I said. Katie looked up, having already engulfed the chocolate. "Now go back to your room, please, there's danger afoot."

"I'm bored of Mario."

"Read a book."

"Mm. Okay."

Katie slipped out again and I waved the phone at Sefu.

"Very good," he said. "Why do you want it?"

"One of her friends said something that made her suspicious about whether Vince was having an affair. I want to see if I can get their number and ask them about it."

"I'll get back to searching Vince's room, unless you need me here?" He left me alone in his room. I could have gone back to my room, but I liked it where I was. I felt safe. It was probably all the swords.

I pressed a key on Mel's phone to bring it to life and saw that it was also PIN locked. What was it with my friends and locking their phones? Where was the trust?

I had three tries. I didn't want to lock the phone, but I also didn't want to just ask her for the PIN, given she was hiding something from me.

I tapped in 1996, Katie's birth year. Access denied.

Melissa wasn't the sort of person who would use her own birth year as her PIN. She also probably wouldn't use mine. What else? The last four digits of her phone number would be too easy to crack. It would be foolish to use the PIN for her bankcard and Melissa wasn't foolish... I found myself tapping in a year, but then I wondered why. The year was special to Mel, but not that special, surely. If you used a year as your PIN, it would be because you wanted to be reminded of it every time you unlocked your phone.

I deleted the numbers immediately. Then I typed them in again. This was stupid. It was egotistical. Oh well, I was both of those things. I pressed the unlock key and was rewarded with the main screen of Mel's phone. She had three notches of battery left and a new message waiting in her inbox.

Well, I'll be shot sideways down a sluice of rainbows and honey.

The number I had typed in had been 2001. The year I chose Mel over my parents. The year I came to live with her. Wow. Either that had meant more to Mel than I'd thought, or she really loved that tedious Stanley Kubrick film.

Kubrick. It had to be Kubrick. There was no way, there was no way – or maybe I was reading just way too much into this. I needed to focus. I needed to focus.

I opened the unread message on Melissa's phone and

saw that it was from Vince. 'Mel,' it said. 'I'm sorry, we can talk about this. It was real to me.'

I blinked at this message. That was the least Vince-y thing I'd ever seen. The guy was vital and confident. He was emotionally open, but I'd never seen him grovel before. Maybe his relationship with Mel was completely different when behind closed doors but... that didn't seem like the sort of thing Mel would put up with. She didn't like secrets or hiding parts of her life. Not since she left our parents' house. The one time I'd seen her really angry at me was when I'd lied to her face about my dalliance with Sefu.

I wondered... should I look at the other recent messages between the two of them? It felt like an invasion, but I was already reading her messages. Ah well, I was trying to solve the murder of her partner. Better to beg for forgiveness than to ask for permission – and see the murderer never caught.

Looking at her inbox, I was amazed to see a message from our parents. I opened it up, and discovered a whole chain of them, going back years. Asking for information, for forgiveness, for acknowledgement... I stared at them for a long time, but I just didn't have the processing space. I went back to the inbox, and to Vince's messages:

> 15:50: **OK C U THERE**
> 15:45: **AN HOUR?**
> 15:39: **SURE, HOW BOUT NANDOS?**
> 15:30: **WHATS UP?**

I flicked through to her sent items – no replies to our parents, so far as I could see – and read the other half of the exchange. She'd texted Vince saying she wanted to meet up because they had something important to talk about, but hadn't wanted to go into details. Frustrating.

Melissa hadn't mentioned Nando's, which was interesting. She'd met up with Vince and whatever they'd talked about, it hadn't gone well. I could carry on backwards reading their messages, but if she'd only just found something out about Vince, as seemed likely, I probably wouldn't get anything useful out of her message archive.

I nodded. Why else had I wanted this phone? Yes, I needed to check on Mel's alibi. I scrolled through the contacts list until I found 'Susan Fletcher's mum'. The name matched Mel's alibi on the wall planner. I scrolled through Mel's text messages with Susan's mum to see if there was anything about her cancelling the tutoring for this kid. There was nothing.

Okay, so Mel hadn't cancelled, but that didn't necessarily mean she hadn't shown up. I needed to find a way to check on the alibi that wouldn't raise suspicion. Sending a message that said "Hi, did I come to tutor your kid today?" wouldn't get me anywhere.

I tapped the phone against my forehead for a few moments before inspiration struck me.

'Hiya!' I wrote 'I think I may have left one of my textbooks behind today. Could you check? It would have been on Susan's desk. It was green with a blue stripe.'

I hit send. If I got a message back saying 'you didn't come to us today, it must be somewhere else' I'd know Mel was lying about her alibi. I ticked another item off my mental list, leaving one more. I worked my way through Mel's contacts, trying to remember the name of the person who'd raised her suspicions about Vince in the first place. I scrolled past 'Ian' and 'I Can't Stand This Guy' before remembering her name: Ifza. I dialled her number.

Ring, ring. Ring, ring. Ri-

"What's up, Mel? I'm busy."

"Ifza," I said, "sorry, it's Phoebe not Mel. Listen, something bad happened. I need to know what you told Mel about Vince."

"Phoebe?" Ifza said. "Mel's sister?"

"Yes," I said. "And I really, really need that information. It's really important."

"I don't know, I don't know you. It's Mel's business and –"

"Vince has been hurt."

A sharp intake of breath rattled through the tinny phone speaker. "How's Mel, is she okay?"

"She's fine, I'm trying to keep her safe, that's why I need to know what you told her. Please, Ifza."

"It wasn't much, you know. I told her I recognised Vince from a protest group I used to belong to over here. She messaged me saying he denied being part of the group, but I'm sure it was him."

"You're sure he was in the group or you're sure you recognised him?" I asked.

"I know I recognised him, but maybe I was wrong about where from."

"And when was this?" I asked. "When did you know him from?"

"It was a while back – he was younger. A lot younger."

"How old are you, Ifza?"

"I'm thirty-five."

"And you and Mel organised that joint action against the war together?"

"Yeah. Look, I'm thinking I may have messed up. He might not be someone I knew from an action. I might have known him from school."

"You're kidding."

"I'm not a kidder. That was what I thought at first, you know, but I thought that must have been wrong because the person I knew at school wasn't called Vince."

"Can you remember what he was called?"

"I can't remember. Just not Vince. But maybe I'm wrong about all of this."

"Okay, okay, thank you, Ifza. Can I call you back if I think of any more questions?"

Ifza paused for a moment before relenting. "Sure, whatever you need."

"Thanks!" I breathed, surprised at the sudden feeling of relief I felt wash over me. It felt good to have a stranger say they'd help me. I heard Ifza hang up.

So, if Ifza was right, and that was a very big if, then Vince was hiding something in his past. Something from Liverpool. Cassie was born in Liverpool. I should see if there was anything else in that room that both the police and I had missed.

Cassie's room was just the way we'd left it – barren and wrong feeling. It made my friend's absence feel sharper. I started searching the room, moving from the desk, to the bed and around past the windowsills. They were empty. Everything had been taken either by the police or by Mel and me earlier. The bad news was this meant I couldn't find any clues. The good news was it meant the search was one of the quicker ones I'd conducted today.

My sinking spirits lifted when I reached the wardrobe, where I'd found that strange piece of paper earlier. I gave the ancient oak monstrosity an experimental tug, but it was heavy enough that shifting it felt like a last resort. Instead,

I lay down on the floor and groped around under it as best I could. After a moment, my fingers brushed a piece of paper. With my face pushed hard against the wardrobe, I carefully inched the paper towards me before finally fishing it out, my heart pounding.

It was a sheet of lined A5 paper, and Cassie's handwriting occupied most of it. It was divided into columns.

Richard Lampart	Vince
Born 1967	In his mid-30s
White guy, brown hair	Yes
Born in Liverpool	Born in Liverpool
Went to High Hopes	?????
Super Serious, Mum said	Pretty fun guy
If my dad knows I exist, should know what I look like	Doesn't know me or seem to care about me. Only talks to me if I corner him.
Is called Richard Lampart	Is called Vincent
Misc:	?????

Could be Vince in the picture. Might not be, though.

Wait, what? Cassie had thought Vince was her dad? Or wondered, at least. I passed a second glance over the sheet and saw that Cassie had mentioned a picture. She'd never said anything about having a picture of her dad. Was there any chance it was under her wardrobe with her other notes?

I scrabbled around underneath, my shoulder stretching in its socket. I felt nothing. I sat back and thought for a moment. I went and knocked on Katie's door, and asked for a ruler when she opened it. She glared at me, her Nintendo held in one hand. I had clearly interrupted some very important plumbing. Still, she disappeared back into her room and returned, carrying a thirty-centimetre shatter-resistant ruler. I thanked her and returned to Cassie's room to swish the ruler under the wardrobe. The scrape of the ruler against the floorboards was interrupted by something smooth. I used the ruler to tease it out. It turned out to be an old-looking photo.

I picked the picture up and very nearly gasped. In the picture were Cassie and a young, stern-looking guy – but Cassie looked odd. She was wearing colourful '80s clothing, had different hair and sunglasses that could have stopped a bullet. But she also had a small scar on her cheek. Cassie hadn't had a scar there, had she? Putting the scar along with the ridiculous clothing was pretty definitive. It had to be Cassie's mum, and so the guy was obviously her dad. She was right, he didn't exactly look like Vince. The face was the right shape for sure, and the hair was about the same colour, but the eyes and the set to the jaw were very serious. The expression in the photo was so alien to how I remembered Vince's face that it was hard to picture them as the same person. Like Cassie's note had said, they could be the same person, but probably weren't. After all, there was no real reason to think that Vince was the man in the photo. He looked like a perfectly ordinary man with few distinguishing features.

I turned the picture over and closed my eyes, wondering exactly why Cassie had come to us. She was young, she was driven, but there was a very strong activist scene in Liverpool. To come all the way to Birmingham was odd. And why specifically to our little group? She'd wanted to fight the referendum campaign, so was happy working with us, but she'd cared just as much about a dozen other causes. Had her search for her dad brought her here?

This was interesting, but it didn't help me with a motive for why Cassie or Vince might have been targeted. I needed more information.

I started double checking to see if I'd missed anything in Cassie's room, but was interrupted by a beep from Mel's phone. I pulled it out of my pocket and saw I had a message from 'Susan's mum'. My head was so full of new information it took me more than a minute to remember that Susan was the kid who Mel had supposedly tutored. My heart leapt and I opened the message: 'Soz. Can't find book. Sure u left it here?'

Mel's alibi held. That was the best news I'd heard all day. I'd known she couldn't have been involved, but it was nice to have proof. I sent back a message saying not to worry about it and that the book must have wound up somewhere else.

I stepped out of Cassie's room and nearly bumped into Sefu. He grinned at me and pointed to his room. I followed him in and we moved into our lips-to-ear conspiracy position. I updated him about Mel's alibi and the notes Cassie had left behind about Richard Lampart.

"Good finds, Phoebe, it feels like we're getting somewhere!" Sefu said. He checked the time on his phone. "We've got about two hours left. We're doing well. And speaking of doing well, I found something in Vince's bin, check it out."

He stepped back and dug a crumpled piece of yellow paper out of a pocket. I looked over his shoulder as he smoothed it out. It had four numbers written on it: 7341.

"Hang on," I said, "how did you know this was significant?"
"What?"

"It was a crumpled post-it note, but you did a whole dramatic reveal thing. You knew this was significant."

"...no I didn't."

"Did you find this clue, open it, note its significance and then crumple it back up again so we could do this little reveal moment?"

"...No."

"Sefu," I said, but then I stopped. I couldn't put this feeling into words. It was warm and it was safe and it was exciting.

I couldn't look at his silly grin without hugging him. Sue me. I felt strange – as if I was being pulled in two different directions. Vince was dead, and I still missed Cassie terribly... but on the other hand, I was enjoying having a puzzle to solve. I was feeling closer to Sefu than I ever had, even closer than when we'd been seeing to each other good and proper. It felt like I was making progress and, hopefully, there'd be tangible results. This feeling was night and day with how I'd felt since that awful referendum.

I held Sefu a little tighter. I didn't want this moment to end. This moment, when we still had a puzzle to solve but we didn't have to face up to the fact that one of our friends was a murderer, was perfect. I wondered if enjoying it made me a bad person.

Sefu seemed to sense my doubt. He stroked my back and shifted so my head could fall onto his shoulder. I closed my eyes and just breathed. I tried not to worry about anything else. I was here and I was alive. I breathed.

"Okay," I said, once I'd released the Clue-Finder General. "Let's see if this code unlocks Vince's phone, shall we?"

I fished the phone out of my pocked and pressed a button to get at the unlock screen.

"Right," I said. "What's the code, Sefu?"

"7341."

I typed in 7 3 4 1 and clicked the button.

INCORRECT PIN

3 INCORRECT ATTEMPTS OUT OF 3

PHONE AND SIM LOCKED

The average age of those saying or writing the phrase, 'You lost, get over it!'

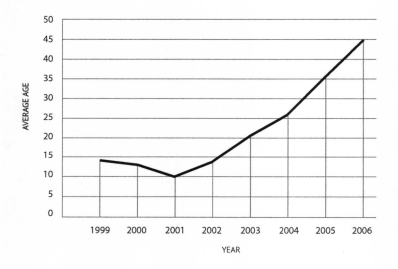

× Chapter Fourteen

We stared at the phone in my hands.

"No!" I said. "No, no, no. What have we done?"

"We've locked the phone."

"Yes, I know we've locked the phone, but how? You found a PIN code in Vince's room! If it wasn't the PIN for his phone, what *is* it the code for?"

I held the phone in my hand. I wanted to stamp on it or smash it against a wall. We'd probably get in trouble for interfering with evidence when the police eventually showed up, but we'd messed with so much evidence by this point it was hard to care too much.

"Phoebe."

What were we even doing? We weren't detectives. We definitely weren't Miss Marple. Xia was right. About that, anyway. Damn it. We should have just cleared out, left the body here and tried to disappear. Well, that wouldn't have worked, but something like that. She should have hidden Vince in the woods for the foxes to eat. Gone to France.

"Phoebe?"

"What?"

"You're panicking again. This is fine. It's a slight setback but we're still going to find the murderer. Focus on me."

I looked up at the Clue-Finder General, and slowly the world straightened around the edges. I found a smile from somewhere for him. I took my thumb out of my mouth and spat out the chewed remains of a nail. "Sorry," I said. "What are we going to do?"

He thought for a moment. "Gus is our prime suspect, right?

"Right."

"So, let's see whether he actually can – and will – climb the pipe if we let him think he's ruled out."

"Er..."

"What's up?"

"You know I'm really fond of Gus, right? We've worked with him for over a year."

"Yes?"

"So... he attacked those Patriots Unite thugs at the protest right before Cassie's death."

Sefu tugged at his earlobe. "He did. He made a bad decision. One relapse doesn't indicate something more sinister."

"No. No, it doesn't. I feel like I'm betraying Gus by even talking about this. He's worked so hard to deal with his past, but someone murdered Vince. We can't ignore what happened at the protest, even though it was probably a one-off mistake."

"He won't attack us if we catch him out, Phoebe."

"Sefu... one of our friends murdered Vince. I'd be cautious about catching any of them out. I know I'm being irrational. Gus is a big softie, but I'm scared."

"You were happy to go and search for fascists, Phoebe."

"Yes, but it's one thing to go and look for fascists when you probably won't find them, and it's part of this abstract..." I waved my hands in the empty air frantically, trying to conjure up what I meant, given my words were failing me.

"And it's another to have one of my friends possibly turn on me because I found out something he did in a moment of weakness. We don't even know *why* he attacked Vince."

"So, if Gus did do this, and we don't know if he did, you're saying we shouldn't make sure? We should just wait for Eryl to get here and say we've sorted it out?"

I chewed me lip.

"Look, Phoebe, this isn't like searching for the fascists. If Gus has… if Gus turns and does something he'd regret, we can run for it. Get away. If we know what happened, we don't need to restrain him."

"What if he turns on everyone else?"

"Phoebe, think about Gus. Think about who he is. Don't let Hollywood twist how you see him."

The python twitched its tail but it couldn't seem to get its fangs into my flesh. Being a detective seemed to be inexorably squeezing the life out of it. I wondered if I should take up detectiving as a career. The first thing to do would be to look up whether detectiving was a real word…

"Okay." I breathed in, then out, and then in again. "You happy to do this?"

"I'm a fast runner. I'm good. You ok?"

"Yup."

Gus was in his room, but wearily agreed to come outside with us for a moment on the promise of being brought in on events. Once we were down in the courtyard, we stopped near the drainpipe.

"The Patriots Unite guy we found saw the murder," I told him. "We didn't want to believe him, but what he said checks out. We think the killer is one of us."

Sefu nodded. "According to him, the killer stabbed Vince,

then climbed up that drainpipe and slipped into the house."

I was watching Gus carefully. No flicker of guilt or unease. No sign of sudden violence, just sadness and fatigue.

"He didn't get a good look at the killer," Sefu continued. "But it was definitely a woman."

Gus frowned. "Mel was out. That means Xia, Paula, or..." His eyes flicked to me.

"Phoebe and I watched it happening together from a window," Sefu said. "It's definitely not her."

I nodded. "But we don't know if it's even possible. Sefu and I couldn't manage it, and with all possible love, I don't think Liam is strong enough. You seem the best person to give it a try, not being a suspect and all."

"If he really saw a woman, then Xia's the obvious candidate." Gus said. "But Liam told me she was with him in the barn."

Sefu leaned towards him "We think he might be covering for her for some reason." Sefu was demonstrating impressive improvisation skills. Maybe he should do stand-up once we were finished here. "But either way, we'd rather you gave it a go if you don't mind."

Gus nodded unhappily at Sefu's lie, but he turned to the water pipe. If he was our guy... if he killed Vince, this was where he'd make up some excuse about not being able to climb it. Or, maybe, just maybe, he'd have a flashback to killing Vince and beat Sefu to a pulp as he relived it. I moved slightly so I was standing in Gus's way if he wanted to attack Sefu, but not so that it was completely obvious to either man what was happening. No one else was going to get hurt tonight, not if I could help it.

Gus didn't turn. Instead, he gripped the pipe and gave it

an experimental tug. He nodded again, placed his right foot on the wall, and grasped the pipe with his hands. He leaned backwards so that his arms were straight. Then, in a flash, he started swarming up the pipe. He didn't use my awkward technique of hugging the pipe with my legs, he walked his feet up the wall like a pro. He was taller than I was, and stronger too, meaning that he was more naturally suited to climbing, but I was still jealous. Still, the relief that Gus wasn't about to do anything he'd regret washed the unpleasant emotion away in an instant.

He poked his head over the roof of the building once he reached the top, then started to descend. He lowered himself more slowly than he had ascended but he was still back on the ground in under two minutes.

"It's a piece of cake," Gus said. He was breathing deeply but not heavily. "There wasn't anything on the roof. Did that help?"

"It did, thank you, Gus," Sefu said.

Gus nodded. "Do you need me for anything else?"

"Not yet," I said. "You can carry on with whatever you were doing. Don't say anything about this yet though, okay? We'll tell everyone everything soon, I promise."

"All right…" Gus said. He disappeared back up the stable stairs.

"So, Phoebe," Sefu said. "What do you make of it?"

"You were right," I said. "Gus was fine, and he climbed that pipe like a champ. No violence, no attempt to hide anything. If he snapped and attacked Vince for some reason, I don't even know what, there's no sign of that now."

"So it might not be Gus. Liam and Xia alibi each other… do we think it might be Paula?" Sefu asked.

"Maybe. Cowardly Winston thought it was a man, but maybe he was mistaken at that distance. We can't say for certain that it's Paula until we've found a way to test her climbing ability."

"Let's not waste any time. Are you well enough to continue?"

"Yes," I said, "but never mind me. Are you?"

Sefu nodded. "I was shaken up for a while. I'm okay, though."

He didn't look okay. He looked exhausted, and sad, and his eyes were haunted shadows. "If you say you're okay, you're okay," I said, as gently as I could. "Are you?"

His expression flashed between a scowl and a smile. "Phoebe, it's great that you're paying attention to this stuff, but you can't spend every conversation we have trying to get me to open up. I'm a human being, not a puzzle box."

I never do anything right.

"I know," I said, "and I'm sorry I was so wrapped up in my own stuff it took me so long to notice. I'm trying to make up for lost time. Sorry, I'll cool it."

"Thanks," Sefu smiled. "Let's go and see Paula. I want to see if she has anything to say about the maintenance as well. I think there might be something there."

I climbed the stairs, surprised to find myself actually quite awake, all things considered. Maybe the fresh air had jolted me into being alert, but not on edge. Sefu and I stopped in front of Paula's door and knocked. There was no reply.

Sefu eased the door open and peered in. He looked back at me. "She's asleep," he whispered.

I shrugged. "Let's go in, have a poke around."

"What? No."

"Why not?"

"Because it's wrong. We're the good guys remember. We don't act unethically."

"We're trying to catch a murderer, Sefu. Eryl is coming. What's the time now?"

"Nearly three-thirty."

"So Eryl will be here in around ninety minutes. Let's get in there and have a poke about, see if we can find anything that might help."

"I don't like this."

"So wake her up if you want."

Sefu thought about this. Finally, he shook his head and stepped into the room.

Most of our rooms are decently sized. Paula took the smallest room, despite owning the building. I questioned the logic of this decision as I looked around the room. A bookcase spilled paperbacks and file cases out onto the floor. There was a desk, piled high with paper. The bed, which currently contained a snoring Paula, was hemmed in by books. A laundry basket occupied one corner. A quick glance revealed that it was empty. Her wardrobe occupied most of one corner. I eased one of the doors open, wincing as the hinges creaked. Inside were a series of meticulously ordered articles of clothing and nothing else.

Paula's room contained little in the way of personal artefacts. I spotted a radio near the bed, but no knick-knacks or photographs.

A scraping noise caused me to turn. Sefu had taken the chair out from under the desk and was placing it so that it faced Paula in the bed. He sat in the chair and crossed his legs. I moved so that I was in front of him and moved my lips next to his ear, in our traditional conspiracy position.

"What are you doing?" I asked.

"You poke about, I'll wait here. If she wakes up, she'll see me first and not you rummaging around. We'll be able to ask her questions without her getting too angry about us being in her space."

I nodded and returned to my search. I checked Paula's bin and found, along with a collection of receipts, the remains of the parcel I had delivered to her this morning. Interesting. The parcel had been quite small, about the size of a few small novels stacked on top of each other. The bookcase seemed like a good place to start. I inspected the shelves. Most of the books were fairly standard revolutionary works: *The Communist Manifesto*, the autobiography of Malcolm X, *Pedagogy of the Oppressed, Manufacturing Consent* and so on.

There was a shelf of A4 exercise books. I pulled one off at random and discovered it was an accounts book. Paula was our commune's treasurer, meaning she balanced the books from the money we fundraised against operational costs and the bills we had to pay for the farm. I put the book back and went through the shelf, trying to find the latest two volumes. I found them and handed them to Sefu.

I took a step back from the bookcase and cast an appraising eye over it. Did any objects look like they'd been moved? Not really. I returned to the wardrobe and rooted around in the bottom of it. Nothing there. How about on top of the wardrobe? No, just dust.

If I was Paula, and I was going to hide a small object somewhere so that I could get at it but no one would suspect, where would I hide it? It was bad luck that I was staring at the wardrobe, because my eyes were immediately drawn to the half open drawer that contained Paula's pants. She wouldn't keep the box in there, would she? That would be weird. But then, no one would want to root around in a pants drawer. My logic was flawless. My hand dove into the pants drawer and rooted around as if it was deep underwater and fast running out of air. I could feel my hand trembling as the seconds passed while it still found no box. It couldn't keep this up much longer. My hand moved assertively from one corner of the drawer to the next, then across the diagonal, before leaping free.

I was close to being forced to face the possibility that I wasn't going to find the object from Paula's parcel. I crossed over to the desk, which was covered with piles of paper. They looked as if the slightest pressure would dislodge them, and yet Paula must have worked on them. What were they all? I picked up the top few documents from the nearest stack and found an application form for a copy of CCTV footage. Paula had half-filled it in; it seemed to be from the die-in we did in Victoria Square the day Cassie died. Other papers were print outs of bylaws and other regulations that we would have had to follow when protesting. There were a series of legal documents concerning different aspects of the referendum and whether it could be legally challenged.

I replaced the papers back on the stack, which caused the teetering tower to collapse across the desk. The noise caused Sefu to shoot a glare at me, and we both swivelled to look at Paula as she snorted and rolled over. We both stayed perfectly still for more than a minute while we waited to see if Paula was going to wake up. She didn't.

I returned to the drift of papers and tried to see if there was anything interesting in there. A scratch of blue ink leapt out at me amongst the sea of black and white. I teased the paper in question out of the drift and found myself holding a plain A4 sheet of paper with handwriting on it. It looked like a letter. Who sends letters to people?

'Hi, Mum,' it said. Well, that answered that question. Still. A letter? Well, Paula didn't have a mobile telephone. There was a landline connection in the stables, but the wire had gone down a few months ago, and the phone company was being a jobsworth about getting it back up.

'Hi, Mum,' said the letter. 'I'm really sorry, but I can't send any more. Things are quite tight for us as well and I think I've sent more than enough for taking on Dad's half. I know that place means a lot to you but maybe it's time to call it a day. You and your activist buddies aren't really getting much done these days, are you? Losing the referendum was a blow but it's over now. Anyway, it was lovely to see you on Saturday. Let's meet up again soon, okay? With Love, Matthew.'

Now that was interesting. Paula needed money. Did she need it enough... to kill Vince? No, that didn't make any sense. Still, it was something we should follow up on. I turned back to the desk and did a quick check to see if there was anything else that jumped out at me. There wasn't, so I turned to Sefu and gently extracted the record books from his grasp. I opened the most recent one and started to work my way through it.

If I had a head for figures, I probably wouldn't have read Philosophy at uni. I tried to focus. It looked like we took money in from fundraising projects and a couple of generous donors. Those of us who lived at the farm contributed towards the upkeep from our jobs.

The farm's outgoings were more complicated. I saw

entries for materials: pamphlets, printers' fees and placards. There were permit fees, bills for the farm, maintenance that needed to be carried out...

There were quite a lot of entries for maintenance.

One, two... three times the water tank had needed to be patched in six months, according to this document. I didn't remember any problems with the water tank but Gus had said it hadn't been repaired for ages. Paula had included an entry for two thousand pounds to refurbish a third shed that didn't exist. There were a number of entries for work that I was pretty sure had been carried out in the refurb back before this place belonged to the dude who sold tractors.

I pointed some of these out to Sefu, who stared at them. I moved into the conspiracy position. Sefu's lips bushed against my ear as I whispered, "This must be what Gus was talking about. Paula's been embezzling funds from our group?"

"Let's wake her up and ask her about that," said Sefu.

"...not just yet. I want to have one last look around. Is that okay?"

"Sure, but be quick. Paula's starting to fidget."

I took another quick look at the wardrobe to make sure there was nothing of interest in there... but no. The bookshelves, similarly, appeared uninteresting. I turned to the desk and –

I had seen something just now, out of the corner of my eye. I let my eyes drift from point, to point, to point. I couldn't see anything out of position, except the massive drift of papers I'd knocked over.

I took a step back and looked again. Nothing. Maybe I'd been imagining things. There was nothing on the desk, there was nothing under the –

There was something under the desk. Right at the back, in between the back leg of the desk and the wall was a shadow that was too deep. I knelt down and scrabbled at the shadow with my hand. It turned out to be a solid metal box. I drew it out from behind the leg of the desk and stood up to examine it.

The box was about the size of two paperbacks stacked on top of each other, unless one of them was a Harry Potter book. Then it'd just be one. Was this what had been in the parcel? It looked like it should open like a clamshell. Two tiny silver hinges occupied one long end, while the other... the other end had a mechanical lock. There was no keyhole. Instead, it looked like it would open if someone inputted the correct four-digit code.

I walked over to Sefu and showed him the box.

He shrugged.

"It needs a four-digit code... and we know a four-digit code."

I looked at Sefu sceptically, then shrugged back. I inputted 7541 and tried to open the lid. The box stayed resolutely shut.

"It doesn't work," I said.

Sefu scowled, then looked at the box. "That's because you entered the code wrong."

"What?"

"Give it here."

Sefu changed the '5' to a '3' and the lid of the box spontaneously leapt upwards. Sefu grimaced in alarm but managed to keep the lid from springing open completely. It was a good thing too, as I found out when Sefu turned the box towards me. It was packed to bursting with fifty-pound notes.

× Chapter Fifteen

It was more money than I had ever seen in my life that wasn't a number on one of my parents' investment reports. I goggled at it. "What is this? What's it for?"

"I want to say drugs," Sefu whispered. "But you wouldn't have £50s for that. I think. Maybe I'm overestimating my knowledge of the drug trade."

"Are we even sure Paula knows what's in there? It was Vince's code, after all."

He shrugged.

"I have an idea," I said. "Shut the lid, we pretend we haven't seen what's inside, and see what Paula claims it is."

Sefu paused for only a moment before nodding. He forced the lid shut and scrambled the code so the lock engaged. "Do we wake her up?"

"Yeah." I moved so that I was standing to Sefu's left and slightly behind him, like this was an American family portrait and I was an overbearing patriarch.

"Ready?" asked Sefu. I patted his shoulder. "Paula?" he asked, out loud. "Paula. Wake up, please." Paula stirred, but didn't wake up. Sefu gave her a poke. "Paula."

Paula's eyes fluttered open. She focused on Sefu's feet, then her eyes groggily worked their way up to Sefu's face, then mine. "What's going on?"

"Well, here's the thing," I said. "We've been chatting to everyone about Vince and we've uncovered some slightly alarming things. We feel we need a bit of background on an item or two concerning you, Paula."

She groaned. "I was asleep." She didn't sound happy about being woken. Go figure.

"To start with," I said, "what was in that package I delivered to you yesterday? I only ask because you looked like you'd seen a ghost when I gave it to you."

"That's personal," Paula said, although her eyes were still unfocused. I got the feeling that this was a rote response rather than a considered reply.

"Personal, was it?" Sefu asked. "It looks like a metal box to me."

That woke Paula up a bit. Her eyes darted to the now empty space under her desk, then up to Sefu's hands, which held the box.

"What – how dare – this is a violation of my space!"

"This isn't a violation," Sefu said mildly.

"Why are you even here?"

Sefu shrugged. "You agreed to us investigating."

"You never told me that the investigation included going through my personal things."

"Personal like a metal box?"

"I don't appreciate being interrogated, Sefu. This is just like during the campaign, when they'd interrogate someone from the 'no' side about exact facts and figures, whilst the 'yes' camp made their stupid WMD claims completely unchallenged."

"We're not talking about the referendum, Paula," I said. "We're talking about you. What's in the box?"

Paula looked from me to Sefu and then back to me again. Eventually, she sagged. "I don't know," she admitted.

"Say again?" Sefu said. "It's your box, why don't you know what's in it?"

"Someone sent it to me," Paula said. She looked at me. "I think you know that."

I smiled thinly and nodded. "So, you weren't expecting it?"

Paula shook her head.

"That's... interesting," I said.

"Why is someone sending you random metal boxes, Paula?" Sefu asked.

"You wouldn't understand," Paula said. "I might as well ask the average voter to understand UN weapon inspection protocols."

"Give it a rest, Paula. There are other things in the world happening," I said.

"Yes!" Paula cried, and hauled herself into a sitting position, "We're supposed to be going down to Fairford today to sabotage the B-52s. We have to gather our gear."

I nodded. "That can wait an hour. That is all this will take. An hour. Sefu and I, we're nearly finished."

"Nearly finished with what?"

"Is the metal box something to do with you stealing money from our accounts in order to pay off something to do with the farm?" Sefu asked. His tone was light and mild. It was as if he was asking for the reason someone had bought semi-skimmed milk instead of 1% fat.

Paula sat bolt upright. "What? What? How do you know about that?"

"Oh, come on, Paula," I said. "It's all in your account books. I'm about as far from an expert as it's possible to get and I still found it."

Her chest inflated indignantly. "Show me! Show me in the books where I stole money!"

Sefu and I looked at each other. Maybe I'd made some kind of awful mistake. It wouldn't be the first time tonight. I opened one of the exercise books and showed Paula the three different occurrences over six months where the water tank had supposedly needed repairing.

"Correct me if I'm wrong," I said, "but the water tank hasn't been repaired since I've been here."

Paula shook her head. It didn't feel good to see her suddenly looking so vulnerable.

"Why don't you tell us about it, Paula," Sefu prompted.

"Are you sure you don't already know about it?" Paula snapped, anger bursting into her eyes. "You sure seem to know about everything else. How do I know you're not the people who've been blackmailing me?"

Sefu and I looked at each other. "You're being blackmailed?" he asked.

"What? No! I mean... what?"

"Paula," Sefu said. "You need to calm down. This is just me and Phoebe talking to you. We're not your enemies. Why don't you tell us about the blackmail?"

She chewed her lip. She sat up straighter but avoided eye contact. She straightened her bed covers, smoothing the wrinkles as best she could. I tried hard not to fidget. Finally, she looked at us.

"I don't own the farm outright. Since my divorce, I've owned half and my husband has owned the other half. A few years ago, he found he needed cash, so he announced he wanted to sell it. I couldn't let that happen, as it would have meant breaking up our commune. We were doing really good work. I paid him what money I had. It wasn't enough, so I started moving money from our accounts to pay him off. He was happy enough with that, and it meant that eventually, our farm would really be ours.

"The only problem was, someone noticed. I don't know who. They never signed their name. I got a letter in the post with a photocopied page of one of my ledgers. Places where I'd siphoned off money were circled. The note said I'd be exposed and possibly imprisoned if my secret was known. The note demanded that I send on information about other activist networks, their leaders and activities. What could I do? Really, what options did I have? I sent information to a P.O. Box. I was never able to find out who'd sent the letters."

"You know," I said, "maybe you wouldn't have needed to do all this if you'd tried talking to us."

"Oh yes, I'm sure that would have gone swimmingly," Paula said. "'Oh, guys, can I just get your attention for a minute. I've been stealing money and informing on my network.'"

"Honestly, it doesn't sound that bad," I said.

She burst into tears.

"I think our parameters for what's normal might have shifted slightly over the last twelve hours," Sefu said, as we watched tears run down the face of the woman who had invited us all into her home, fed us and provided us with direction.

Her hands...

I turned to look at Sefu. 'I have an idea,' I mouthed. Sefu cocked his head at me. I rolled my eyes and pointed at the box. I gave a 'gimmie' motion with my right hand. Sefu handed the box over.

"Paula," I said, "if that's the worst of it, I think you're in the clear. There's just one more –"

"That's not all," said Paula, "there's something worse."

I blinked.

"Mhm," Paula said, then lifted her head from her hands. "I argued that we should have the referendum when it was first being talked about."

"We know," Sefu said. "You didn't know it would turn out like this."

"I thought I was being democratic!" Paula wailed. "I said to people that we shouldn't be scared of a referendum. It's democracy! We live in an unbelievably stupid first-past-the-post system, we should take more democracy wherever we can get it. Plus, I said those people saying it was too complicated an issue to trust to the people were being unbelievably patronising. I thought we could win! I didn't know the 'yes' camp was going to lie constantly and consistently. I didn't know the meat of their campaign, the real substance, the one core idea they'd get people to unite behind was going to be a lie written on the side of a bus.

"I assumed that they would play the game by the rules. I didn't know they were going to break the law multiple times to win. I didn't know the official 'no' campaign was going to be so lacklustre. I didn't know that people would just ignore our complex reality and retreat into sloganeering. I thought people were better than that!"

"Paula..." I said gently, "I don't care that you thought the referendum was a good idea. We've all done stupid things."

"Not even stupid," Sefu said. "Just naïve. You thought people were going to examine the facts. It's not your fault that they didn't."

Trying to wrestle this interrogation back on track, I asked, "Other than the embezzling and the championing the referendum, that's the darkest stuff lurking in your past?"

"Well, there was this one time in the 60s when I was off my face on acid –"

"Nothing relevant to the events of the past twenty-four hours?"

Paula shook her head.

"Okay," I said, holding out the metal box, "then you can have this back."

Paula grasped the box with both hands, gratefully. She gripped it tightly and tried to take it, but I wouldn't let it go.

"You know what," I said, "I've changed my mind. I'm going to keep this."

"What? No!" Paula half-shouted. "It's mine!"

"Tough." I said. I pulled on the box slightly. Paula responded by trying to rip it from my grasp. Her hands were thin and shaky. I pulled with slightly more force and the box popped from her grip.

"Give it back, Phoebe!" Paula said, her eyes desperate.

"Why? Why do you care if you don't know what's in it?"

"There will be something important in it! It came from the blackmailer. It's probably more instructions or, I don't know, something equally horrible. If I don't deal with what's in the box, there may be serious consequences."

Sefu and I looked at each other. "Satisfied?" he asked.

"Yes," I said. "With a grip that weak, I don't think Paula could have climbed the water pipe."

"What?" Paula asked. She looked utterly baffled now.

"Paula," Sefu said, "We will explain as soon as we can, I

promise. I just want to know if there was a note that came with the box."

"There was, yes. It said the box was a reward for my long service and the code would follow on in a separate letter."

"Huh," I said. "That's interesting."

"Isn't it," Sefu agreed. "Paula, the code is 7341. We found it during our investigation. We'll leave you to open it yourself. Don't worry, I think you'll be quite pleased with the contents."

Paula had the box open before Sefu was out of his chair. Her eyes widened and a shaky breath shuddered out of her lungs. She pulled the notes out of the box and started to count them. We paused to watch, and she looked up at us once she was done counting, her eyes wide.

"This is the exact amount I need to pay off the farm," she said. "Why would the blackmailer be sending me this?"

"Crisis of conscience?" I suggested.

"Come on, Phoebe," Sefu said. "Paula, we'll leave you to it. Sorry for waking you up."

We went back to his room and got into our conspirator position to take stock.

"What on earth was Vince doing blackmailing people?" I hissed, barely able to contain my anger.

"We don't know it was him."

"We found the code in his room."

"It could have been planted there."

This made me pause, but it still felt wrong. "Okay, let's say it was planted. So, the blackmailer knew we'd find Paula's box, they knew we'd search Vince's bin, they knew we'd find the code and make the connection and come to the incorrect conclusion that Vince was the blackmailer. Is that more likely than Vince blackmailing people?"

"If it wasn't Vince, then it was someone else in this house. Blackmail? Murder? Who exactly do we live with?" He twitched next to me.

"It's okay, Sefu," I said, "I feel the same way. This is scary. Do you need to take a moment?"

Sefu shuddered and let out a worried, tight noise. "No, let's focus on getting this solved," he said. "I'll feel better once we've found the reasons behind the murders. Do we think it could have been Gus?"

"Not sure."

"And Paula is unlikely because her grip is too weak."

"Yes, although it's not impossible. Her grip was weak but she might still technically have been able to make it."

"And it wasn't me."

"Yes. You were with me when it happened. Besides, you'd be quite a phenomenal actor if it was you."

"I did play Othello in the school play."

"That's a tough part."

"Yeah, but I didn't get it because of my talent."

"Ah. Were the demographics in your school not great?"

"Amongst the people who enjoyed acting, definitely."

"If we're eliminating Gus and Paula, we're saying Xia and Liam lied to us?" I asked.

"Why would Xia lie for Liam?"

"I don't know. We don't know it was Liam that Xia was lying for. Maybe it was the other way around. Maybe something else is going on."

"So we need to try them again," he said.

I shook my head. "There's only so far we can get with talking and talking to these people who have already lied to us a bunch of times. There are other ways of getting

191

information. How's your phone signal?"

Sefu checked his phone while I fished the small bottle we found in Xia's sanctuary in the barn out of my pocket.

"I've got three bars and the barest scratch of a mobile internet signal," said Sefu.

"Great, can you look up Silver Haze room odorisor for me?"

He tapped away at the keys on his phone. Whilst he was doing this, a memory poked at me. Those notes Cassie had been making about her dad... I wondered if Mel's friend Ifza could shed any light on them given she might have known Vince when they were both young. I took out Mel's phone and dialled Ifza's number. It only rang three times before she picked up.

"What's up?" she asked, without pre-amble.

"Random question," I said, equally direct. "The person you knew at school, the person that might have been Vince, was he called Richard Lampart?"

"What?" Ifza shouted. I heard a crunch and a rattle, before a scraping noise. "Sorry," she said a moment later. "I dropped my phone. You shocked me. Yes. That was his name. Your Vince was Richard Lampart."

"How sure are you, Ifza?"

"I'm absolutely sure."

Mel's partner and Cassie's dad. One and the same. And he had a fake name, which was bad news.

"What school was this?" I asked.

"High Hopes, it's in Croxteth." That name was familiar as well. I fished out Cassie's list of reasons Vince might or might not have been her dad. Under the 'Richard Lampart' column were the words 'went to High Hopes'.

192

"And this guy calling himself Vince... did he recognise you?"

"I don't know, maybe."

"Ifza, I need to trust you here. Can I do that?"

"You don't know me from Eve, Phoebe, but I'll do what I can. What do you need?"

"Can you track down someone who would still know Vince? I need details of his life that he's been hiding from us. Actually, sorry, I don't need details about Vince. I need details about Richard Lampart."

"I can probably track down some of his old school friends, if they haven't moved," Ifza mused, "but most of them will have. I might see if his parents have moved house. I think I went there for a party a long time ago. Don't worry, Phoebe, I'll get on it. This will help Mel, right?"

"Absolutely," I said. "Thanks, Ifza, you're the best."

"Yeah, I am," she said, and hung up.

I held the phone in my hand. Vince wasn't Vince. If Vince wasn't Vince, who the hell was he? Who was Richard Lampart? Was it innocent, and he was just running away from something? Or... was he an infiltrator?

"What's up, Phoebe?" Sefu asked, looking up from his phone.

"Vince... that wasn't his name. He was Cassie's dad. Richard Lampart. He didn't even seem upset about her murder. Everything he said..." I trailed off.

"W-what? Who was he?"

"I don't know! He was from Liverpool. Mel's friend, Ifza, went to school with him. Whoever he was, he came here for some reason. Maybe he had a good reason for using a pseudonym?"

"Maybe. Xia vouched for him and she doesn't do that for just anyone. But if he was here covertly... maybe he did send those blackmail letters. No, I'm not ready to believe that yet. People have reasons for using pseudonyms. Maybe he was hiding from someone. I met someone from Campaign Against the Arms Trade who used a pseudonym because her activism had caused death threats from Patriots Unite. Let's focus up."

Sefu looked around as if he was trying to remember what he'd been doing before someone dropped a building on him. He looked down at his hand and saw his phone. "Ah, yes. I found Silver Haze on a website. It's categorised under 'poppers'."

"I've heard of those."

"Me too. Can you remember what they are?"

"Not in the slightest. Is there any more information?"

"Yes, there's an about section, hang on. Blah blah blah, isopropyl nitrite, blah blah blah, increase blood flow.... Oh."

"Oh what?"

"Well, they're not for human consumption but this website is basically winking at me about that. Anyway, it sounds like these things are a marital aid."

"Ah."

"Yup. And it feels like that's a more likely reason for the scene we found in the barn that we've used ourselves for romantic purposes than Pilates doesn't it..."

"And Xia and Liam aren't..."

"They are 100% not, no. Liam once described himself as 'gay as the day is long'."

I clapped my hands together. "Okay, *now* we go and talk to Liam."

Together, we walked to Liam's room and knocked on the

door. The door opened. Liam stood on the other side. He looked tired, and like he had been crying. He looked at me. He looked down at my hand. I realised I was still holding the popper. He nodded. "Figures," he said. "Come on, Gus, we need to tell Phoebe and Sefu some things."

"Sorry, what?" Sefu asked. Liam pushed the door a little more open, to reveal Gus, who was sitting, looking tired, on the edge of Liam's bed. He nodded, got up and followed Liam, who stepped around Sefu and me, before walking down the corridor. Sefu and I glanced at each other, suddenly worried we were about to do something awful.

Still, we couldn't exactly stop now. I followed Sefu, who followed Gus, who followed Liam. Together, we wound up in the stable under the house. As I entered, I saw that Liam was leaning up against the printing press, whilst Gus was standing next to our piles of leaflets. His arms hung by his sides, and I could see he was tapping the fingers of his left hand against his left thumb in sequence over and over again. Thankfully, I took a moment to think before I opened my mouth.

"We just have some questions, lads." I said. "Neither of you are in trouble and we don't want anyone to say anything they're not comfortable with. No one is–"

"Yeah, that would be nice," Gus said, "but it's just a matter of time now. Better to do this here and now."

"Do what?" Sefu asked.

Gus looked at Liam, who nodded, his face calm and his smile genuine. The moment held a second longer. A very long second. Then Gus hooked his thumbs in the pockets of his trousers and said, "Liam and I have been seeing each other on and off for a while."

There was a silence that lasted a just a trifle too long. I

kept waiting for Gus to explode. For there to be something else, something violent. But there was only a silence that held.

"It's none of our business," said Sefu. "But thank you for telling us."

"Were you together before Vince's death?" I asked.

Gus nodded.

"Was Xia with you?" Sefu asked.

Gus shook his head, his eyes moves from me to Sefu and back, curiously.

It wasn't Xia's sanctuary, I thought, the pieces finally clicking into place, *it was theirs.*

"Okay," I said. "That's all we need. Sorry if this hurt, I realise we stumbled into this a bit and that's my fault. I'm really focused on getting this thing solved... anyway, we'll leave you two alone."

I turned to go.

"We're not done," Gus said. I turned back and saw that Gus was smiling slightly. Liam had walked to his side and was holding his hand.

"Gus, mate, you can tell us anything you want," Sefu said, "but we're not asking anything.."

"This morning, Liam came to see me. He told me that someone's been trying to blackmail me over an... incident in my past, as well as the fact that... I'm gay." Gus paused and breathed. He looked up at us. "As well as the fact that I'm gay," he repeated. "Anyway. Liam wanted to know what he could do about it. He'd been intercepting blackmail letters to me for months, giving them information about other organisations like ours, just so I'd be left alone. I said that wasn't right. I said to tell this blackmailer where to go."

Liam smiled. He squeezed Gus's hand.

"Okay," I said. "Thank you. Did you keep any of the blackmail letters?"

"Only the last one," said Liam. "I had to show Gus. One moment."

He nipped off, leaving Gus with us. Our friend closed his eyes and scratched his scalp. He opened his eyes and frowned, looking up at nothing in particular. Given my tendency to shove my oar in and row where it wasn't necessary, I kept my mouth shut. After a few moments, Gus seemed to reach a conclusion.

"So, the reason for the blackmail..."

"We haven't asked, it's none of our business," said Sefu.

"The reason for the blackmail," said Gus, "was because I've spent time inside, for GBH. Some guy came at me in a club. He pulled a knife on me."

Sefu winced. "How did that go?"

"I took the knife off him, didn't I?" Gus said, "It's not the first time it's happened neither. People think because I'm not the tallest or, because I'm not rippling with muscle, they can try all sorts of things out with me. Anyway. I took the knife and, in the process, I buried it into his stomach." He looked at us, possibly expecting us to look shocked or outraged at his actions.

"Seems fair," said Sefu.

I nodded.

"Maybe," said Gus, "but we're not supposed to do stuff like that. Us who have been trained are supposed to show restraint. We're supposed to retreat at all costs. That being said, my old instructor always used to say 'if there's nowhere to go, take 'em down. You can only spend time in prison if you haven't been stabbed. Better to not take the chance and not hold back'. They went pretty easy on me, mostly because I stopped the guy from dying, called an ambulance and stayed with him. I cooperated with the police. I still spent time in prison... but there it is."

"Do you want a hug, mate?" I asked.

Gus's face cycled through a strange series of emotions, before he nodded. I hugged him from the front. Sefu hugged him from behind. Together, we made a Gus sandwich.

"Pfffff," said Liam from behind us. We jumped apart. I was relieved to see an amused expression on our friend's face.

Liam flashed a sheet of paper at Sefu, who set to examining it.

"What's going on?" Gus asked.

"You're not the only person who's been blackmailed," I said.

"What?"

"I know. Someone's been busy."

Sefu looked up, "I'm going to need some time to process this. Okay, thanks, lads. Unless there's anything else you need, we'll let you get back. Sorry again for all this, but thanks for telling us, Gus. We love you."

"We love you," I echoed.

Gus smiled and walked out of the stable, next to Liam.

"Did you see that?" I asked.

"See what?"

"I think we didn't do too much damage. Gus just left here holding Liam's hand."

Sefu let out a breath, which turned into a smile. "Okay then," he said. "It probably wasn't either of those two. If it was, they must have been in it together. We think Paula is too weak and Mel has an alibi. So it must be Xia."

"It's most likely to be Xia. We're working balance of probability here unless we can find definitive proof. Xia has been trying to shut us down all day. She's a climber. She knows where your swords are. The only thing we're missing is motive. Why did she kill Vince? She's a pacifist."

"She is a pacifist, yes, but everyone has their limits. Remember when we protested that Patriots Unite rally? Some thugs broke through the cop line and rushed us. A strict pacifist would have run or refused to move. Xia saw one of the thugs grab Paula and slugged him in the face, buying Paula time to get away. She's not afraid to get her hands dirty if it'll prevent greater violence."

"I remember that. She said something afterwards. What was it?"

"'Pacifism is fundamentally the most moral and ethical position a person can take, but it cracks in the face of fascism, because it lets the fascists get what they want. If you are being literally attacked by literal fascists, shutting them down by any reasonable means isn't just moral, it's necessary.'"

"Maybe that's what she thought she was doing this time. Maybe she found something out about Vince."

Sefu clicked his fingers and bolted out of the stable. He returned a few moments later. "I just asked Gus and Liam to distract Xia in the kitchen for a bit," he said. "They're going to help plan the Fairford action with her."

"Okay, why?"

"It'll give us a chance to search Xia's room, and it means that the three of them are watching each other. They can't all have been working together to murder Vince."

I nodded. "Good idea. How long have we got until Eryl gets here?"

"Less than an hour."

"Okay. Let's do this."

I heard Xia's voice from the kitchen as we crept upstairs. "The real trick is going to be getting over the wire and onto the airfield. We'll need to coordinate with the other groups once we're there. We might need someone to distract the military police so they move to the other side of the base."

Sefu reached Xia's door first, opened it and slipped inside. I followed, my heart thumping. Given how far we'd come it was ridiculous to be scared, but I really didn't want Xia to catch us in here and get upset with us. Particularly if she was a murderer.

I'd occasionally been in Xia's room before. It wasn't a particularly nice place to spend time in for anyone who wasn't Xia. Xia believed in minimalism in her private space. Her bedroom contained these things: one bed. One pillow. One duvet. One wardrobe, in which were her clothes. One cupboard, in which were her personal effects. One lamp. One rug, which lined the floor. That was it. No sound system, no posters, no family pictures. Xia lived an uncluttered life.

This did mean, however, that there were only a very small number of places to search. I peeked under the bed and found dust bunnies, but nothing else. All that remained were Xia's wardrobe and her cupboard. Sefu hovered indecisively, so I took the decision out of his hands and opened the wardrobe.

Inside the wardrobe were four dresses, four tunics, four pairs of trousers and a pair of jeans I'd never seen Xia wear. Four pairs of shoes lined the base. Inside the drawers at the bottom of the wardrobe were underwear and a small box, which, when opened, revealed a few pieces of cheap jewellery. I rooted around in Xia's underwear drawers unenthusiastically.

I didn't find anything I didn't expect, except a book titled *Venus Envy* by Rita Mae Brown. I took the book out and rifled the pages. Nothing seemed particularly relevant, it mainly being about some art gallery owner in Virginia. I returned the book to the drawer and continued my search. I didn't find anything else, except a zip lock bag containing some pills which could have been MDMA, or possibly some upmarket herbal remedies, it was hard to tell without sampling them.

I turned around to see how Sefu was doing. He'd found a small box of correspondence in Xia's cupboard and was working through it. Suddenly, he dropped the letters he was holding in his left hand, and focussed on what was in his right – a postcard. He looked round to me. "Got something!" he hissed. "Let's get out of here before Xia comes back."

I kept an ear out whilst Sefu replaced the letters in their box and returned the box to the cupboard. We slipped out of Xia's bedroom at a choice moment, when the conversation about Fairford seemed to be in full flow. We crossed the corridor as quietly as possible and dived into my room, which was closer than Sefu's.

Once inside, Sefu handed me the postcard. It was postmarked Dovecot, Liverpool, and had been dated three days ago. It read as follows:

'DEAR XIA. AGREE, V SUSPICIOUS. TRYING TO TRACK HIS PROVENANCE. SEEMINGLY NO INITIAL REFEREE. TROUBLE. CALL WHEN POSSIBLE.'

"I don't remember a postcard arriving recently," I said, turning it over in my hands. But then, Mel nearly always got to the post box before me.

"It might have come in an envelope. Still, 'V suspicious'. Do you think that means 'very suspicious' or 'Vince is suspicious'?"

"It could be either, but still, Xia found out something that was suspicious. What if it was about Vince? Why didn't this person just write 'suspicious'? Xia found something out. Did it make her angry, I wonder? Is this a motive?"

"It's more of a motive than we've got for anyone else. Should we go and talk to her?"

I made a face. "She'll just try to shut us down again. There are a few more threads I want to pull on first. We haven't had a chance to search Mel's room."

"Why would you want to do that?"

"She followed Vince. She might have noticed something and written it down. She might have some information on Richard Lampart and not know it's significant because she hasn't connected Vince and Lampart. It's not a massive priority but it would be good to check. Ifza was checking into Lampart for us as well. I could give her a call back. There's something else… Oh yes, Cowardly Winston said his mate was going to do something to our cars. We should check on those whilst we're working out what to do next."

Sefu nodded. We left my room, descended the stairs to the courtyard and started walking towards our cars. The clouds overhead had started to darken again but the rain had drained away from the gravel, so at least it was dry underfoot. Sefu went to inspect his car whilst I went to check on my Almera. Mel's car was in between ours, and it looked fine, although mud spattered its lower half.

The interior of my car looked okay and it didn't look like any of the doors had been messed with. Then I squatted down to check the wheels. The driver's side looked okay. I scuttled around to the passenger side. Three large nails had been hammered – or possibly driven with a nail gun – into the rear tyre. Two more were in the front tyre.

I knelt down to see how deep they were in, and whether they could be pulled out. My knee went down on something soft that didn't feel like gravel. It kind of gave way a bit beneath my weight. I raised my knee, expecting to see a chunk of tyre that had been ripped from the wheel.

It was a hand.

The Liberal Democrats:

"We must pull out of Iraq at the first possible opportunity"
Nick Clegg, leader of the Liberal Democrats

"Liberal Democrats reject Gordon Brown's call to make him PM with signature policy of withdrawing from Iraq"
Politics Home

× Chapter Sixteen

The back of someone's hand – their arm – stuck out from under my car. Feeling the terror python uncoil, dreadfully slowly, I bent down and looked under the car.

Eyes.

A face. The face of someone who I had last seen swinging a knife at Vince. Racist Carl. The eyes were open, unblinking and unfocussed. His face was slack. Pale.

The terror python slithered slowly up my throat, causing coldness to spread out from my stomach to my chest to my limbs to my head. The python opened its mouth with the speed and cold calculation of a hunter stalking a woodland creature. It sank its teeth into my brain slowly, and with a certain amount of familiarity.

I didn't give in to the python. I didn't have the time. I gritted my teeth and tried to get my breathing under control. I opened my mouth to call for help. Nothing emerged the first time, but on the second try I managed a strangled "Sefu!"

"What? What's up?"

"Get help."

"Why?"

"Get. Help."

I heard running feet behind me. I moved my body so that I was mostly blocking the view of what was lying under my car. The shock of finding Racist Carl had nearly made me lose myself. No one else needed to go through that.

"Phoebe, what are you doing?"

"Racist Carl," I rasped, over my shoulder, not moving. "He's hurt."

"What?"

"Sefu, please get help. He's lying under my car. I'll try and get him out."

"I can get him out, Phoebe, you should go and get help."

I half turned to look at my friend. I saw him glance over my shoulder, and his eyes widened. "Get help," I said. "Trust me."

Sefu sprinted off towards the house. I turned back to my car and tried to not look at what was under it. I reached down and gripped the hand, which was stiff, cold and wet. A breath shuddered out of me. I pulled the hand towards me. The arm moved but not the body it was attached to. I groaned and stood, still holding the hand. I braced a foot against the passenger door of my car and hauled. I felt the body move jaggedly against the gravel that lined the courtyard. I couldn't look down. I pulled again and the body slid further out. I couldn't look down. I couldn't look down.

I looked down.

There was a mass of blood just below the collarbone, slightly to the left of his sternum. Shaking, I reached down to his neck to search for a pulse. I couldn't feel anything, so I held my other hand over his nose and mouth to see if I could feel air leaving his lungs.

There was nothing. I looked down and saw Racist Carl's eyes staring up at me. I felt like his gaze was trying to drag me home. Not my real home, not the home I'd made on the farm, but that other home. The home I was worried I'd never truly be able to escape.

Whatever the terror python had injected into my brain finally got some traction.

I was lost to it.

I heard running feet approaching from the house. My name was called. Hands gripped my shoulders and I was ushered into the house. I found myself being led to my room and then lowered down onto the edge of my bed. My shoes were slipped off my feet and my blazer was peeled from my back. I looked up and saw Mel's face. She embraced me.

"You shouldn't be here," I said, "I can't trouble you now, you've had far too much –"

"Shush your face, little muffin, and budge over."

I squiggled back in the bed until I had my shoulders to the wall. Mel climbed in as well and wrapped her arms around me. I buried my face in her shoulder and started to cry.

I couldn't believe I'd deluded myself into investigating Cassie's death. Voices rose within me, voices that I should have listened to for these last three years. They hissed fundamental truths to me, calmly but with such lacerating contempt it made my eyes screw ever tighter shut. I wasn't strong enough to see the case through. Maybe if this had all happened years ago I could have done something, back when I still had potential.

Another person was dead. Another and another and another. It was too much. I'd never solve the murders. I couldn't. Who was I kidding? I was just a care worker surrounded by people better than me. People who'd taken me in, who'd made sacrifices for me, and how had I repaid them? I'd spent hours trying to prove one of them was a murderer. Why hadn't I just fled the farm? That's what I normally did when things got too tough. I'd fled from my parents' house,

I'd fled from Sefu. If I stayed here, I'd have to step up. One of my friends was a murderer, and I'd probably have to sacrifice more than one friendship in order to get to the truth. Was I strong enough to do that?

No. No, no, no, no, no, no.

With that one, horrible syllable echoing round and around in my head, my consciousness crumbled in on itself. The walls were the silver and white of my old house. Dead eyes stared out from behind glass. I knew these eyes. Spots I'd hide in, though nowhere was safe, I found myself in, waiting, listening for the tread of feet. I felt the cracks in the world. White rage breathed through the cracks and into my hiding space. I could only ever hope to not be found, and to emerge hours later, hungry, cold, icy inside and out, pretending certain things had never happened. I felt the places where my hair had been ripped out. I felt the scars on my arm. I felt the deep well that had been bored within me. I felt the terror snake that had been forced down my throat.

I felt plaster and glass and plastic and ceramics shatter as I walked past their homes. Shards spiralled around me in a blizzard of contempt. I backed away, lightning sharp fragments crunching under my bare feet. I needed to hide. I couldn't let the seraphs see what I'd done. I gathered up the shards, blood running between my fingers-

A hand took mine. The hand squeezed. A feeling flooded through me and in that moment, I knew that everything was going to be alright. I gasped and found myself back in my bedroom – my real bedroom. I was in the farm, and I was safe. They couldn't get to me whilst I was here. I opened my eyes and saw that it was Mel that was holding my hand.

I felt another surge of panic rise within me. "How long was I out for?"

"Less than half an hour."

"Is Eryl here yet?"

"Not yet."

I sighed in relief I hauled myself to my feet. "I've got to find the murderer before she gets here."

"You need to look after yourself."

"I need to focus. I can't believe I fell apart again!"

"Recovery from what we went through is a process, you know this. You're going to have setbacks. Especially after a day like today. Come here."

Mel held out her arms. I hesitated, wanting to run out of the room and back to my mystery solving, but I was shaking and having trouble thinking straight. I hugged my sister. She slotted neatly into place under my chin, and suddenly everything was all right again.

I breathed in, then out.

"Thank you for looking after me," I said.

"You looked after me earlier. Besides, I'm not sure I can ever look after you for long enough."

Faintly, in the distance, I heard a sob. It was high and lonely. It sounded like Katie. Mel stiffened briefly in my arms. She'd heard it too. I started to release her but she hugged me tighter. "Sorry about Katie. She knows something's wrong and it's stressing her out. Are you sure you're okay, Phoebe?"

"I am now, yes, thanks love. Go on, see to the kiddo."

Mel let me go and smiled up at me. She nodded and walked to the door. A thought formed in my head as she reached for the door handle. "Enough for what?"

Mel glanced back at me.

"Mm?"

"You said you couldn't look after me for long enough. Enough for what?"

"Enough to make up for seeing what they were doing to you, and not doing anything about it."

She was out, and through the door before I could reply. It clicked shut behind her. I stared after her, feeling cold. Mel had looked after me rather than immediately going to check on Katie. Maybe Katie wouldn't have got overwhelmed by whatever had caused her tears if Mel had been there and not in here with me.

I clapped my hands to my cheeks, like I'd seen characters do in Sefu's cartoons. I couldn't afford to fall apart again. But I just didn't know if I could hold it together either. The terror python had swallowed me whole and I'd only just managed to wiggle free. I didn't know if I had the strength to stay out of its jaws again; if I didn't, I'd make things worse for both Katie and Mel. I'd make this less of a home for them, make it less...

I thought about Gus. I thought about Liam and Xia. One of them was a murderer. One of them made this place less of a home for all of us, less safe. Not one of them was behaving like a murderer. If I'd just killed someone, and I knew that by sticking around I was putting all of my friends in danger from the police, I'd have run away. I'd have taken Sefu's sword and just fled. That way there would be no murder weapon. Without the sword, no one would reasonably think that someone would go up that downspout and across the barbed wire and slip into the side window. It was too bizarre. No bloody sword meant no smoking gun.

There was something to that thought and I couldn't quite get a grip on it. A knock on the door jolted me out of my train of thought. I opened the door and found Sefu on the other side. "Good to see you're up and about. Sorry you had to find the body like that," he said.

"Are you okay?"

Sefu shook his head. "Not really."

"Do you want to carry on with the investigation?" I asked. I needed him. But if he needed some time...

He smiled. "No, I want to see this through. So, the body. Gus and Paula stashed him in with Vince. Also, Cowardly Winston wasn't lying about nobbling most of our cars."

"Not all of them?"

"Vince's is untouched, and Mel's is just really filthy."

That was something, at least. "I was having this thought about how everyone was behaving but it's not quite there yet. Do you have any ideas for what we should do next? We don't have masses of time."

Sefu reached into his jacket and pulled out a bundle of papers. "I searched Mel's room while she was in here with you," he said.

My eyes widened and my mouth split into a grin. "You genius!" I hissed. "What have you found?"

"Nothing that really helps but given a theme of today is uncovering secrets, I thought you might want to see these."

He handed the papers over. They were all letters, some to Mel, some to me... in the unmistakable hand of my mother. I flicked through them, phrases jumped out at me. "Please, Melissa, Phoebe won't talk to us. Will you talk to her?" "Are you stopping our letters reaching her?" "Phoebe, I'm so sorry." "Melissa, I can only apologise..." "I know you came to our house, the furniture was moved." "Did you steal the letter opener from your father's study?"

"Ah," I said. Something had just clicked in my mind. "That explains why Mel started the game to get to the mail before me."

"Was she trying to make sure you didn't forgive your parents?"

I shook my head. "Probably just trying to make things easier for me. We see them at Christmas and birthdays, it's not like we've cut them off." I waved the papers. "They're just being dramatic. This is nothing."

I shook my head, a little puzzled. "Probably just trying to make things easier for me. We see them at Christmas and birthdays, it's not like we've cut them off." Mel was shielding me from some scheme they had. And that was fine with me.

Sefu looked disappointed.

"It was still a good find, thank you."

Sefu smiled.

"So what now?"

Sefu had already thought about this. "Now that we've – you've – found Racist Carl, it means that Cowardly Winston is still stuck up in that loft. I want to chat to Cowardly Winston again. He was sure the attacker was a man, and we're not sure about that, right? Before we accuse Xia of anything, I want to make sure Winston was wrong. It could be we've been way off base this whole time and it wasn't one of us after all."

"Should we go and get our weapons?" I asked, without much enthusiasm.

Sefu pointed over to the sword he kept propped in a corner of my room. "That will be plenty for intimidation purposes. Come on, let's go."

We retrieved his sword, clumped down the stairs out of the house and strolled up the gravel path towards the barn.

We seemed to be walking slightly closer together than we had when we'd last walked this way.

"How long did it take you to come back to yourself after finding the body?"

Out of the corner of my eye, I saw Sefu shudder. "Ten minutes. It was horrible, Phoebe. With Vince, there was the attack, and I was running on adrenaline for ages. This one just came out of nowhere. I thought I'd grown used to unpleasant surprises, but that one cracked me a bit."

"I'm really sorry to hear that. That sounds awful."

"Yeah, yeah, it wasn't great."

"Want to talk about it?"

I turned my head in time to see Sefu smile at me. "I'm okay. Thank you for asking. I think I need to just work through things a bit. Let everything slot into place in my head. It's good to have you here. Everything feels a bit more normal now."

"It didn't feel normal until I was here?"

Sefu shook his head. "I tried to carry on the investigation while Mel was looking after you. I couldn't keep everything straight in my head. I started shooting off at odd angles and covering old ground. Maybe we're good at keeping each other focussed?"

"Huh," I said. "I like that."

Sefu snapped his fingers. "That reminds me. I didn't tell you. I had a blackmail letter as well."

I rounded on him, "You *what*, bab?"

"I know! I didn't think anything of it at the time, but I just remembered when Paula was talking about hers. It's crazy. This isn't the 1940s. Who tries to blackmail random people?"

"Sefu, please, start earlier in the story."

"Right. Right. It was yonks back, when we were seeing each other. I got a letter saying that the author had heard about you and me, and that I needed to be careful because some people might not like it."

"What?"

"Yeah. It detailed some of the places we'd been seeing each other – my room, my sister's flat, in the stables when we were sure no one was about, but they missed that one time we were feeling fancy and we got a room at the Radisson."

"You've got a very good memory."

"Thank you. Anyway, it said that some people might have a problem with a black man and a white woman together."

I knew this only too well. A friend of mine had seen some white men standing outside a pub in King's Heath shouting 'race traitor!' at an interracial couple. This was in 2001. I'd found it appalling. What I found even more appalling was how unsurprised some of my friends were because they'd experienced similar things first-hand.

"Now," Sefu said, "so far, so patronising, right? 'Dear Mister Sefu, did you know… some people are… racist!' But then it got to the actual blackmail bit. The person who wrote the letter wanted me to send information about other groups to a P.O. Box. The splashier the details were the better. If anyone was planning any actions that sounded like they'd cause trouble or capture a lot of media attention, they wanted to know about it."

"What did you do?"

"I threw the letter away."

"You weren't worried about the consequences?"

"What consequences? Who was the blackmailer going to tell? My parents? They wouldn't care."

"And you thought if I cared about word getting about us then I wasn't worth your time?"

"Pretty much."

"Smart man. Still, one blackmail victim under one roof is unusual. Two is a stretch. But three?"

"We'd had a few visitors to the compound before the letter came, I'd assumed it was one of them."

"Maybe, but would a random visitor have time to steal one of Paula's books, photocopy a page and then put it back without Paula noticing?"

Sefu snapped his fingers. He drew the Gus blackmail letter from his pocket and handed it to me, before patting his pockets frantically.

"What are you doing, mate?"

"Looking for that piece of paper that had the combination for Paula's box on it..." Sefu said, before yelping in delight and drawing the scrap of paper in question out of his pocket. "That must have come from the blackmailer, because the parcel did as well. Does the handwriting match, that's the question..." He squinted at the two pieces of paper. "One's a letter, one's only numbers," he said, "but there's an address for a P.O. Box on Gus's letter and there are numbers. Yes. Yes, I think the handwriting matches. Look."

He showed me the letter, and the numbers in particular. I nodded.

"Vince was blackmailing multiple people in the farm," Sefu said.

"Okay, but it's not proof, right?"

"No. We need something from Vince that shows he sent... the..."

"Why did you trail off? Sandwiches? Were you going to say sandwiches?"

Sefu ignored me. He dug about in his pocket and flourished a piece of paper. "I went through Vince's pockets and found some receipts, remember? One of them was for the post office. The amount here... this is about what I'd expect to send a parcel the size and weight of Paula's money box first class. It's dated from three days ago, which is about right. The parcel wasn't tracked, was it?"

"No," I said.

"Shame. It's still not conclusive, but it's pretty close. But we still don't know why Vi – Richard Lampart – would blackmail us."

"And why did he send Paula money?" I said. "That's also interesting."

"That could have been someone else," Sefu mused. "We don't know for sure it was the blackmailer. Or how's this for an idea: Richard was getting information on other groups from Paula and Liam. He'd failed to get information from me. Let's just assume he just couldn't get any dirt on you and Xia, and he didn't need to blackmail Mel to get information from her. Then Liam suddenly turns around and tells him to get lost, and Paula is clearly right on the edge and about to lose the farm. He knows that because he's going through her bookkeeping and her letters regularly. Richard really needs this information and his continued residence here on the farm for some reason; perhaps it's absolutely crucial to his continued wellbeing, more valuable than money. What does he do?"

I clicked my fingers and beamed up at the Clue-Decipherer-General. "He tries a little of the carrot on Paula to make up for the threat of the stick, and to make absolutely sure she doesn't have to sell the farm."

"Yeah?"

"That's a thought, isn't it. So why would information on activists be worth more than money? We live in a capitalist system, nothing's more important than money…"

"Unless it's a route to more money, or to more status, which is just another way of saying more money. Where was the information going once Richard Lampart had it? We're pretty open about what we believe in, what we do and what we plan to do. We live in a different kind of community with a lot of openness."

"Not always." I hesitated. "We're about to trash some bombers. That's a pretty good secret. It's worth selling to the military-industrial complex. Assuming that Richard knew anyone in British Aerospace or somewhere like that. And Paula was sending him information on other groups. That information would probably be far more valuable than what our group was getting up to."

We approached the barn that should contain our prisoner. It was only then that it occurred to me that the weaselly little fascist might have managed to get down from the platform unaided. It was a long way, but he might have been desperate enough to try it.

"You still up there?" Sefu called as we entered the barn. Silence echoed back. "He's not up there, P," Sefu said to me. "Let's bring down the platform to see if he left anything behind."

"No, wait!" called Cowardly Winston from up on the platform. "I'm still here!"

"Good," Sefu said. "We want to have a chat with you.

Have you been blackmailing any of us?"

"What? No."

"Why would Patriots Unite be blackmailing us?" I whispered.

"Costs us nothing to ask," Sefu shrugged.

"What are you whispering about?" Cowardly Winston asked. He stuck his head over the platform and, for the first time, I saw his face. I'd thought he sounded like a weasel, but I was surprised to see he looked like one as well. He wore a grey suit with a white shirt and had short hair slicked back, with a buzz cut on both sides. His eyes were staring and untrustworthy. "Hey," he said, looking at me. "Hello, gorgeous."

I glared up at him.

"You know, you'd be a lot prettier if you smiled," he said.

"I'll give you a smile if you tell us how you know the person who attacked our mate was a man," I said.

"What? Of course, he was a man!" Cowardly Winston grinned, as if my poor feminine faculties had overheated. "He stabbed a guy with a sword!"

Sefu and I looked at each other.

"Okay," said Sefu, passing a hand over his face.

"What's your name, mate?" Cowardly Winston asked, that grin remaining in place.

"Sefu."

"Alright, Sefu, I'm Mark. Where are you from, Sefu?"

Sefu's jaw tightened. "Hall Green."

"And what's your name mean?"

"Nominative determinism."

"Could you describe the man who attacked our friend?" I asked, before Cowardly Winston said anything else that would stretch Sefu's sorely depleted reserves of patience.

"Slim. Black hair. Had a sword."

I glanced over at Sefu and could see the same thought in his eyes. Xia. "Helpful. So, we have something you might want to hear. We found your mate."

Cowardly Winston's grin froze. "He didn't make it out?"

"He's dead."

"What did you do? What did you *do*?" Cowardly Winston raged up on the platform, which started to creak alarmingly. We waited below to see which would give first: the platform or the temper tantrum. Cowardly Winston stiffened and stilled with impressive speed.

"The same person who killed our mate also killed yours," Sefu said. "So I need to ask you, is there *anything* you can tell us that might help us find the person who killed your friend? Anything at all? Maybe you've been holding something back, or maybe –"

"My mate was one of the group who taught your friend a lesson – the one in the pub." Cowardly Winston's voice was cold.

"What?" My head reeled. "Why? Why did he do it? Cassie was just a sweet kid, damn it."

"He was told to. Our boss told us to follow her and teach her a lesson. He said she was asking questions she shouldn't be asking, that it was okay, she was a leftist and a saboteur. Just like you." Cowardly Winston spat at us.

"Anything else?"

"No. Now are you going to let me down so I can get out of here?"

"No." I turned on my heel and walked out. Cowardly Winston's shouts followed me, as did Sefu.

He nodded. "At least we know who killed Cassie and why."

"We don't know why! Cowardly Winston said she was killed for 'asking questions'. Find someone on our side who doesn't ask questions. That's what we do. That's why they hate us. They don't want a thinking, questioning citizenry. So Cassie was asking questions. What questions? Was she asking about Patriots Unite? We already know they're fascists! They try to hide behind dog whistle politics like patriotism and they deny, deny, deny what they are at every opportunity, but anyone with two brain cells to put together can see what they are! The people that agree with them either don't care or are in denial. Was Cassie supposed to be asking questions about their secret donations to LGBTQ+ charities or something?"

"Fair point."

"He had to have seen Xia," I said. "Slim, black hair, that's her."

"But we don't know why..."

I nodded. "Maybe she was being blackmailed as well, and she worked out it was Vince?"

He shrugged. "Perhaps."

"My problem with it being Xia is that thought I was having earlier. Xia is still here. Why hasn't she just gone? She could have faked a family emergency. Wait, no – she could have just said she was fed up with our nonsense and that she was going to go to Fairford. That would have been entirely plausible. But she's still here. Why?"

Sefu thought about this. "I have no idea."

"Exactly! There must be a reason she's still here. Maybe –" I was cut off by a ringing noise from my pocket.

I didn't recognise the ringtone. It was a strange thing to suddenly have an unfamiliar noise coming from my right kidney. As the second ring sounded, I realised I still had Mel's phone. I fished it out of my pocket and saw that it was Ifza calling. I answered. "Hello, Ifza?"

"Hi Phoebe, yes. Look, it wasn't super easy, it was pretty inconvenient actually, but I've tracked down Richard Lampart's parents."

"Oh, wow. Thanks, Ifza, you're the best."

"That's right, I am. Now I'm outside their house, do you want to talk to them now?"

"Sure, yeah, let me at them." I made my way across the courtyard to the shed where Lampart's body was. Enough light was spilling into the shed that I could clearly make out his features. I'd loved that man, the way that a sister loves it when a good man comes into their lives and makes her sister happy. I mean, I really loved him for that. But also his endless good humour and the way he could charm anyone anytime to do anything. When you have eight people living together, there can be friction. And a man who could negotiate agreements between sides, create a working compromise, and still have everyone thinking he was their friend, well, let's just say that I'm pretty sure our fractures will rip us apart now.

"Okay," Ifza said, "I'm ringing the doorbell."

Silence followed for a few moments, but then I heard Ifza speaking, faintly, before saying into the phone, "Okay, Phoebe, I'm passing you over."

"Who's this?" said a new voice. She sounded like a middle-aged woman. Probably Lampart's mum.

"My name is Phoebe Green, I've found someone, a man in his mid-thirties. He's unconscious. The ID in his wallet said his name was Richard Lampart. I've been trying to get hold of someone who knows him so I can let them know."

"Richard's been hurt?"

"Yes, don't worry, I've called an ambulance. Now, I need to know I'm calling the right person, there are several Richard Lamparts out there and you're linked to just one on the list. Can I describe this person to you and you can tell me if it's your Richard?"

"Y-yes, of course. Erm…"

I looked down at Vince's body, which was lying face up next to the body of Racist Carl, their near identical chest wounds glistening in the half-light.

"This man is white, he has a beard clipped quite short. His hair is also clipped short and is receding. His eyes are dark brown and his eyebrows are quite thick. He has small ears. He's about five foot eleven inches tall and is maybe 70 kilos. Does that sound like your son?"

"Yes, yes, that's our Richard. Oh God, is he hurt badly?"

"Quite badly, yes, but the ambulance operator said he should be stable until the ambulance arrives. Don't worry, I'll let you know what hospital he's going to be taken to."

"Where are you?" Lampart's mum asked.

"Just outside of Birmingham. Would you expect Richard to be out here? It's pretty remote."

"I'm not sure. He works in Birmingham, I know that, although he's not allowed to tell me where."

Not allowed to?

"What does your son do for work, Mrs Lampart?"

"He's a police officer."

Chapter Seventeen

I fought back the urge to scream.

"A police officer?" I said. "As in he's still one right now?"

"Yes!"

"When did you last see him?"

"Three weeks ago, he came back for the weekend."

Vince had been gone that weekend... "And he said work was going well?" I asked. "Is he a beat cop or..."

"No, he said he can't tell us what he does. Look, why are you asking so many –"

"Oh, the ambulance is here!" I cried. "Look, give me your home number and I'll call you straight back as soon as I know where they're taking Vince."

"Who's Vince?"

"Richard, sorry, I'm a little shaken up by this."

"I understand." Lampart's mum rattled off a number, which I pretended to write down.

"Okay, great. I'll call you in a little while. Can you give the phone back to my friend now please?"

I heard the phone be passed over. "Phoebe?" Ifza's voice.

"Ifza," I said, "get out of there right now. Richard Lampart was a cop."

If Vince... if Richard Lampart was a cop, then he was here to spy on us. Where was Richard Lampart when the BNP were wandering around randomly attacking people? Where was Richard Lampart when Patriots Unite murdered Cassie?

I lurched out of the shed and over to Sefu. I told him what I'd learned.

That was when it sunk in. Vince had been a cop. Our friend – Mel's partner – was a complete lie. A smiling paper-thin mask over the snarl of an enemy. He was one of the people who had attacked Sefu. He was one of the people who illegally detained us when we counter-protested fascist groups. He was one of the people who detained and deported people to countries that would execute them, all because they weren't born on these shores. He was one of the people who refused to investigate hate crimes because it was more important to prevent people shoplifting vodka from Tesco. He was one of those sworn to uphold the status quo. The status quo that worked to crush the poorest and most vulnerable members of society for longer than anyone could remember, and that was before we got on to the subject of Iraq. Vince had never been one of us. He hadn't been against us. He'd been working to destroy us.

I wanted to throw up. I would have, I think, if I hadn't been so totally exhausted. I hugged myself as the terror python ripped and tore at me. Everything about Vince was a lie.

Just like the government had lied and cheated its way through a referendum, it had sent its police force to lie and cheat on us. He was a spy. He wasn't an activist. He didn't work as a landscape gardener. He didn't believe what we believed. He was a monster we'd welcomed into our home.

Getting us to love him, getting Mel to love him, knowing all our secrets both personal and professional, was beyond slimy. It was traitorous to common decency. We do precious little that's illegal, fewer drugs than most top politicians and certainly less alcohol. We protest, organise, agitate and proselytise, and those are all legitimate democratic activities. And yet, here we were. With a government agent. Lying and cheating on us.

I saw Sefu walk stiffly into the stables. I wanted to follow him, but then I saw him punch a bundle of banners perched on top of a crate. He was still for a moment after this, but then I heard him exhale. Without warning, he exploded into motion – he rained blows down on the banners, the thumps of his hands striking the thick canvas booming out into the courtyard. A scream ripped out of his throat as he rammed fist after fist into the canvas. I don't know how, but with each strike, the python eased up, just a fraction. Like he was punching my agony into the fabric.

After maybe a minute, he dropped his hands and slumped a little. He breathed heavily. He was still facing away from me. When I could move, some little while later, I walked up behind him and rested a hand on his shoulder. "How are you feeling?" I asked, my voice hoarse and shaky.

He laughed unhappily before replying, "Been better."

I hugged him and felt some of the tension flow out of him.

"This certainly explains why Lampart was killed," Sefu said, once we'd calmed down.

"We have to find a way to get Xia to talk to us about this. That postcard we found really makes it seem like she found out about Lampart. Maybe it made her angry enough to do something like this."

"We need proof," he said.

"We need proof and we need to know why she's still here. And did she mean to kill Racist Carl? Do we even know how he died?"

"A stab wound to the chest."

I cast my mind back to finding the body, the wound was high on the chest. Higher than I'd expected. It was strange. If I'd wanted to stab someone, I'd have chosen basically anywhere except high on the chest where I might hit the sternum or collar bone. I felt anxiety rise inside me as I remembered the sight of Racist Carl's body. I fought it down, now wasn't the time. Mel had been right yesterday, fighting the anxiety away wasn't usually the answer, but we only had about twenty minutes until Eryl got here. Now was definitely a time to lock my anxiety up in a little box until this was done. I only had to do this for twenty minutes. Then I could fall apart. I really wanted to hug Sefu so I could centre myself but there wasn't time for that either. I focussed on the memory of hugging Mel. How safe she made me feel now we'd escaped. I felt the anxiety drain away.

Then my eyes snapped open.

"We need to check the dead fascist, right now."

Sefu blinked. "We do?"

"We do indeed. Quick!" I ran to the shed, Sefu following just behind me.

"Look," I said, pointing at Racist Carl's chest. "Carl is basically the same height as the cop but the wound is higher on Racist Carl's chest than it is on Lampart's. They're nearly identical but..."

I slipped my tie from my neck and measured from the cop's foot to the wound and did the same thing on Racist Carl. "We need to roll the cop over!" I cried, my mind fizzing. Sefu joined me as we rolled Lampart onto his side and I measured the wound on his back.

"The wound on his back is lower than the wound on his

chest, which is lower than the wound on Racist Carl's chest! You realise what that means?"

"You're analysing a pair of corpses?"

"I think they were killed by the same sword-strike. Deliberate, accidental, who knows. But it was the same blow."

"That'd be very difficult... but it looks like it dodged the sternum. To get a strong stab like that, with the blade nearly straight out, you have to strike from the shoulder. There are plenty of other angles with force behind them, but none that come out like that."

I looked at the bodies finally. "Xia's the same height as the cop," I said. "If she was going to do a thrust straight forward from the shoulder, would that angle be possible?"

Sefu shook his head. "I don't think so. To get that angle she'd have had to hold the hilt down by her belly button and thrust up, which isn't likely. But if she didn't, why did she lie about doing Pilates with Liam?"

"She probably just wanted to get to Fairford as soon as possible. She didn't want us investigating because to her Vince was dead and there was still work to be done. I got her all wrong."

I needed a little more time, but I'd run out of that. Eryl was minutes away. I turned to Sefu. He still looked worse for wear, as if he'd been damaged from inside out. I supposed I must have looked the same. But I needed him.

I explained what I wanted him to do, and he ran off to see to things. Sefu had gone through so much tonight, and he was still willing to do what was necessary. Was I?

Sefu had given up his career as a lawyer to come here. Mel had come here out of desperation, but she'd stayed because it was the right thing to do. Paula had loved the farm so much she'd sacrificed her principles to keep it running. Xia was driving herself into a frenzy for the greater good. Gus had been so messed up by the army that he felt he needed to hide a part of who he was, but he always showed up to every action. Liam had forgone a public relationship to help Gus.

I'd come here, but only because Mel was here. I'd stayed, but only because it was easier than finding my own place. I'd gone to actions because my friends were going. I believed in the cause, but so far I hadn't sacrificed anything. I was helping the cause, but I wasn't doing nearly enough. Not yet.

There were only so many ways this could all pan out. Was I going to run away, or was I going to stand up for what I believed in? For an end to hierarchy. For everyone doing their part and no one being crushed by a system determined to preserve the luxury of the few at the expense of the many. For justice for all, not the rich. For an end to war between states, and between the state and its people.

I stood there, in the courtyard, for a long moment, before I made my decision. It was time to stop running. From the terror python. From the past. From myself.

I felt odd. I couldn't feel the constant, squeezing terror I had felt for as long as I could remember. I felt certain. I felt determined.

I checked on a number of details, made a phone call, sent a text and received one back, and then, when Sefu returned, I told him my plan. He disagreed. We didn't have the time for that. He had to get on board and fast.

A little later, I entered the house and did what little remained to be done. I then walked to my bedroom, had a bit of a cry, cleaned myself up and changed into my most comfortable suit.

Someone knocked on the door. "You ready, Phoebe?" asked Sefu from the other side.

"I'm ready."

I walked through to the kitchen, while Sefu knocked on our friends' doors. Xia was the first to emerge. She glared at me as she entered the kitchen. "Five minutes, Xia," I said. "Five minutes, and then we can go to Fairford."

She hesitated, clearly wanting to object, but her better nature won out. She sat down at the table, smoothing down her shirt as she did so. Xia had been pretty foul to be around for most of the day, but I understood. If she'd killed Lampart, I'd cover it up. The movement needed her. Plenty of people marched for peace, but marches were rarely successful. Xia did more than march. Xia, working by herself, had stopped arms manufacturers exporting weapons to repressive regimes. The next day she'd chained herself to the gates of an arms fair, shutting the entire thing down. When she got a team behind her, she was practically unstoppable. She'd known about Lampart, the question was exactly how much she'd known. Even if she was a murderer, I wouldn't let Xia go to prison because of a cop.

Paula walked in, saw Xia and sat next to her. "What's going on Phoebe?" she asked.

"We need to have a quick chat with everyone before Eryl gets here. She might get struck off if she hears too much, so we have to be quick."

"I'm going to need a cup of tea for this," Paula muttered. She got back up and started fussing about the kettle. Paula had given me a home when I'd fled my parents. She'd cared for everyone who lived here, made sure we were fed and healthy. She worked with countless groups to plan actions.

She wasn't as spry as she had been, so her direct action days were mostly behind her, but still, she lived to make the world a better place. Lampart had blackmailed her. He'd made her turn against what she loved and I'd never forgive that. I wouldn't let Paula go to prison because of a cop.

Gus and Liam walked in, hand in hand. Paula looked up at the sounds of their approach. She then glanced down at their hands and smiled, before turning back to the kettle. The two lads had been working tirelessly to fight the referendum. They'd canvassed on doorsteps and distributed leaflets to try to counter the spread of propaganda. Before they'd come to us, they're tirelessly promoted workers' rights. The cop had threatened Gus's freedom. The cop had blackmailed Liam. If either of them had snapped and done something they'd regret, I'd have understood. I wouldn't let either of them go to prison because of a cop.

Sefu walked into the kitchen and shut the door. Mel wasn't coming. She shouldn't hear what would come next. Mel had probably worked less hard for the cause than the other four. She had a kid to care for, after all. That being said, she'd been the one to recruit Gus and Liam. She'd brought me along. Mel was responsible for our group being as large and hard working as it was. The cop had raped her and emotionally abused Katie. I wouldn't let Mel go to prison because of a cop.

Sefu's training as a lawyer meant he was invaluable to our group as a public face. He was regularly interviewed by local newspapers and the occasional radio show. He demolished any bad arguments put to him in seconds. He clearly and concisely explained to anyone who would listen what our group was fighting for, and why it was right. Our group needed him.

When I took a mental step back, it was pretty clear that there was only one person that our group didn't really need.

Sefu walked to the head of the table and stood with his hands clasped behind his back. Our friends were seated around the table in a rough U shape, looking up at him. I leaned against the kitchen wall, next to the sink, which meant I was the only person who could see how tightly Sefu's hands were clasped. He wasn't happy about what he was going to have to do next.

Sefu coughed. "Three hours ago, our good friend Vince was murdered, ostensibly by a member of Patriots Unite. It was most perplexing. My assistant Phoebe and I searched the courtyard and found the knife that we supposed had caused the wound in Vince's chest. The only problem was the knife was too large to have caused such a hole. There was a cut on Vince's cheek that matched the knife, but what of the wound in his chest?

"My assistant and I searched the grounds and encountered a lone member of Patriots Unite lurking in a barn. We interrogated him and he spun a preposterous yarn about a ninja attacking Vince with a sword."

"A ninja?" Liam asked.

Sefu nodded. "Yes. What imaginations these fascists have. We did not think much of it at the time, but we decided to test his story anyway, just to be sure. I immediately cast my eyes to the water pipe that lines the north corner of this very building. Scaling it in a few quick pulls, I found myself on the compound wall. From there, I spotted a strip of cloth attached to a barb of the wire, and a sword, lying discarded in the woods. One of my swords. My most precious sword, in fact."

Sefu started to pace back and forth at the head of the table. He kept his voice level, but he seemed to be on the edge of calling a halt to this scheme. I held my breath. He'd promised but it had been grudgingly made. I wasn't entirely sure he would keep that promise.

He started again.

"Now, we knew that there was another fascist on the grounds somewhere, as that person had attacked Vince. Because of this, Phoebe was convinced that we should devote our time to locating the missing miscreant. I, however, wasn't so sure. I was concerned about the discovery of my sword, covered with blood. I was concerned that the murderer was, in fact, someone in this room."

I had hoped for my friends to turn to each other and pass hushed whispers between themselves, but instead they just stared at Sefu.

"You'd better have a good reason for saying that, Sefu," said Gus.

Sefu didn't stop pacing. "Oh, I'm very afraid that I do. Still, it seemed impossible. What reason would any of us have to murder Vince? I turned to this question. I soon uncovered that Vince was young Cassandra's father. He had blackmailed many of those present here. He was, it turned out, no angel. But were any of these facts a motive for murder?

"I spoke to poor Melissa and asked her a few delicate questions. I tracked down an old school friend of hers, a woman from Liverpool. I asked her to search for Vince's parents so we could establish a few key facts, then I turned to our suspects."

He stared at the people sitting at the table, one by one. "Paula, you had a motive, but we soon established you could not have climbed the pipe to escape the courtyard as you're not strong enough. Gus, your motive was strong, you are literally strong, but the technicalities just did not fit. Liam, of course, had an alibi, as did Xia."

"You said one of us did it," said Liam flatly.

"I'm sorry to say that I did not," said Sefu, "I said someone in this room did. The truth is that my assistant Phoebe is the guilty party."

My friends' gazes locked on to me. I couldn't meet them. I had to sell this, and sell it hard. I looked up at Sefu, and I drew in a breath.

"But... surely you can't mean me, Sefu?" my voice fluttered like the first gasp of a maiden after a dive into deep water.

"I can indeed! It was you who stole a sword from my room, who stabbed poor, innocent Vincent, who climbed the outside of the building like Spiderwoman, and who discarded my sword in the woods."

Liam looked at me, his eyes wide. "Is this true, Phoebe?"

I sagged for a moment, then put on my best evil face. "Yes, Liam, yes. I'm afraid it is. Yes, it was me who killed Vincent – or, should I say, Richard Lampart."

"Who's Richard Lampart?" asked Gus.

"But, Assistant Phoebe, I don't understand," Sefu said, wrestling control of the conversation back, "why take Vince's life?"

I folded my arms, evilly. "Because Vincent – or Richard Lampart, to use his true name – was an undercover cop sent to investigate this activist group. You see, it was not enough for Richard Lampart to infiltrate and spy on us, he also blackmailed several of us, extracting vital information on our sister groups. Finally, to make the illusion perfect,

Richard Lampart had to take a partner while he was here."

"Oh, God..." Gus muttered.

"Just so, Gus," I hissed. "Richard Lampart seduced my sister and pretended to be a loving and devoted partner to her and step-father to her child over the course of *two years*. That is called rape by deception. Only one person has ever been convicted of rape by deception in the UK, and that person wasn't a cop. There was absolutely no chance that Melissa would get justice. On top of this, we learned that Lampart was also indirectly responsible for Cassie's death."

"What?" growled Xia.

"Yes, indeed. There was no possibility that Lampart would have faced justice for these crimes. He was a cop. He wouldn't have even been arrested; he'd have been shuffled off to another department and told not to be a naughty boy. But he had to pay. In the absence of a just state and an unaccountable police force, I acted. Someone had to."

I hoped desperately that my friends wouldn't question this turn of events.

"I don't condone this, Phoebe," said Paula, her voice like stone, "but I understand. What are we to do about this?"

"I shall tell you!" Sefu announced, slipping back into his detective voice. "Phoebe is going to go to the newspapers and tell them everything that happened here. After that, she is going to go to prison. Debts must be paid, after all, particularly when a cop is dead."

I nodded.

A chair scraped against the floor. Xia had stood up. Her hands were on the table, as were her eyes. "Can we please go to Fairford now?" she asked. Everyone else looked at Paula, who nodded.

I collapsed into a chair, utterly exhausted. I felt awful for the deception, but it was for the best that the fewest possible people knew the truth. The maddening thing was, even after Sefu's speech and my performance, I was pretty sure from watching people's expressions that only Xia and Liam had been convinced. Hopefully, the others in the commune knew enough to keep their mouths shut.

Everyone except Sefu filed out of the room. Outside, in the courtyard, I heard the noise of a car. My friends were still in the corridor. Eryl must have finally arrived.

Sefu caught my gaze. "I'll catch Eryl up," he said. "You'd better finish this."

I nodded, and stood. My limbs felt heavy, but my heart was beginning to slow back down. I walked down the corridor and opened one particular door without knocking.

Except from an article published on The Guardian website on 11ᵗʰ April 2019

COURT OVERTURNS REFERENDUM AS VOTERS WERE POORLY INFORMED ... IN SWITZERLAND

Switzerland's supreme court has overturned a nationwide referendum for the first time in the country's modern history, on the grounds that the information given to voters was insufficient.

× Chapter Eighteen

Mel sat on her bed. She had obviously been crying. She looked up at me as I entered. I smiled at her. "It's done."

She looked up at me. "You never even asked why..."

"We didn't have time," I said. "Eryl was on her way and we had to get the theatrics done before she got here. If she heard all the details, she'd be at risk of being struck off because she'd be complicit in the deception. Or at least that's how Sefu remembers it from law school. Sefu's just explaining our situation to her now, so we still have some time. So let me tell you what I think happened:

"You took a lift with Vince on the way to his 'work', along with Katie. You told Katie you were playing detective. I don't know exactly what you found, but I can guess. You messaged Vince and told him you wanted to meet. He suggested Nando's so you dropped Katie off at the farm and then went to Commercial Street for some tasty chicken. I rang every Nandos in Birmingham a few moments ago and the staff at the Mailbox remembers you clearly because you confronted Vince in the Nando's. He confessed to being an undercover police officer. You were furious. There was an argument. The staff had to ask you to leave.

"You went to your tutoring gig but only stayed there for a few minutes. I texted Susan Fletcher's mum and she said you had some emergency and had to leave early. Maybe you always knew what you were going to do next and you'd planned to leave early. Maybe you hadn't planned anything. But I think that all the stress and pain was too much for you, so you made a decision in that moment and have just been acting on instinct since then.

"Either way, you came home, feeling angry and scared. Given the state of your car and your tyres, you must have parked it up a track nearby so he wouldn't know you were home. You might have been trying to hide from him. You might have been planning. You slipped into the house when no one was around and grabbed one of Sefu's swords. You had a think about how to get about the building without being seen and found an old carpet in the spare room. You might have even placed it on the barbed wire then, who knows, maybe that's when you put on a dark beanie.

"You watched Vince from the stables as he was pacing around the courtyard. You saw him, but he didn't see you. Racist Carl from Patriots Unite came in and attacked Vince. You heard Sefu call to Vince from the window in the north wall. That shout probably saved Vince's life. Sefu's sorry about that, by the way.

"You saw that Racist Carl had lost his knife in the struggle with Vince. He wasn't going to do the job for you, more's the pity. As soon as you heard us heading away from the window, you ran out into the courtyard and stabbed Vince with Sefu's sword. You accidentally stabbed Racist Carl too, but who's counting."

"I didn't know about that..." Mel whispered. Fresh tears welled up in her eyes.

"He ran from you but was in too much pain to get far. He hid under my car when he heard me and Sefu coming, where he passed out from blood loss. He died sometime later. Good riddance.

"Once you'd stabbed Vince, you fled to the corner of the courtyard. You must have been running quite fast, because you touched the wall of the compound with your free hand – a hand that had become quite bloody, thanks to you burying a sword into Vince's back. You climbed the water pipe, which must have been difficult whilst holding the sword –"

"I'd sheathed it," Mel said. "The sheath has a thick bit of string attached to it. I clamped that in between my teeth."

"You're a quick thinker, sister of mine. Anyway, you moved along the barbed wire as I raised the alarm, sorry again. The shirt that you were wearing snagged on the barbed wire. It left a scrap behind.

"You hid on the east wall of the house for your moment. You then climbed into the house, pulled the carpet in after you, changed your shirt, and put Sefu's sword back in his bedroom. You didn't do a great job of cleaning that, I'm afraid.

"In the chaos, you slipped back out on to the wall and dropped down on the far side, by the woods, where you'd left your car. My guess is you took your shirt and dumped it somewhere along the way. In the woods, probably. Then you got to the car and drove round and home, so we'd know you couldn't possibly have done it because you'd been out. The others told you what had happened, and you retired to your room to have a cry. I came in to check on you a little while later. As I was leaving, you saw that there was a large bloodstain on my back. You realised that I must have pressed my back up against the area where your bloody hand hit the wall. You knew I'd wonder about it so you decided to get out ahead of the matter. As soon as the coast was clear, you rushed downstairs and cleaned the bloody handprint from the wall.

"Once that was done, you listened to us run around like muppets. You could have taken Katie and left, but you didn't. You didn't leave, because you knew it was unlikely you'd be caught. Also, and this is just me speculating, you didn't leave because you couldn't. If Gus or Xia had done this thing, they could have packed their bags and left. Even Paula could have left her home, but I'm wondering if you couldn't leave because, in your head, you would be abandoning the person you'd failed to save once already. It was only a matter of time before I fell apart again. So you lay in bed thinking about what you did, and about what Vince had been doing to you for the last two years. Am I right?"

"A few details here and there were off but who's counting." She looked up at me, her eyes wide. "Phoebe... you can't take the blame for this."

I patted her hand. "It's already done. But I'm curious. How did you find out about what Vince was?"

"I slipped my phone into his pocket at the climbing centre and set a sound recording going. I've got it somewhere."

Mel opened the drawer on her bedside table. "My phone's gone..."

"Oh yes, sorry." I handed her the phone. She pressed a few buttons.

A sound like rushing air burst from the phone's tiny speaker. This went on for several minutes before I made out muffled voices. Mel turned the volume up.

"There's something I would like to discuss," said Vince/ Richard Lampart's voice.

"What's that, Vince?" said a voice that sounded like it had a smug grin on its face.

"Last time we all met, I mentioned that a certain someone was living with me. Then that someone turned up dead. I want to know if any of you know anything about it," said Lampart.

"Of course, we don't, mate," said a voice that sounded like it would roll over and beg if told to by someone in authority.

"Right," said Smug Grin. "Not a clue."

"My daughter is dead," growled Lampart. "This is not a game. Now, do any of you know anything about it or not?"

"I heard something," said a new voice, who sounded like she got into fights for the fun of it. "I heard some of Tommy's crew did it."

"What?" Lampart roared. "You did this, Tommy?"

"Hahaha, you got me," said Smug Grin, now identified as Tommy. "But don't worry mate, it was for your own good."

"For my own good?" Lampart shouted.

What followed were sounds of a scuffle.

"Look, leave it out, you two," said Fighter, who sounded like she had done pretty well out of the matter. "Look, Tommy, you'd better have run that by someone upstairs before doing something that… improvisational."

"Murderer!" Lampart said.

"Of course, I got permission," Tommy whined. He sounded like he had a broken nose.

"Really?" demanded Fighter, "You got the head of the SDS to sign off on a murder?"

"Well no, not exactly, but he gave me the all clear to take care of it."

"Those were his words? Take care of it?"

"Murderer!" Lampart yelled again.

"Vince, you need to leave,' said Fighter. "The point of these meetings is for us to blow off steam and meet other people in our... circumstances. You're not helping. Go and cool off, okay? I'm sorry about Carrie—"

"Cassie!"

"Cassie, but Tommy is right. She could have exposed us if she'd dug any further. Now, Tommy, you were told to 'take care of it'."

"That's right, I was given a lot of leeway to interpret that instruction."

I heard flesh strike against flesh. Fighter didn't sound like the sort of person to slap someone, so I guessed she had just face palmed.

"Vince, what are you still doing here?" Fighter asked.

I heard the roaring, rustling again, which, in context, I recognised as cloth rubbing against a phone's microphone. I'd heard it a couple of times when friends had pocket-dialled me.

Mel clicked the recording off. "The recording after that is mostly blank apart from when I 'accidentally' bumped into Vince a little while later and retrieved the phone."

"You're going to need to make a copy of that and send it to Eryl."

Mel nodded, silently.

"I have a question," I said.

Mel couldn't look at me. "Given what you're doing for me, you can ask me anything you want."

"Did you worry about what might happen to Katie if you got caught?"

"Katie..." said Mel. He voice was faint but saturated with pain. "She's part of the reason I did it. I'd worked so hard to get her away from people who might hurt her. People like our parents, who would have abused her just like they abused us.

I got her out and away from them, and then I came here, and Katie had a family. It wasn't easy, and I haven't been a great mother a lot of the time, but we were doing okay. And then I found out about him. What would have happened if Katie found out that the man she thought of as her dad had come here to destroy us? Can you imagine what that would do to a child's mind? She might not be able to trust anyone ever again. Even going back to our parents would be better than that."

"Do you know what you'll do now?" I asked. "I'm guessing you're not going to go to Fairford."

Mel shook her head. "I can't stay in Birmingham. When this all comes out the press is going to try and talk to me. I don't think I'd be able to cope with that."

"Where will you go?"

"I'll stay in Liverpool. I have friends there."

"I'm sure Ifza will take care of you. She seems reliable."

Mel's lip wobbled, then she threw her arms around me. "I'm sorry," she sobbed. "I'm so sorry."

I hugged her back. "It's okay, bab. I'm not going to let the state punish you for something the state did to you. They should be buying you a house and Vince should be in jail, but we both know that'd never happen. I don't know if this is the best outcome, but it's not the worst. Just promise me one thing?"

"Anything."

"When Katie grows up, if she wants to get involved with activism, promise me you won't try and stop her. We'll need bright little angels like her if we're ever going to change things. It'd be great to get out of prison and find a young firebrand niece waiting for me."

"I won't stop her," Mel said. She sounded like she was barely holding herself together.

From outside, I heard the bellow of an outraged lawyer. "She *what?*"

"I'm going to have to go before Eryl kills Sefu," I said.

Mel wrapped her hands around my neck and squeezed. "I'm sorry."

"I love you," I said. "And I'm happy to be doing this. Surprisingly happy."

Mel sobbed, but eventually let me go. I rose and stepped out into the corridor where Sefu was waiting for me. "How did Eryl take the news?" I asked.

"She's furious."

"How furious?"

"She's got through five cigarettes in the last three minutes."

"Yeesh."

We stood in silence for a long moment.

"I didn't want things to wind up like this," I said.

"I know."

"I wanted to have a conversation about whether we were going anywhere with…"

Sefu reached forward and took my hand. He drew me slowly towards him. Our lips met and I felt a shivering warmth work its way up my spine.

The kiss only lasted a few seconds. "I'll wait for you," said Sefu. "I'll wait until you get out."

I shook my head. "I don't want you to wait. I might be some time. If you're still single when I get out, then we can talk."

Sefu nodded. He leaned forward and kissed me again.

Once we were done, we rested our foreheads together. "I've got to go," I said, after maybe two minutes.

"I know."

"Come visit when you can."

"Okay."

"Thank you for everything today, Sefu."

I turned and walked down the corridor. I clumped down the stairs and out into the courtyard. Paula's Land Rover and Gus's Honda were gone. I smiled. I hoped I'd be able to hear about them on the news, if I'd be able to get the news where I was going.

Eryl was leaning up against her BMW, which was parked at a bizarre angle near the sheds. She was smoking a cigarette but threw it aside when she saw me. "Get in," she snapped.

I walked around to the passenger door and followed what was, presumably, her official legal advice. Eryl rummaged in a glove box until she found a miniature tape recorder. "Sefu filled me in. I'll get your version of events in a minute, but you should know I've called the police. They're on their way with the coroner. I've warned them about the fascist you've got in the barn. They'll pick him up if he's still there when they arrive. I've told Sefu to make himself scarce."

"Great, thanks."

"We need to discuss what legal strategy. Do you plan to plead guilty?"

"Yes."

"That will help. You've got no previous convictions. There were also mitigating circumstances, so we have got a shot at something between five and ten years, depending on how sympathetic the judge is. Out in two thirds with good behaviour. So three to seven years inside. Are you prepared for this? It's not going to be pleasant."

"*The Daily Mail* told me that UK prisons are basically holiday camps."

"Judging by some of the holiday camps I've been to in Jersey that might not actually be far off. You look strange, Phoebe."

I smiled at the lawyer. She raised an eyebrow but when I didn't say anything, shrugged. "I'm going to get you to dictate a statement that I'll release to the press tomorrow. Ideally, we'd take some time to work through it together but we don't know how difficult the police are going to be about you yet. Best to get it out the way now. So..." Eryl pressed a button on the side of the tape recorder. "Phoebe Green, tell us about Richard Lampart. In your own time."

I thought about the years ahead of me. I'd be close to thirty by the time I got out of prison. It was going to be tough. Still, Mel had done her part by making sure Richard Lampart couldn't hurt anyone ever again. I'd take whatever happened to me gladly if it meant she and Katie were safe.

I told Eryl and her tape recorder about Cassie, my darling sweet friend, and how Vince had got her killed. I told her about following Vince after we left the climbing wall and planting a phone in his pocket. And how I bumped into him later, all accidental like, and took the phone back. And listened to it.

I saw Sefu drive away from the farm with Mel and Katie in the back seats. I breathed a sigh of relief.

I told Eryl about returning to the farm, knowing what Vince was. I told her how betrayed I'd felt and how I'd snatched up a sword in an impulse of sudden rage.

Soon, I heard sirens in the distance. Then, I saw blue and white lights. Moments later, I was hit by the strangest of feelings – satisfaction and relief upon seeing an approaching police car.

Afterword

The Special Demonstration Squad (SDS) was set up by the Metropolitan Police in 1968 to infiltrate left-wing British protest groups. The SDS was shut down in 2008 and its duties were taken up by the National Domestic Extremism Unit. A public inquiry into undercover policing, and the SDS in particular was announced in 2015 by then Home Secretary Theresa May. It is due to report in 2023.

As of April 2020, the enquiry has published the names of 69 undercover officers, while the names of hundreds more remain restricted. Collectively they spied on more than 1,000 political groups, such as Greenpeace, Anti-Fascist Action and the Greenham Common Women's Peace Camp. They also investigated the family of Stephen Lawrence.

Multiple officers had sex with activists while undercover. At least one officer fathered a child. Because the police officers deceived the activists about every aspect of their personality and history, in my opinion, consent is impossible in these circumstances. One activist survivor said she would never have consented to having a sexual relationship with undercover police officer, Jim Boyling, if she had known his real identity. Sadly, the law did not agree. In 2018, the Crown Prosecution Service decided not to prosecute Boyling for offences of rape, amongst others.

Several police officers were sacked for gross professional misconduct due to actions they undertook while working for the SDS. To the best of my knowledge, none of them saw any real consequences for their actions beyond this. Scotland Yard said it "unreservedly apologises for any pain and suffering" adding that "the Metropolitan Police Service has never had a policy that officers can use sexual relations for the purposes of policing".

Not In My Name is a work of fiction and any similarity to people or groups living or dead is entirely co-incidental. Richard Lampart is fictional, but he is based on a collection of real police officers who infiltrated real organisations and hurt real people. With that in mind, I should mention one key inaccuracy in my story. According to reports, when activists have discovered that they have been infiltrated by an undercover police officer, they usually asked the officer to leave. I have been unable to find a single report of activists assaulting spies, no matter what the spies did to them. The real people this story is based on are almost all far kinder and more merciful than my fictional characters. In my defence, having Mel find out about Lampart and then simply asking him to leave, before going through a protracted and ultimately unsuccessful legal battle would not have made for a very interesting novel.

For more information on the SDS, I recommend reading *Undercover: The True Story of Britain's Secret Police*, written by Paul Lewis and Rob Evans. If you would prefer something less dry, the stand-up comedy show, Cuckooed by Mark Thomas, details how his close friend was spying on him for Britain's biggest arms dealer. It is available from GoFasterStripe.com

Throughout this book, quotes are attributed to various public figures. These quotes have been edited to change the subject of the quote to the Iraq war. I am indebted to Deborah

Frances-White, who gave permission to use her speech for the 'Anger' segment. This speech is adapted from *The Guilty Feminist Podcast episode 14: Anger with Lolly Adefope*. Ms Frances-White wished that I make it perfectly clear that the quote has been changed, which I am very happy to emphasise. The original speech can be heard on the Guilty Feminist website under the above episode at timecode: 00:18:30. Other quotes and statistics have been edited as well, although every attempt has been made to maintain the spirit of the originals.

Finally, just in case anyone thinks I've been a little bit harsh on right wing activists, I should mention that Patriots Unite is based on a real group as well. Cassie getting attacked in a pub was also inspired by multiple real assaults, one of which happened after a protest I attended.

COMING SOON

a new Democracy and Dissent mystery
by MICHAEL COOLWOOD

To stay informed about the next book or for other exciting
new publications from CLARET PRESS

like **Michael Coolwood** (author) on **Facebook**

or **Claret Press** on **Facebook**

follow **Claret Press** on **Twitter @ClaretPress**

subscribe to the **Claret Press** website

www.claretpress.com

Lightning Source UK Ltd.
Milton Keynes UK
UKHW041130300620
365804UK00001B/46